"You're to become a holy sister, Lady Elizabeth?" Prince William asked in a slow, drawling voice. "Are you certain that's your destiny?"

She looked up at that, startled. Merciful Saint Anne, he had the most wicked eyes she'd ever seen. *All the bloody saints of Christendom!* She didn't want those dark, unsettling eyes on her. You could almost drown in them. If you were a susceptible female, which she certainly was not.

"Accompany me to my room, Lady Elizabeth," he said suddenly, not waiting for her reply.

"I'd be happy to find you a comely serving wench——" she began.

"Come, my lady," he said, his voice brooking no opposition.

The torches cast a flickering light over the darkened hallway outside his rooms. There was no one to rescue her, nothing but her own wit to set her free from the murderous prince. Maybe she'd become another of the dark prince's victims, making her way straight to sainthood, skipping the convent altogether.

His grin was slow, wicked, dangerous. He put his hands on her bare shoulders and started to draw her closer. "If I weren't atoning for my sins I'd be sorely tempted to drag you into my chamber and commit a great many more." She couldn't move, so she simply closed her eyes as he brought her closer, and his lips settled on her...forehead. Then he let her go, turned and disappeared into his room.

Not even good enough for a desperate lecher, she thought, the feel of his mouth on her forehead, taunting her.

Anne Stuart

Hidden Honor

RECYCLED PAPER · RECYCLED PAPER

ISBN 0-7783-2065-0

HIDDEN HONOR

www.MIRABooks.com

Printed in U.S.A.

Hidden Honor

1

Elizabeth of Bredon strode through the great hall of her father's castle, keeping her pace determined and her chin high. Her heavy skirts flapped around her long legs, her unfortunate red hair was already escaping from the thin gold circlet that kept it in place, and her mood was far from hospitable. Prince William's men were even more disgusting than the usual members of his benighted sex, and she'd already had to rescue two serving wenches and a scullery boy from their determined lechery. And she hadn't yet come face-to-face with the notorious princeling himself. Probably off despoiling her father's dairymaids. Or perhaps the cows themselves.

One more night, Elizabeth reminded herself, and then the safety of the household would no longer be her responsibility. The journey to the Shrine of Saint Anne was a mercifully brief one—no more than two nights on the road—and then she'd be free of men and their ignominious appetites for the rest of her life.

Well, perhaps not, she reminded herself, glancing at the huddled group of monks in the corner. The holy brothers didn't appear to be much better than Prince William's roistering knights, though so far they'd stayed away from the serving women and the live-stock. There were six of them, ranging in age from a youth too young to shave to an ancient who moved with such slowness and pain that Elizabeth itched to try one of her herbal remedies on him. It had helped the complaints of Gertrude, the elderly laundress, and she had little doubt that it would ease the old monk. Little doubt he'd refuse to take anything from her hands, as well. In her experience men were unlikely to listen to her.

The remaining monks were in no way remarkable. Two of them were pale, soft, and ordinary enough. One seemed young and strong, clearly new to his vo-cation and the limits imposed by it. Only the sixth seemed the epitome of quiet, chaste brotherhood, from his demure, downcast blue eyes, his glossy blond curls and his soft, almost feminine mouth. He'd smiled at her earlier, the sweetest smile imaginable, and if there'd been men like him around, men not promised to other women or the church, then she might have reconsidered her long thought-out plans.

Ah, but that would have been a mistake. No matter how gentle, how pretty a smile or how soft a glance, once men became husbands, women became chattel. It was the way of the world and always had been, and Elizabeth was too wise to waste her energy railing against preordained fate. She merely intended to avoid it. She had no intention of devoting herself to a brief life of producing babies and dying from the effort as her mother had. She wanted solitude, strength and power, and a convent could provide just that for a woman unsuited to married life.

Still, Brother Matthew had a very pretty smile, one that almost made her rethink her decision. She had no use for men, but children were a different matter. And children with Brother Matthew's sweet expression would be wonderful indeed.

"Daughter!" Baron Osbert bellowed from across the hall, and Elizabeth slowed her pace out of habit. The herbal concoction she'd discovered and slipped into her father's wine may have dampened his carnal appetites, but it did little for his choleric disposition. Her only defense was to take her time, which helped convince her father of the imbecility of females in general and his only daughter in particular.

She stepped over a snoring body, skirted a flea-ridden dog and made her way across the hall, scuffing the rushes with her feet as she went. Her feet were too big—so everyone had always told her—but they went with her overtall body, and were very useful for kicking, as her five younger brothers and their assorted friends had quickly discovered.

Her father was sitting at the table, but not in his accustomed place of honor. He was off to one side, and not looking any too pleased about it. "You overgrown half-wit," he said with paternal pride. "Where have you been?"

"Seeing to the comfort of your honored guests, Father," she said in the patient voice she reserved for her sire. At this point in her life he was the only one who dared hit her, and she had no fond memories of his meaty hands. She stayed out of his way as best she could, and when forced to converse with him she kept the simple mien of a witless woman. It was what he expected, and far easier that way.

At times she found her own stratagems amusing. Her father was firmly convinced she and all those of her sex were half-wits, while she, of course, was certain the opposite was true. If her own family was anything to judge by, men were slow, spoiled and stupid.

"Seeing to their comfort, eh? Much ease a bag of bones like you would provide," her father said with a snort.

"Were you wishing I offer our guests more personal pleasure, sire?" she asked in innocent tones.

"No one would want you. Besides, you're promised to the convent. Best place for you, even if it's costing me a small fortune I can ill afford. Worst mistake I ever made was to marry your mother. Skinny wench, and too damned smart for her own good. It's not right for a woman to be clever. At least you were spared that burden."

Elizabeth smiled sweetly. "Praise be," she murmured softly. "In that one way I take after you."

Baron Osbert had no notion he was being insulted, but there was a stifled laugh from the man to his right, the man in the place of honor usually reserved for the lord of the castle. Elizabeth had been doing her best to ignore him, but now she had no choice. She turned slightly, to get her first good look at the notorious Prince William.

She'd heard the stories, of course. His title was no more than a courtesy at that point. William Fitzroy was King John's eldest son, but there'd been no marriage to sanction his birth. John Lackland's first marriage had produced no children, only a divorce, but now he had a new wife, a French child he'd married when she was twelve. Three years later there was still no legitimate offspring, and people were beginning to wonder if William might be named the royal heir.

It would be an unfortunate day for England when that happened. The stories about William Fitzroy were legendary and disquieting. He was a spoiled lecher, a whoremonger whose current act of penance was occasioned by the accidental death of a young woman who shouldn't have been in his bed in the first place, and so Elizabeth would have told her if she'd happened to have been there. Not that Elizabeth would have been anywhere near a prince's bedroom herself, but she could always imagine what she might say.

In any case, it wasn't the first unfortunate incident involving Prince William's unpleasant habits. This time, however, the girl was of minor aristocracy, and her father, one of King John's supporters, wasn't as easily placated. So William was headed for the Shrine of Saint Anne to do penance, accompanied by an armed guard to protect the royal personage and a group of clerics to make certain he was cleansed of sin. And Lady Elizabeth had the dubious privilege of joining their party, to be delivered safely into the hands of the reverend mother.

She'd been wise to avoid the prince—she knew at first glance he was trouble. It was little wonder he'd managed to cut a swath of lechery across the countryside—what woman would have said no to him? Though apparently the problem lay in the fact that several women had done just that, and suffered the brutal consequences.

Sprawled lazily in her father's chair, the dark prince was every inch the royal personage. He was long-limbed, she could tell that much, and his black hair was shorter than was the custom, though it curled about his strong face like a lover's caress. His eyes were opaque, dark, almost black, and his skin was the golden color of a man who spent a great deal of time in the sun. Maybe he despoiled virgins in the light of day, Elizabeth thought critically.

He dressed in almost gaudy finery, with gold chasing on his tunic and his leather boots, a large ruby ring on his left hand, chains of gold hung around his neck, so many that a lesser man might bow beneath their weight. Not Prince William.

He didn't have the mouth of a lecher. No thick, pink lips, no lascivious smile. It was a strong mouth in the midst of his clean-shaven face, almost stern, and she wondered if the spoiled prince ever smiled. He looked older than his years—old in the ways of sin, perhaps. He probably only smiled when he was molesting innocents.

"This is m'daughter," Baron Osbert said, introducing her carelessly. "Not much to look at, but she's quiet and biddable and won't get in your way on the journey. Tell the prince what a great honor it is, to have his protection on your trip to the convent.''

"It is a great honor, my lord," Elizabeth repeated dutifully.

But Prince William was looking at her with far too much interest. "Quiet and biddable, is she?" he murmured, and Elizabeth felt an unwelcome shiver run across her backbone. He had a deep voice, with a faint rasp to it that tickled her skin. "Just the way I like my women," he added.

Baron Osbert hooted with laughter. "Not this woman, my lord. She's hardly worth your time and attention."

"All women are worth my time and attention," he said in a slow, drawling voice. "Your name, my lady?"

All the bloody saints of Christendom! She didn't want those dark, unsettling eyes on her, and she certainly didn't want her existence to mar the even tenor of the prince's self-indulgent life.

"Elizabeth," her father answered for her. "Approach the prince, you dullard, and make your curtsey."

Elizabeth had no choice but to do as she was bid, keeping her head meekly lowered. She'd perfected the gesture for a variety of reasons. Keeping her head low diminished her height, and it prevented people from reading the expression in her eyes. Even the dullest of her brothers would be unsettled if they realized just what their sister was thinking.

"You're to become a holy sister, Lady Elizabeth?"

the prince asked in his remarkable voice. "Are you certain that's your destiny?"

She looked up at that, startled, and found herself meeting his gaze. Merciful Saint Anne, he had the most wicked eyes she'd ever seen. You could almost drown in them. If you were a susceptible female, which she certainly was not. She stared up at him, dumbstruck. There was no joy in those eyes, or evil. But there were ghosts.

"She hasn't much choice in the matter," her father answered for her once again. "She's too tall and too slow to provide much use as a wife."

"I'd never heard that wit was a desirable trait in a woman," the prince murmured, watching her.

Her father bellowed with laughter. "True enough. But who'd want to warm himself with a bony creature like her? Give me a plump woman any day, one with curves and something to hold on to."

"Whereas I'm a great deal more broad-minded. There's untold pleasure to be had in the most unexpected of places, if a man has the wisdom to look."

Enough was enough, Elizabeth thought, lifting her chin to risk the prince's unsettling glance. "If I may be excused, Father? I have work left undone, and I wish to say goodbye to my brothers. God knows when we'll see each other again— I don't expect they'll be traveling to Saint Anne's to visit me anytime soon."

"Not unless they're forced to, and they're too smart to get caught," Osbert said carelessly, ignoring the fact that the powerful man beside him was at that moment paying the price for being caught. "I doubt you could find them. They're healthy young animals, and tonight is a night for celebration, and I have little doubt they're off enjoying themselves. They wouldn't wish to be found by their elder sister. I'll convey your farewells to them.''

''Celebration?'' Prince William murmured.

''The honor you do our home,'' Osbert said with unexpected smoothness. ''And the departure of my daughter.''

''That bad, is she?'' There was a thread of laughter under his deep voice and Elizabeth jumped. She'd always had a weakness for a man who laughed, but not at her expense.

She spoke up. ''To give a child to the church is always cause for rejoicing.''

''Particularly when she's no good for anything else,'' her doting father observed.

''I'm not convinced of that,'' the prince said, causing that shiver of unease to dance down her spine once more. His voice was almost worse than the intense gaze of his dark eyes. He made her want to squirm, to run away. To melt.

Running away was the most practical response. ''I'll just see to the brothers, then, and retire...''

''Which brothers? Yours, or the monks?''

''You've already assured me that my brothers are nowhere to be found, and of course you are right, Father,'' she said. ''I wish to make certain the holy friars are provided for.''

''Keep away from them.''

Prince William's deep voice had lost its compelling

edge. It was the voice of a royal, expecting to be obeyed.

And supposedly dim-witted or not, she didn't dare countermand such an order.

Elizabeth sank into another curtsey. "As your lordship wishes," she said demurely. She cast one glance over her shoulder, at the small group of monks in the corner of the great hall. Several had already stretched out on the rushes, sound asleep, but Brother Matthew, with the sweet smile and beguiling blue eyes, was still awake. Watching her.

"Perhaps you're not that well suited to the convent after all, my lady," William said slowly. "You seem to find certain men far too distracting."

That made her jerk her head back in surprise. There was almost a touch of displeasure in his voice, as if he didn't like the fact that she kept staring at the gentle monk. Surely a man such as Prince William didn't have to have every woman fawning over him?

Apparently he did. "Accompany me to my room, Lady Elizabeth," he said suddenly. "I find I've grown unexpectedly weary, and after your father's fine wine I doubt I could find my way on my own."

"I'll be happy to find you a comely serving wench, my lord," she began. In fact, she'd be happy to do no such thing. Entrance into Prince William's bed was a dangerous thing, and she had no intention of sacrificing any of the women who would likely tempt his appetite, not even to save herself. And in truth, she couldn't believe she was in any danger. Prince William was a notorious lecher, a connoisseur of beautiful women. She was hardly the sort of female to interest a man like Prince William.

There wasn't time to dose him with her father's herbal concoction—it took several days for it to take effect. It was a good thing she was safe from any stray lust on the part of the king's son.

"A visiting prince deserves the company of the daughter of the house and no less," he said, rising.

She'd been right, he was very tall indeed. Not as huge as some of her father's best fighting men, nor as brawny. He had a lean, wiry grace to him, and he came around the table and took her hand in his, and there was nothing she could do about it.

"Come, my lady," he said, his voice brooking no opposition. "Bear me company. You can tell me of the pleasure to be found in this uncivilized place."

Her father was still sitting in his chair, dumbfounded. He hadn't even had the sense to rise when his honored guest had done so, but remained motionless, openmouthed in dazed shock.

The prince's hand was surprisingly rough in hers. She would have thought a prince would have soft, babied skin. But then, word had it that Prince William was a fighter, as well as a lover, and the long hours of training with weapons would toughen him.

He certainly didn't lack for strength. Before her father could utter a protest, or more likely a warning for her to please his guest, he'd drawn her from the smoke and heat and light of the great hall, into a darkened corridor, out of sight of everyone.

"Which way are we going?" the prince asked in an even voice.

"Where am I taking you?" Her own voice didn't waver, a small miracle when in fact she was as close to panic as she'd ever allowed herself to feel. The man beside her was bigger, stronger than she was, and he was known for his unexpected brutality. She had no interest in bedding a tender lover, much less a monster.

"To my rooms. Where you will leave me, to spend one more chaste night under your father's roof before you throw your life away with the holy sisters. I mean you no harm, Lady Elizabeth." She might have believed him if it weren't for the irony in his voice.

The torches cast a flickering light over the darkened hallway, and she looked up into his face, trying to read his expression. The shadows playing across his skin made him look as dangerous as he was rumored to be, and she wasn't reassured.

There was nothing she could do at that moment—his grip on her hand, while not painful, was determined. She had no choice but to lead him to the solar, and hope that something might distract him along the way.

"Of course, my lord," she said meekly. She started forward, in her nervousness forgetting to take the small steps that were considered proper in a female. She covered ground quickly, and he kept pace with her long stride, moving with an almost leisurely grace.

She had little doubt the prince would command the

best rooms in the house, the warm and well-appointed solar in the south tower. It took no time at all to traverse the long corridors of the castle, and there wasn't a soul in sight to impede their progress. No comely serving wench, no mischievous brother, no disapproving monk. They moved through the halls unwatched, unheeded. There was no one to rescue her, nothing but her own wit to set her free. If she was, in truth, in any danger, which seemed very unlikely.

The door to the solar was closed, keeping the heat inside, and she halted, her mind working feverishly. She could topple to the floor in a faint, and despite his height he'd still have a difficult time hauling her limp body into the room. Though doubtless he'd have no trouble finding someone to help him. He was, after all, a prince, albeit one by courtesy rather than law.

She could kick him in the shins, surprise him into releasing her hand, and make a run for it. He'd probably move faster than she could, but she had the advantage of knowing her ground, and there were numerous hiding places in the castle where she'd spent all her life.

Or she could simply accept her fate. It wasn't anything worse than most women had been enduring for centuries, and there were countless martyrs who'd been ravaged and murdered. Maybe she'd become another of the dark prince's victims, making her way straight to sainthood, skipping the convent altogether.

For some reason the notion didn't appeal. She was

still trying to come up with some plausible means of escape, when he simply released her hand.

"I told you, Lady Elizabeth, you have nothing to fear from me," he said, his deep voice curling down her spine. "I have no interest in raping you."

She felt her face flush, but it wasn't with the gratitude that she would have expected. How mortifyingly foolish, to think someone like Prince William would prove any kind of threat to a skinny, overgrown redhead with a tongue like a razor. She wasn't even woman enough to appeal to the most desperate men in her father's household—why in the world should a dedicated lecher want her when there was far more abundant pleasure to be found? And why was she feeling faintly aggrieved rather than gratified by her close escape?

Perhaps because it hadn't been that close. She couldn't quite summon the vacant expression she usually reserved for irritating men, but she nodded. "If you desire anything you have only to ask one of the servants," she said, starting to move away before he could change his mind. Not that he was likely to.

But to her shock he reached out and put his hand on her shoulder, halting her escape. Strange, but the feel of his hand against her shoulder, bare flesh against bare flesh, had been oddly disturbing. This time the weight of his hand through solid layers of clothing was even more unsettling. Hands touched all the time during the course of the day. Seldom did people touch any other part of her body. Particularly tall, handsome males. And there was no disputing that Prince William was very handsome indeed.

"I won't be needing anything. As doubtless you've heard, this is a journey of penance." There was a faint distaste in his smile, though she wasn't sure whom it was directed at. Himself, or the powers that had decreed he must atone. "You would be wise to seek your bed as well, my lady. We'll be making an early start of it, and my guard tend to be impatient."

"Yes, my lord."

"And the friars will see to themselves. They've taken a vow of poverty, remember? They're perfectly adept at taking care of their own comfort. They don't need you hovering around them."

"I don't hover."

"You looked as if you wanted to," he said. He hadn't lifted his hand from her shoulder, and the weight of it was warm, heavy, spreading through her body in a most disturbing manner.

"I'm mistress of the castle," she said. "That's been my purpose in life, to see that my father's guests are well taken care of."

"Then it's a good thing you'll be putting your talents to something more useful," he said. "Do I have your promise?"

She jerked her head up to look at him, honest surprise wiping every other consideration from her mind. "Promise, my lord?"

"To keep away from the great hall?" he said patiently. "To seek your quarters and stay there till the morning light? The men I've brought with me aren't trustworthy when it comes to women.''

And you are? she wanted to ask, but she decided she'd already pushed her luck to extremes. And he was letting her leave, untouched. She should be wise and grateful.

It was easy enough to agree, when it was exactly as she had intended. ''I promise, my lord. Though I must say you greatly overestimate any effect I might have on susceptible males. I have found that I am entirely safe from such things.''

His grin was slow, wicked, the complete opposite of Brother Matthew's saintly smile. And far more dangerous. ''I think you greatly underestimate susceptible males, my lady. And if I weren't atoning for my sins I'd be sorely tempted to drag you into that room and commit a great many more.'' He put his hand on her other shoulder, and he started to draw her closer, and she looked up into his dark, dark eyes, letting him do it, wondering if he would kiss her. She would have liked one last kiss before she took her holy vows, though she'd be much better off being kissed by Brother Matthew than the most dangerously lecherous man in the entire kingdom.

But no one else would want her, so it didn't matter. She couldn't move, she simply closed her eyes as he brought her closer, and his lips settled on her...forehead. A brief benediction, and then he let her go.

Not even good enough for a desperate lecher, she thought. Thank all the mercies of heaven for that. She stepped back, and if she didn't know better she would have thought his release was reluctant.

"Sleep well, my lord," she said, turning to leave, hiding her intense and totally irrational annoyance. "I'll be ready to go whenever you wish. Have peaceful dreams."

"I doubt it," he muttered. And a moment later he'd closed the door of the solar behind him, leaving her alone in the hallway, with the feel of his mouth on her forehead, taunting her.

An hour later he was sprawled in a chair in the solar, watching the fire, when he heard the faint scratching on the door, the creak of the leather hinges. He allowed himself a stray hope that it was a certain tall, skinny, redheaded creature who wasn't anywhere near as meek or as witless as she'd have everyone believe, and then relaxed when one of the monks ducked inside, closing the door silently behind him.

"Did anyone see you?"

Brother Adrian shook his head. "Not a soul. I already had an excuse ready—you were in need of spiritual counseling and my Christian duty was to aid you."

"And I would have turned to the youngest monk in my retinue? Somehow it seems unlikely."

Adrian flushed. "I didn't think…"

"It's all right, Brother Adrian. They would simply assume I'm extending my debauchery to those of my own sex. It wouldn't be the first time."

Brother Adrian frowned. "But you wouldn't. You don't…" he faltered.

"I don't," the man said. "But Prince William does. Is the prince safely settled for the night?"

"He is."

"No women anywhere near him?"

"None."

The man sighed. "This is harder than I expected. Keep watch on him, Adrian. He cares nothing for atonement."

"And you care too much," Adrian was bold enough to say.

2

Elizabeth was up early. She'd always been impatient with too much sleep, and on the day she was to start her new life she could barely wait. Excitement bubbled in her veins, and even though her meager belongings were packed and her goodbyes said, she still rose before the first light, pulled her loose-fitting dull brown gown over her shift and laced it herself, and then sat by the window as the sun climbed over the eastern hills. It would be the last time she would see it from this window, and she wondered that she felt no twinge of sorrow. There would be other sunrises, in other places. She'd seen enough of this one.

She leaned her head against the cool stone wall and watched as the household slowly came alive. The milkmaids straggled into view first, and Elizabeth could tell even from that distance that the household guests had found amiable company among them. They were followed by the stable help and then the rest of the household servants, one by one, as they set about their duties. There was no sign of the visitors, either knights or monks, even as full daylight spread over her father's keep.

It was an orderly, well-run household, despite her

father's slovenly ways, and she had always done her best to make it so. God only knew what it would look like when next she saw it—if she ever did. Even a small castle such as Bredon required a strong chatelaine to order the multitude of servants necessary. In the few years since her father had discovered daughters, even plain ones, had a use after all, she had been kept at a run, overseeing even the merest details of a household that required a small army to run. She seldom had time for her own interests, her study of the stars and the curative effects of roots and herbs. However, she'd become quite masterful at feeding and caring for the fifty or more members of her father's household.

Who would see to them after today? With no woman to see to the running of the place it would most likely fall into disrepair and decay.

Of course, who was to say there wouldn't be a woman? Once her father was free of the restraining effects of Elizabeth's potion, he'd doubtless find himself married once more, and her younger brothers would doubtless follow suit. In truth, there would probably be too many women rather than too few. Another good reason for her to leave—she wasn't the sort to peacefully relinquish what little power she had.

But that would no longer be her concern. She might never return, never see her family again, and while she'd miss her monstrous younger brothers, she wouldn't mourn. She would have a new family once she arrived at the Shrine of Saint Anne. A new family, a new name, a new calling. And no regrets.

The first of their guests strode into the courtyard, and Elizabeth watched in astonishment as Prince William himself headed toward the stable. He was fully dressed in his elegant clothing, the gold chasing glinting in the early sunlight, but he had no cap on his head, and she realized with some amusement that he was prematurely balding. His dark hair had been carefully combed over his skull, but it only just covered the crown of his head. He was almost as bald as a monk. It was a good thing he was so tall—most people wouldn't have the vantage point she had.

Then again, it probably wouldn't matter if he was fat and ugly, as well as bald. He was the only son of the king, powerful and privileged, and no one would dare say no to him. She couldn't imagine how he could have killed a woman, or more than one if gossip were to be believed. What woman would dare to resist him, even one of high birth?

She could watch him quite safely, hidden away behind the thick walls of the castle, and she indulged herself for lack of something better to do. He moved with surprising grace for a man so tall, and his long legs made quick work of the expanse of the courtyard. He'd either spent the hours in such debauchery that he hadn't bothered to get any sleep, or unlike his fellow travelers he'd spent a chaste, well-rested night in the solar. He didn't look particularly chaste—there was too much knowledge in his eyes, but there'd been no screams in the night, and she could only assume that everyone had made it through safely.

Even Prince William. He passed the stable, heading

directly toward the small chapel, and then he disappeared inside.

Elizabeth leaned back, astonished. Prince William's current atonement had been forced on him, and if even half the stories were true, he was a heedless, cruel man with little regard for man or God.

Though he hadn't looked particularly cruel last night. And cruel men didn't kiss plain women on the forehead, did they?

It made no sense to her, and she liked things to make sense, but in the end it was the least of her concerns. The household was truly awake by then, and more of Prince William's entourage had appeared, looking a great deal less sprightly than the prince himself. It was time to go.

There was no member of her family waiting to see her off—only the servants. Gertrude, the elderly laundress, was weeping openly, and even Wat the stable lad was blubbering. She hugged them all, fighting back her own tears, and approached the weary nag that her father had grudgingly given her for the journey with only minor trepidation.

The men were already mounted. The monks were on particularly fine animals, a surprise. Most holy brothers rode donkeys, not high-strung chargers. Poor old Melange would have a hard time keeping up with even the slowest of them, but it was the best she could hope for. Wat dragged the mounting block over, but before she could move the dark prince spoke, startling her. She hadn't realized he was so near.

"You're not riding that pathetic old nag," he said flatly.

She'd forgotten his voice. She looked up at him, and tried to remind herself that despite his eyes he was nothing but a horrible, wicked, balding man. "It's the only mount I have."

"I've seen your father's stables. He takes better care of his cattle than he does his women."

"Don't most men?" she responded, then bit her lip. Being outspoken was always a failing, and she didn't want his dark, unnerving eyes on her any more than necessary.

"Brother Adrian!" he called over his shoulder, his eyes never leaving hers. To her surprise, it was the youngest, baby-faced monk who slid off his horse and came running.

"Yes, my lord?"

"Find milady a better mount. If she tries to keep up with us on that poor beast she'll be left behind in no time."

"I don't know if Baron Osbert would be willing—"

"Baron Osbert has no say in the matter. He would scarce want to inconvenience his prince, would he? He is singularly lacking in wisdom, but even he can't be shortsighted enough to offend those in power."

"Indeed," Brother Adrian said, advancing toward Wat, who stood trembling in his manure-stained boots.

"I don't know what I can give you," Wat said in a wavering voice. "The baron has never let her ride much. She's such a hopeless rider that he was afraid she'd ruin any of his decent horses.''

Prince William was still looking at her. "You really are a disgrace, aren't you?" he said softly.

"So I'm often told." She wasn't about to defend herself. She would ride whatever they put her on, just as long as it took her to her new life.

"Bring her Anthony's mount. He won't be needing it."

Elizabeth allowed herself a brief moment to worry about poor Anthony's fate before she spoke. "I'm certain Melange will be fine."

"And I'm certain she won't. Are you planning on arguing with me?"

That was exactly what she wanted to do, but she thought better of it. One didn't argue with the king's son, particularly when he was known to possess an uncertain temperament. "As you wish, my lord."

He nodded. "A sensible decision. I knew you were wiser than your father. We're already late in leaving." He should have moved away. His huge black horse was restless, breathing heavily in the early morning air, ready to jump ahead, but he kept the beautiful creature under control with almost imperceptible effort as Adrian returned with a freshly saddled chestnut mare.

Elizabeth eyed the creature warily. The horse was bigger than Melange, and much livelier. But she certainly wasn't about to waste her time thinking she had any choice in the matter. Life wasn't about choices, it was about making the best of what was forced on you.

Riding a strange horse was bad enough, but going through the awkward business of mounting with the prince's dark eyes on her was worthy of argument. Until she glanced at him and knew he wasn't going to budge.

The mare held still with surprising patience as she scrambled onto her back, a good sign. Melange, for all her torpor, wasn't as well behaved. Elizabeth sent a silent prayer of thanks heavenward. If she hadn't managed it she had little doubt the prince would have put his hands on her again, in front of everyone, and that was the last thing she wanted.

And then they were off, their cavalcade moving with stately grace through the early morning mist. Elizabeth looked back, one last time, at the assembled servants, the familiar shape of Bredon Castle, where she'd spent her entire seventeen years. And then she turned her back on it, facing her new life.

It was a matter of great pride for Elizabeth that she never cried. Not when her father boxed her ears, not when her brothers called her a maypole, not even when she'd overheard two of the women of the castle discussing her total lack of feminine attributes. Not even when her only chance at married life was destroyed before it even began, when the man she'd been betrothed to chose another. When she looked in a mirror, even in the wavering reflection she could see herself well enough. Red hair—a sign of the Devil. Pale skin that freckled and burned in the bright sun. Way too tall—she towered over most men. Way too skinny—her hips were narrow, not made for childbirth, so what good would she be to anyone? She had breasts, but their relative abundance was more of an inconvenience than a boon. They had no use but to get in her way and occasionally excite the attention of some idiot male. At least in the convent no one would notice.

She never cried, and she prided herself on her strength and resilience, but by the time the sun was high overhead she was ready to sob with pain and frustration.

In seventeen years she'd never traveled more than half a day away from the castle, and then only once, to her aborted wedding. Her mother had no family left to visit, and Baron Osbert certainly never sought out her company on his occasional journeys. But now she'd been in the saddle longer than she'd ever been in her entire life, and her body screamed at each step the horse took.

"My lady?" The soft voice penetrated her self-pity, and she lifted her head to look into Brother Matthew's pale blue eyes. "Are you ill?"

She cast a nervous glance ahead, but Prince William was well in front of the caravan, almost out of sight. She gave the gentle monk a brief smile. "Just travel-weary," she said with at least a modicum of honesty. In fact, she was so wretched she could scream from it, but it would do her little good. "You're very kind to worry," she added. "I'll be fine once we stop to rest."

Such a shame to have such a pretty face lost to a monastery, she thought absently when he smiled back at her. A few more sweet men like him in the real world would certainly improve the quality of life. Instead, most husbands were bullying brutes, and the thoughtful men were devoted to celibacy. As was she, she reminded herself swiftly.

"I'm not sure the prince has any intention of stopping before nightfall," Brother Matthew said in a wry voice.

Elizabeth couldn't help her tiny moan of despair.

"I can see to it that he does," Brother Matthew said, eyeing her with great sympathy. "Just a word in his ear and I'm certain he'd stop. After all, he could hardly expect a frail woman to keep up this kind of pace."

"I'm not a frail woman," she said between clenched teeth. There was a time in her life when she would have given anything to be a frail, helpless flower of femininity. God had ordained otherwise, and she had no choice but to take pride in her strength and endurance. Even if it seemed to have abandoned her when she most needed it. "I'll be fine. I'm just not used to riding such long distances."

"The journey's only just begun. There's no need for him to set such a pace."

"Perhaps he wants his penance over and done with," she suggested, shifting around to try to get more comfortable. Her horse took her restlessness with comparative good grace. Melange would have made life pure hell.

"I would imagine he does," Brother Matthew said. "Celibacy sits very hard on a man like Prince William. Be careful of him, my lady. It worries me that your father couldn't even spare a kitchen maid to bear you company. As the only woman in this group of men it makes you very vulnerable."

"I think they'll manage to restrain themselves," she said, tossing an escaping strand of red hair over her shoulder.

"I think you trust too easily. You must promise to come to me if you ever feel you're in danger. I will do what I can to protect you."

She looked into his pale, troubled eyes and melted. Why weren't there men around like him? Peaceful, kind, handsome men with light, soft voices that soothed rather than disturbed? Why waste such a paragon on a monastery?

Blasphemy, of course, but at least she'd been wise enough not to speak it out loud. Who more deserving than the mother church? It wasn't as if she herself weren't taking the only chance she had. It was an honor to serve God.

Brother Matthew leaned over and put his hand on hers. Soft, beautiful hands, with a heavy gold signet ring on one finger. "Promise you'll come to me," he said urgently.

His hands were cold. Surprising, because the sun was bright overhead. Her own blood tended to run hot—a convenience in a drafty, ill-heated castle, but she knew she was unusual. It only made sense that a holy brother would have cool skin. Maybe the heat that plagued her blood would still and cool once she joined the holy sisters.

He had taken her hand and held it, forcing their horses close together as they rode forward. Brother Matthew's mount was a great deal more high strung, and Elizabeth could feel her own horse's distress at his closeness. An anxiety that mirrored her own, though she wasn't quite certain why. She could think of no way to pull her hand away from the well-meaning friar, and she squirmed in her seat again.

"Brother Matthew!" The youngest monk had ridden up to them, his voice urgent.

Brother Matthew released her hand, slowly, reluctantly, and turned to face the young man with almost insolent leisure. "Yes, Brother Adrian?"

"Prince William wishes to converse with you."

"We'll have more than enough time to talk when we stop," he said, still keeping pace with Elizabeth. "We can discuss atonement and sin at length over dinner."

"He says now, Brother Matthew."

Brother Matthew's smile was exquisitely charming. "The prince will have to accept the fact that he is on a journey of atonement, not of pleasure, and his desires no longer come first. I will join him later."

Brother Adrian wheeled away, clearly annoyed, and Brother Matthew laughed softly.

"Was that a wise idea?" Elizabeth asked. Just because she was unreasonably enchanted by his sweet smile didn't mean she'd lost her good sense. "Prince William doesn't seem the sort of man it is wise to defy, no matter how penitent he's supposed to be. Isn't that how he came to be on a pilgrimage in the first place?''

''Indeed. And part of his atonement should be to hear and accept the word *no* each day.''

''Are you in charge of his penance?'' she asked, curious.

''That surprises you? It does me as well—a prince of the land should have his soul under the guidance of an archbishop at the very least, not a simple friar from a small monastery.'' There was an unexpected tone of resentment in his voice.

''You must feel very honored.''

Brother Matthew's opaque blue eyes swept over her, and his smile was angelic. ''An honor I could well do without,'' he said, reaching for her hand again.

She was a better horsewoman than anyone suspected, and it was a simple matter to make her horse skitter away as if she were poorly controlled by a clumsy novice. Out of reach of his cold, gentle hands and his melting smile.

And then she realized the others had stopped, and all those around her were dismounting. The wretched prince had decided he was human after all and in need of a rest.

There was no mounting block. In normal circumstances she was agile enough to slip down off the back of a horse, but her current mount was higher than Melange, her skirts were wrapped around the saddle, and her muscles screamed at the very thought of it. Maybe she'd just stay where she was. If she got down, she'd simply have to get up on this instrument of torture once more, and that was one thing she wasn't certain she could do.

Maybe Brother Matthew could help. She turned, but he'd slipped away without a sound. And there was no mistaking who was advancing on her, tall and dark and oddly menacing.

No, there was nothing odd about his menace, she corrected herself. Prince William was a danger to all women. And all the predawn trips to the chapel and penitential journeys wouldn't change that. Not if you looked into his eyes.

Brother Adrian accompanied him, and when Prince William slid off his horse with effortless grace he tossed the reins to the young friar and advanced upon Elizabeth. The horse skittered back, feeling her nervousness.

He reached out and caught the reins, putting his hand on the neck of her mount, soothing her with only a touch—an unspoken communication that made Elizabeth even more nervous. He must truly be an instrument of the Devil. She firmly believed that animals had better instincts than humans did, and yet her horse trusted him. If he could trick animals he could deceive anyone.

"Time to dismount, Lady Elizabeth," he said. "If you stay too long in the saddle, you'll stiffen up."

Too late, she thought miserably. "I'm fine, thank you," she said. "My lord," she added hastily.

Her skirts were brushing against the fine wool of

his cloak, and she could feel the warmth of his body, even through all those layers of clothing. She should have felt stronger, more powerful, looking down at him from her high perch. She didn't.

"Get down, Elizabeth." It was an order. No one was around except Brother Adrian, and he was trying his best to pretend he couldn't hear their conversation.

If she tried, she'd fall at his feet. And she wouldn't do that for any man. She looked down at him, wondering if a plain "no" would do any good. She had grave misgivings that it would.

"I don't want to."

"Get down."

"I can't!" she said finally. "If I try to climb down off this wretched animal I'll fall on my face, and then there'll be no way you can possibly get me back on her. I'm better off just staying here until we stop for the night...." The words trailed off in a whoosh, as he put his hands around her waist and lifted her down off the horse.

She was right, there was no strength in her legs. But he was holding her with just the power of his strong hands, so that she wouldn't collapse, and slowly the trembling in her knees stopped and she could stand on her own. If only she could stop the rest of her body from shaking.

"She's not a wretched animal. She's a very fine horse, and you know it as well as I do," the prince said in a mild voice that should have reassured her.

"You can let go of me now."

"I don't want to." She wasn't certain if she heard

him clearly, since he released her even as he spoke and took a step back. She grabbed the horse's reins for additional support, and ran her hand down her neck in apology before she realized she was touching her just as the prince had touched her. She pulled her hand away hastily.

"No, she's not a wretched animal," she agreed. "I'm just a bit…unused to riding for such a long period."

"Indeed." He nodded his head toward a stretch of woods. "You can go over there."

"Why?"

"To relieve yourself," he said bluntly. "Unless you've managed to control your bodily functions as well as you control your father's household, you should be in need, and I doubt you want to join the men."

She could feel a blush suffuse her face. Now that he mentioned it, she did need some privacy. "You could have put it more delicately," she snapped. And then remembered to add "my lord" in a meek tone.

"You don't strike me as particularly delicate, Lady Elizabeth." He took the reins from her. "Go ahead."

She'd overestimated her strength. She was fine standing still, but the moment she tried to take a step forward her knees began to buckle.

And the moment they did, his hand came under her arm, keeping her from falling.

He was closer now, much too close, as he had been the night before. "I beg pardon," she said breathlessly. "I'll be fine in just a moment."

"Do you want me to carry you?"

"No!" The thought of the dark prince carrying her into the secluded woods was beyond unsettling. "I'm fine." To prove it she pulled free from him and took a step forward.

Her body obeyed her. She managed a cool smile and headed for the patch of woods designated for her use, moving with all the grace she could muster.

Until she was out of sight, when she hobbled, groaning and moaning into the bushes.

She would have liked nothing more than to curl up in a ball and stay there, but she knew it was out of the question. If she tried it, he'd send his men after her. Or even worse, come and find her himself.

She had no choice in the matter. At least the day was more than half over. If she could just get herself onto the back of that horse one more time she'd survive the first day. Barely.

They were already mounted when she emerged from the woods. All of them, sitting on their horses, watching as she slowly made her way into the clearing.

She straightened her spine and approached the horse. No mounting block this time, and Prince William was on his own charger, holding the reins, watching her.

She never cried, and she wasn't about to start now. Maybe if she managed to get her foot into the stirrup she could haul herself up that high...

"Give me your hand." Prince William's voice was peremptory. He was next to her horse, and she couldn't quite see how he was going to get her on it from his high vantage point, but she held up her hand, anyway, blindly obedient.

It was a grave mistake. He pulled her up, effortlessly, and plopped her down in front of him.

His horse startled nervously at the added weight, but there was no question that the dark prince was an excellent rider, controlling him with seemingly no effort.

Controlling her, and she didn't like it. Before she could squirm, protest, slide down, he'd moved forward, fast, the horse leaping ahead with restrained energy. The others followed, and any protest Elizabeth could have made was drowned out by the noise of the hooves on the dry road.

And the panicked racing of her heart.

3

This was not good, Adrian thought, keeping his head down to hide his doubts. There were few things he trusted in this chaotic life, but the strength and purity of Brother Peter's vocation was one of them. He knew little of the details, only that something in Peter's past made his need to atone all-consuming. It made no sense that he would flirt with danger like this.

In theory Peter's plan had been eminently practical. Prince William was a man with many enemies, not the least of which were the powerful Baron Neville of Harcourt and his well-trained men. His only daughter had died at the prince's hands, and while the king had done his best to help conceal his son's brutality, in the end William was forced to face the consequences of his behavior. That those consequences were relatively trivial—a journey of repentance, a large tithe at the Shrine of Saint Anne, and then freedom to return to his debauchery—did not sit well with Baron Neville. If Prince William were to reach the remote shrine alive it would require more than an armed guard. It would require strategy, as well. And fortunately the monks at Saint Andrews had among their fold an excellent strategist.

Once they reached their destination they would all be safe enough. Prince William would be shriven of his sins, and no one, not even a vengeful father, would be fool enough to murder a man in a state of grace, thus ensuring his swift ascent into heaven.

No, Neville would wait until William sinned again, knowing the wait would not be long. But by then the prince would no longer be the responsibility of the monks of Saint Andrews, and if he met his bloody fate it would be no more than he deserved.

Brother Peter would admonish him for his lack of charity, Adrian thought, insisting that even the most unregenerate of sinners could be saved. Even if in his heart he knew that William had been lost to the Devil long ago, and no amount of penitence and prayer could bring him back.

Adrian looked ahead to the tall, straight back of the man leading the caravan. Brother Peter had the woman up in front of him, an arrangement that would fail to concern the others. But Adrian knew him better than anyone, and he knew what a struggle would be warring in Brother Peter's heart.

He glanced back at the other monks, riding closely together except for Brother Matthew. He played his part well, Adrian thought critically. Anyone would be fooled by those chaste, downcast eyes and his sweet smile. Doubtless that was how he'd managed to get away with his wickedness for so long. All he'd need do was turn to his father, the king of England, and smile that dulcet smile, and all would be forgiven.

But not this time. And the only way to ensure that

he stayed alive long enough to atone for his many crimes was to have him travel incognito, in the garb of a simple monk, surrounded by brothers of the strictest order in all of England.

And up front, tall and strong and commanding, rode Brother Peter, a moving target for any assassin out to end the prince's life.

It had been Brother Peter's plan, and the abbot had agreed with its practicality, even if he loathed the necessity. Before joining the order Brother Peter had been a knight, a trained fighter, a soldier of the Holy Crusade. He was taller than most, stronger than most. In a righteous battle there would be few who could best him.

With Brother Peter leading the caravan, the devious, charming bastard prince of England would live to sin another day. Perhaps kill another innocent. The knowledge of which would weigh heavy on Brother Peter's soul.

But that innocent wouldn't be Baron Osbert's long-limbed daughter. Peter was making certain she was kept safe, as he'd pledged to protect all innocents. And it wouldn't concern Adrian at all, if he hadn't seen the look in Brother Peter's eyes as they rested on the tall, skinny young woman.

They said red hair was the sign of the Devil, but Adrian didn't believe in such nonsense. But looking at Elizabeth, he couldn't help but wonder how such a plain girl could entice a determined ascetic like Brother Peter when he'd shown no interest in far greater beauties who'd thrown themselves in his way.

Or perhaps it was simply that Brother Peter was and always had been a mystery.

Either way, he'd never betray his vows. For all the ways his eyes lingered on Lady Elizabeth when she wasn't looking, nothing would come of it. She would be delivered up to her convent, a bride of Christ. Prince William would be shriven, throw off his monk's robes and return to his life of sin. And Peter, Adrian and the others would return to Saint Andrews, away from the temptations of the great wide world.

They were but a few miles from the household of Thomas of Wakebryght, one day closer to the holy shrine of Saint Anne. God willing, they'd reach journey's end without disaster.

He could see nothing of Lady Elizabeth but the occasional flutter of her drab clothes or the occasional strand of devil-red hair. All would be well, he told himself.

But he was beginning to have a very bad feeling about this.

Elizabeth slept. She wouldn't have thought it humanly possible—the gait of the horse beneath her was smooth enough, but bouncing around the countryside was hardly conducive to slumber. And the solid body behind her, the warmth of his breath stirring her hair, the feel of his legs beneath hers, the rise and fall of his chest, his arms around her, holding her captive…

She couldn't bear to think of it. No man had touched her in three years, and that man had disillusioned her forever. The man holding her on this huge horse was far more dangerous. Lethal, in fact.

And still, she slept. When she woke it was growing dark, and every bone in her body was stiff and aching. She jerked awake as she realized where she was, and the horse beneath her startled, increasing her uneasiness.

The horse was brought under instant control with a brief murmur, and she remembered who held her. The dark prince, the Devil incarnate, with the mouth of a fallen angel.

"Be still," he said, and she stopped squirming, more afraid of the fall from such a huge horse than the man behind her. Perhaps.

"Where are we?" She sounded breathless. Absurd, when she'd been sound asleep.

"'Where are we, my lord William?'" the man behind her corrected her in a lazy voice.

"My lord William," she amended, silently adding, *my scum-sucking, hell-spawn lord William.*

"At our destination for the night. From now on we'll be sleeping in the forest, but tonight you'll be assured of a warm bed to ease your weariness."

"Who says I'm weary? My lord," she added hastily when she heard the sharpness in her own voice. The prince was not known for his tolerance, and he'd killed women before.

"You could barely stand. I'm expecting someone will end up carrying you to your bed." There was a faint undercurrent of amusement in his voice, one that increased her annoyance.

"Not you!" she said before she thought better of it.

She almost thought he laughed, but she couldn't twist in the saddle to see his face, and in the growing darkness it would most certainly reveal nothing.

"No, not me. I have servants who take care of menial details, such as carting argumentative women around."

She stiffened. "Then why am I riding in front of you? Wouldn't I be better off riding with a servant?"

"You're no tiny flower, Lady Elizabeth. My horse is the only one capable of holding you and another man. Besides, I am inclined to be generous toward all. Part of my penance."

She controlled her instinctive snort of derision, more afraid of startling the horse than annoying the rider. The man behind her was an enigma—she had no doubt he was a dangerous man, capable of violence. She had no doubt he was possessed of strong carnal appetites, strong enough that they even appeared to spill over onto a plain creature such as herself.

But he didn't strike her as a cold-blooded killer, one to lash out in rage and brutality. But the plain, ugly truth belied her own instincts, and if she wanted to make it to the Shrine of Saint Anne in good order she needed to curb her random tongue.

Leaving the prison of her father's house had lured her into thinking she had more freedom than in fact she truly had. She would be much better off reassuming the mantle of a faintly witless woman.

"Yes, my lord," she said in the slightly breathless voice she used with her father. "And you'll be truly shriven, by our Lady, and go on to live a life of peace and justice."

He was the one who snorted with laughter. "You think so?"

"But how else could it be, my lord? My father has told me so, and a good daughter knows the wisdom of her parents."

She wasn't expecting him to put his hands on her. He transferred the reins to one hand and took her chin in the other, turning her face up to his. It was too dark to see him, too dark for him to see the banked anger in her dulcet gaze. "And you're such a good daughter, Lady Elizabeth, are you not?" he said lightly. "A fine housekeeper, a dutiful child, with a gift for herbs and healing. You'll fit well into a convent, serving our Lady and keeping a still tongue in your head."

"A still tongue in my head?" she echoed nervously, still looking up at him.

"You're aware that Saint Anne's is a silent order? Devoted to meditation? Most days you won't be allowed to speak a word that isn't in Latin. You'd best get all your arguments out ahead of time."

She turned her head away from him, and he dropped his hand. In truth, the feel of his long fingers on her stubborn jaw had been almost as unnerving as the information he'd imparted. An order of silence? Where her only conversation would be the words of holy orders? She'd go mad.

And trust Baron Osbert not to have apprised her of

that fact. If he had even a particle of wit she'd suspect he'd done it on purpose, but her father hadn't the brains for such treachery. Besides, she kept her conversation to a minimum in his presence—he wouldn't think silence would be a particular burden. He tended to think all tongues should be stilled except his own.

It would have served him right if she'd poisoned him before she left. A miscalculation in his calming draft could do wonders.

She wouldn't have done it, of course. No matter how great the temptation, her gift with herbs and remedies was only to be used for good, not evil. Tampering with her father's carnal desires had saved the servant women, though unlikely as it was, some didn't appear to want to be saved. Tampering with his life would be unforgivable, and no journey of penance would wipe the stain from her soul.

She would deal with life as it happened. She had every intention of becoming abbess of the small order in record time—with her wit, learning and fierce determination she had little doubt she could do almost anything she wanted. She would find a way to relax the strict rules of the order. Or start talking to herself in her cell.

"I have no arguments, my lord William," she murmured in her best, placate-her-father voice.

He muttered something under his breath, and she almost thought he said "like hell," but she must have misheard. The wind had picked up, the warm spring day was growing cooler, and the ramparts of the small castle loomed ahead, looking ominously familiar.

It couldn't be. Thomas of Wakebryght's home was in the opposite direction of Saint Anne's Shrine. They would have had to spend the day traveling away from their destination in order to reach it, a detour that would make no sense.

No, many castles looked the same, built as they were to keep marauders at bay. And the shadows were growing long, making things hard to see. She'd only been at Wakebryght once in her life, on her betrothal day. The day her humiliation had been complete, and she'd sworn she'd never return.

"You might know this place," the prince continued, unmindful of the thoughts racing through her brain. "It belongs to a neighbor of your father's. Wakebryght Castle."

"No!" She couldn't help it, the word came out sharp and definite.

The man behind her seemed unfazed. "No?" he echoed. "I assure you, it's most definitely yes."

"Wakebryght Castle lies in the opposite direction of Saint Anne's Shrine."

"So it does. A little subterfuge for those watching who might wish to cause harm to the king's beloved son." There was a strange note in his voice. "No one will suspect us of doubling back. There's no need to fuss, Lady Elizabeth. One day more or less won't make a difference when the whole of your life stretches ahead of you, devoted to God and good works. And silence."

"I won't go."

He seemed unfazed by her flat refusal. "I did rather

doubt your vocation, but it's not for me to question a father's judgment. I suspect you'll cause the good abbess of Saint Anne more trouble than you're worth.''

''I mean I won't go to Wakebryght,'' she said flatly. ''I'd rather die.''

''My dear Lady Elizabeth, neither choice is yours. We're already here.''

They were at the front gate, and she could see the welcoming committee awaiting them. Including Thomas of Wakebryght's harridan of a mother, Lady Isobel. Her reaction was instinctive, unwise and immediate. She tried to jump off the horse.

She'd taken the prince unawares, but he was still too quick for her. One moment she'd seen the ground looming up from a great distance, in the next she was pulled back against his hard chest, clamped there by strong arms, so tightly she could barely breathe. ''Not wise, my lady,'' he murmured in her ear. ''Suicide is a mortal sin. Not to mention an overreaction. If you dislike your host so much you needn't worry. His wife was entering childbirth when we left yesterday— most likely he'll either be at her side or celebrating his new heir. The man is thoroughly besotted.''

She knew that, far too well. ''Please don't make me go,'' she whispered. ''I'd rather sleep in the forest. You don't even need to leave anyone with me to guard me—as you well know I'm not the kind of woman to tempt men into dangerous behavior.''

She didn't understand his sudden laugh. ''You'll sleep beneath Thomas of Wakebryght's roof, my lady. And if you give me any more arguments I'll have you tied to my bed.''

Not a pleasant proposition. Though if it made Thomas think she'd become the treacherous prince's leman, then he might wonder at his own rejection.

No, he wouldn't. As children they'd played together, betrothed in the cradle, good friends as they'd tumbled in the grass. But at age fourteen, when she'd been brought to marry him, he'd looked up into her green eyes as she towered over him and simply, flatly refused.

The bride gifts were returned. As was the bride, who traveled back to Bredon Castle in an uncomfortable cart, veiled to hide her shame, while Thomas of Wakebryght married his tiny, buxom, flaxen-haired cousin Margery.

And now she was back. ''I'd rather be fed to dragons,'' she said under her breath.

''Unfortunately there are none around. What have you got against Thomas of Wakebryght? Did he break your heart?''

She stiffened, saying nothing, but it was answer enough. She'd forgotten how unnaturally observant the dark prince was. ''Ah,'' he said. ''Well, you needn't worry about it. He's unlikely to even realize you're here. His wife's confinement has been quite difficult, and she's yet to be brought to bed with a living child. I imagine he'll be too busy worrying, celebrating or mourning to pay any attention to you.''

''God willing,'' she muttered.

''Then again, if he's mourning this might be your

chance. If his lady wife isn't up to the task of delivering an heir, perhaps she'll die in childbed and you can take her place. A happy ending for all.''

She looked up at him, but it was full dark by now and she could only see his silhouette against the night sky. ''That's a foul thought,'' she said fiercely. ''I would never wish misfortune to fall on an innocent.''

He said nothing, urging the horse forward into the brightly lit courtyard.

He was right—Thomas of Wakebryght was nowhere in sight. His mother, a sour-tempered shrew with an unlikely smile of welcome on her face, and Thomas's uncle Owen were the only ones welcoming them. There was no way they could miss seeing her, trapped as she was in Prince William's arms, but their eyes slid over her politely to settle on their exalted guest.

''You honor our household with your return, Prince William,'' Lady Isobel said in her cool voice. ''We had no idea we were to enjoy the pleasure of your company so soon. I regret that my son isn't here to greet you. His wife is still suffering greatly. I've sent word, however, and he should join us for dinner.''

''There's no need. Expectant fathers are extremely tedious.'' The prince slid off the horse with surprising grace, then reached up for her. For a moment Elizabeth hesitated. If she grabbed the reins and drove her knees into the horse's flank, he'd take off, carrying her away from this wretched place and the wretched man who'd held her and taunted her.

But that would require turning the horse, who'd

doubtless be in a panic, or else she'd simply ride deeper into the courtyard, and nothing would be accomplished...

She didn't have time to finish the thought. The prince put his strong hands on her waist and lifted her down, wresting her away from her grip on the saddle, her skirts flying up in an immodest fashion before he set her on the ground. He didn't release her—a good thing, since she still wasn't sure she could stand.

"You are already acquainted with Lady Elizabeth of Bredon, are you not?" he said smoothly.

Lady Isobel looked as if she'd seen a snake. "Of course," she murmured. "Welcome to Wakebryght." Her eyes went straight back to the prince. "I'm afraid we won't be very festive— I expect by the time you leave we'll be a house in mourning. Lady Margery is not expected to last the night."

"And the child?" Elizabeth asked.

Not a snake, a garden slug. "The child will die with her," she said. "There is nothing to be done."

Lady Margery and her unborn child would die, and Elizabeth would be there, to comfort Thomas, to aid an unwilling Lady Isobel, to perhaps change her life to what it should have been. All she had to do was remain silent.

She could feel the prince watching her, and she had the uneasy feeling that he knew everything that went through her mind. She lifted her head, looking down into Lady Isobel's hard, dark eyes.

"I have a gift for childbirth," she said flatly. "I've helped the women of Bredon through many a hard labor. Take me to Lady Margery and I will see if I can be of any assistance to her.''

It wasn't a request, but Lady Isobel looked as if she were about to refuse. Until the prince spoke.

''Take her to the poor lady,'' he said. ''I grow weary of arguing in a stableyard.'' And he gave Elizabeth an obnoxious little shove.

Peter watched Lady Elizabeth disappear into the depths of Wakebryght Castle, her slender shoulders squared beneath the veil of bright hair that cascaded down her back. He recognized that cool posture—it was the gait of someone marching into a battle they weren't convinced they wanted to win, but knew they had no choice but to try.

He knew, because he'd been in that very position too many times. Trapped in the midst of bloody battles for a land already awash in human suffering, and he was never sure for what. The desert was scorching and inhospitable, the wealth that had accumulated there of little value when measured against the lives of innocents.

A Holy Land, to be sure, but a Holy Land to all faiths. And he was no longer certain that his own God wished him to kill and plunder in order to wrest it from other poor souls who happened to follow a different God who, in the end, was not so unlike his own.

She would fight for Lady Margery and her unborn child, just as he'd fought for the Holy Lands. And she wouldn't find her sword red with the blood of those who didn't deserve to die.

The real prince was watching him with that faint, knowing smile on his pretty mouth, as if he could read Peter's thoughts. He was a dangerous man who'd been free to roam and ravage for far too long. For as long as he'd known him, William Fitzroy had been a vicious, dangerous man. The Crusades had suited him well—slaughter was his great pleasure—and life back in England must have paled without infidels to butcher. He'd had to turn to English innocents. It was simple enough to see how he'd managed to get away with it for so long. His enchanting smile tended to make women forget the brutalities he was capable of, and his knowledge of human nature made him far too wise when it came to getting what he wanted. William would know what plagued him. And knowing, William would use it as a weapon.

Which meant that Peter needed to redouble his efforts to keep Elizabeth away from him. To his knowledge William had never touched any but the most comely of women, but he wasn't fool enough to think that made Elizabeth of Bredon safe. She might not be a fragile beauty, but her very strength would be an affront to someone like William.

Adrian was watching him, a troubled expression on his face. In his own way he was just as knowing as Prince William—he could sense Peter's unexpected weakness.

It made little difference in the end. Peter had no choice but to protect Elizabeth, and if being near her brought up unexpected, long-dormant desires, then it was nothing more than fit punishment for his sins. The more he wanted her, the more painful her presence was, and he was a man who embraced pain as a means to salvation. He would welcome the torment of Lady Elizabeth's clever tongue, knowing he would never taste it.

In the end it wouldn't matter. In the end Brother Peter suspected he would pay the ultimate price, and it was up to his God to judge him. The sin he contemplated was far greater than the sin he was avoiding.

He was afraid he was going to have to kill Prince William. Cut his throat and let him drown in his own blood, rather than let him live to murder another innocent. There were too many women and children weighing on Peter's soul. If he had to give his up in order to save even one, then he would do it. If he must.

He would give him time to truly repent. There was always the chance that Prince William would attain a state of grace, though he doubted it would last long. Peter had killed before, so many times he'd lost count of the corpses that had lay at his feet. He'd killed innocents and villains, women and men, aging crones and young children. In war, death was impartial.

He would break his vow and kill the man he'd been charged with protecting, kill when he'd prayed never to kill again. He would do what he must to keep one more innocent from dying.

And God have mercy on his soul.

4

For the past three years Elizabeth had been unable to think of Margery of Chester, Thomas's chosen bride, without bitter feelings. Margery was everything she was not—small, plump, blond, docile, with a silvery laugh and an enchanting smile and the intellect of a dairy stool. Thomas had taken one look at her and forgotten his duty, his promises, his honor.

Not that Elizabeth would have wanted him against his will. But it still smarted, painfully, and while she was determined to do her Christian duty and help Margery through the dangerous journey of labor and delivery, she didn't have to like it or her.

There were no loud screams as the servant led her through the winding halls of the small castle to the room where Margery lay. Which was either a good sign or a bad one. Perhaps all was silent because the pain had lessened and things were progressing as they ought to.

More likely Lady Margery was probably too weak to make much noise. The servant pushed open the door and Elizabeth stood still, surveying the tableau. A fire was burning brightly, so that the room was miserably hot, and a crowd of people huddled around the bed so that the occupant couldn't be seen. There were at least of dozen of them, maybe more, including Thomas of Wakebryght, and they were arguing noisily over the bed. The smell of blood was ominous in the room. Perhaps it was already too late for mother and child.

And then the crowd parted, revealing Margery in the center of the huge bed. She was no longer the great beauty that Thomas had chosen. Her belly was swollen, her face tear-streaked, puffy and totally without color. The ankles protruding from her shift were swollen, as well, and her blond hair was a dark, tangled mess.

There was no blood on the shift or the bed, praise God. The man who was presumably the doctor was bleeding her, only making matters worse. Before the night was through the lady would be losing more blood, and she was so pale she didn't look as if she had much to spare.

"Get out of here!" Elizabeth said in her firmest voice. "The poor woman can't breathe, and all this noise must be driving her mad. One of the women can stay, but the rest of you must leave."

Thomas looked at her, his eyes shadowed from lack of sleep, and for a moment he didn't seem to recognize her. "I won't leave my wife," he said simply, turning back to Margery.

He was holding her hand, looking down at her pale, wretched figure with total adoration mixed with deep fear. He knew he might lose her, Elizabeth thought. It might already be too late.

But that didn't mean she wouldn't try. "This is women's work, Thomas," she said in the kind of voice her nurse used to use with her. "She wouldn't want you seeing her like this...."

"I don't care! She's beautiful to me no matter what!" he cried.

The beauteous Lady Margery looked like a sow in labor, miserable and bloated, and the last trace of bitterness vanished from Elizabeth's heart.

"Of course she is," she said in a kinder voice. "But you'll be in the way. Go and get something to eat, and take the rest of these people with you. I promise I'll send for you if...if you need to be here." Tact had never been her strong point, but she couldn't come right out and discuss the awful possibility that each childbirth brought.

For a moment Thomas didn't move. And then he brought his wife's pale hand to his mouth and kissed it, and Elizabeth could see the impressive ruby ring that had, for a few short hours, belonged to her. And then he set it back down on the bed.

"You'll save her for me, Bethy?" he said in a pleading voice. He was the only one who'd ever called her that, and she had actually found it quite annoying, but now she simply nodded.

"I'll do everything I can, Thomas. Just take these people out of here and let me work in peace."

"I'm staying, my lady," a stout, aproned woman announced in a forbidding voice. "She's been in my care since the day she was born and I'm not leaving her now."

"Have you any experience with childbirth?"

The woman laughed derisively. "Eleven of my own, all living, and I'm none the worse for it. And I've helped with countless others. If anyone can help my lady it'll be me."

"Let Berta help," one of the other women spoke in a measured voice. "She has more wits than the rest of the household women put together."

Elizabeth surveyed the woman who'd spoken. She was a stranger to her, a newcomer to the household since her aborted marriage, but judging by the fineness of her silken garments she was one of the family. Not in her first youth, and so beautiful she put Lady Margery, in her prime, to shame.

"She may stay," Elizabeth agreed. "And you, my lady. You seem to be possessed of calm good sense, as well."

The faint smile on the woman's beautiful mouth was faintly sorrowful. "You'd be the first to say so, Lady Elizabeth."

"I don't think my mother would approve...." Thomas began, but Elizabeth interrupted him, taking secret pleasure in her ability to order him about.

"Your mother's wishes in the matter have nothing to do with it. Between Berta and this lady we may just save your wife and child. But if we're to have any chance of it, the rest of you need to leave here. Immediately!"

They scampered away like mice, some clearly relieved, some disappointed at missing the high drama.

Thomas was the last to leave, and he stood in the open door, lingering.

Elizabeth went up to him, putting her hands on his arm and pushing him gently out the door. "I'll do my best, Thomas," she said. "Go and pray."

"Save her, Bethy," he whispered. "If it's a choice between her and the babe, save her. I can't live without her."

Elizabeth didn't blink. "We won't have to make such a choice, Thomas. Go." She closed the heavy door behind him, turning to survey the scene.

The room was bigger than it had appeared with all those people in it, but Margery lay pale and still in the bed, too weary to even cry out at the pain that was lashing her body.

"Open the window a bit, Berta," Elizabeth ordered, stripping off her cloak and rolling up the sleeves of her gown. "We need fresh air in this place. If she's cold we'll layer more covers on her."

She half expected the nurse to object, but Berta did her bidding without comment as Elizabeth approached the bed. "How long has she been like this?"

"In labor?" the well-dressed woman asked. "Two days. She stopped crying out this morning. I'm afraid the baby's dead."

Elizabeth put her hands on Margery's distended belly, and felt the flutter of life within. "It's not dead. I've seen worse than this and both mother and child survived." Not many, but she wasn't going to admit that. Her tiny army needed courage going into the battle.

"Then let us pray you'll work your magic this time, as well," the woman said.

"Not my magic. God's," Elizabeth said.

"That's right, you're on your way to becoming a nun," the woman said in a cool voice. "I'm Dame Joanna. I belong to Thomas's uncle Owen."

"He married?" Elizabeth murmured in surprise. Owen of Wakebryght was a rough, lecherous man in his fifties who'd shown no inclination to marry in all his years.

"I'm his leman, Lady Elizabeth," Joanna said calmly. "His whore. Would you rather I found someone else to help you?"

Elizabeth took a closer look at her. The dress was cut too close to her body, and jewels glittered on her hands and throat. She was well kept, very beautiful, with a distant look in her fine blue eyes that Elizabeth couldn't quite read. And couldn't waste the time trying.

"Take off your rings," she said, stripping her own modest ones off her hands. "We won't want them getting in the way of our work." She half expected the woman to blanch, but Joanna simply stripped off the heavy rings as if they were tin and dumped them in the small bag tied to her waist.

"Tell me what to do," she said, some of her distance vanishing. "I have a fondness for Lady Margery, and I'd as soon save her."

Elizabeth looked down at the still, wretched figure.

Margery had taken everything that should have been hers, but it hadn't been her choice, it had been Thomas's. And Elizabeth could have fought, but instead she'd simply run away, back to her father's wrath.

She might be too tall, too clever, too tactless, and have hair like the Devil, Elizabeth thought, but she could save lives. She'd seen five stepmothers give up their lives bringing sons into the world, and she was determined to learn what she could to save those she could. And she would save this one, and the child within her, if she had to die trying.

It was a long night. Endless, it seemed, after the day Elizabeth had already endured. Margery emerged from her exhausted torpor to scream in unrelenting pain, and the three women at her side fought grimly.

"You'll have to cut the baby free," Berta said at one point, her eyes dark with desperation. "She'll die, anyway, if you don't, and this way you might save the baby. Some women survive such an ordeal."

"Not many," Elizabeth said. "I'm saving them both."

"You said it was God's will, not yours, my lady," Berta admonished her.

"His will is that we fight for their lives and not give in," Elizabeth snapped back. "If you have nothing more to offer you may leave."

Berta subsided in silence. Joanna looked up at Elizabeth from across Margery's thrashing body, and her expression was faintly amused. "God explained that to you, did He?" she said.

Elizabeth was too weary to watch her tongue. "I assume that God has the good sense to think as I do in these matters."

She heard Berta's indrawn breath of shock at such blasphemy, but Joanna only smiled. "We can only pray that that is so, my lady. The God I know is capricious and cruel. He would not think twice of destroying the only happy marriage I've ever seen."

Not even a twinge, Elizabeth thought, marveling. It no longer mattered that Margery and Thomas were happy in their marriage. In truth, it made her only more determined that she shouldn't lose this battle.

She almost thought she'd lost. It was dawn, the early light spearing into the room, and she was so weary she could barely move. The babe was coming, face down, feet first, and there was nothing she could do to turn it. The movements were getting weaker, Lady Margery had barely life left in her, and there was no choice but to try.

"Push, Margery," Elizabeth ordered, but Margery simply shook her head, dazed with pain and exhaustion, not listening.

Joanna was holding tightly to her hands, Berta was at her feet, trying to help the baby, but the last of Margery's energy had left her, and if she didn't push there was no chance for either.

Elizabeth moved up to the top of the bed, bent down and whispered in Margery's ear. "If you don't deliver this babe and live I'll take Thomas back and make his life a living hell. I'm a vengeful woman, and I'll make him sorry he ever chose you."

Margery's eyes fluttered open to focus on Elizabeth's determined face. In her exhausted state she believed her, and she summoned her last ounce of strength, rising up in the bed, gripping Joanna's hands and pushing.

The scream that rent the air was awe-inspiring. Almost as much as the sound of a strong baby's cry that followed. Lady Margery was delivered of a healthy baby boy.

Elizabeth gave the babe a swift glance. He kicked his tiny legs, as strong a baby as she'd ever seen, even after such a hard, long labor. God willing, Margery would survive in as good condition. There was no way to tell if the baby had torn her inside, beyond repair, or whether she'd survive in the same miraculous manner her child had. They could only hope.

Joanna was busy cleaning her up with a calm efficiency that belied her beauty, and Berta was cooing at her new charge as she washed the blood from him. Elizabeth turned back to look at the new mother, and saw a faint blush of color had begun to tinge her deathly pale face. There were tears flowing from her closed eyes, another good sign, and her lips were moving in silent prayer.

Elizabeth leaned closer, to make certain she wasn't making her last confession or offering her soul up to God or some such nonsense, and her thick braid brushed against Lady Margery's face.

Her eyes flew open, swimming in tears, but there was no spectre of death in their depths. "You can't have either of them!" she whispered fiercely.

Elizabeth laughed, too tired to hide her feelings. "Your son and Thomas are yours with my blessing. Just stay strong enough to keep them." And then she left the room, closing the door behind her and collapsing against the thick stone wall, closing her eyes as weariness washed over her.

They would make her get on a horse in a matter of hours. Perhaps she could find an open window and jump from it. Anything was preferable to another day riding, with no sleep, no rest to smooth her way.

The hall was deserted. Maybe no one would know where to find her, and she could just slump to the floor and sleep. Sooner or later someone would come in search of her, but right now they were probably all too terrified to hear what they were certain would be tragic news.

She closed her eyes, sinking back against the cold, hard stone. She could sleep standing up, like a horse, if no one came to disturb her. Just a few moments...

The door beside her opened, and she jerked upright to face Dame Joanna's calm, beautiful face. "Let me take you away from here," Joanna said, surveying her. "You'll need to wash, and a few hours' sleep wouldn't come amiss. I'll tell them you're not to be disturbed."

"You'll tell Prince William? And you think he'll listen?"

Dame Joanna smiled. "I don't usually have trouble making men do what I want. Within reason. If need be I'll offer him up a few hours' distraction while you rest. Owen won't object—he's already shared me with lesser worthies."

"No!" Elizabeth said, horrified. "You don't have to do that."

"I have to do it every night, my lady. And your prince is very striking. He would be if he were just a stable boy."

"Not my prince!" Elizabeth corrected her, then realized how ridiculous that sounded. "And you wouldn't want to bed him. Perhaps you haven't heard, but he kills women for sport. During the act of love."

"No, he doesn't."

"I beg your pardon?"

"Your party spent the night here before they went on to Bredon, and I had a conversation with the prince. There are men who equate pleasure with pain, both in the giving and the taking, but he is not one of them."

"He told you so? And you chose to believe him?"

"He told me no such thing. You think a prince would confide in a whore? But I know men, my lady, far better than I would wish. Prince William is not the man people say he is."

Elizabeth shook her head. "That is always a possibility, I suppose. I really don't care to find out what kind of man he is."

"Don't you?" Joanna's voice was faintly disbelieving. "I know women, as well. Don't look at me like that, child. Concentrate on happier things. Such as how powerful you feel, having wrested Margery and her child from the grip of death."

"It was God's hand..." she began dutifully, but Joanna interrupted her.

"You and I both know it was your skill, and whether you choose to admit it or not, you're filled with triumph. The convent will be good for you, my lady. You'll be out of the reach of men's stratagems, and you'll learn to use your power."

"But I don't—"

"Don't bother trying to argue with me, Lady Elizabeth, you're too tired. You're a clever girl, but I'm a wise woman, and right now you're no match for me. Just come along and let me get you settled, and then I'll tell Lord Thomas he's a father. Unless you'd rather be the one who imparted that particular news? There's old business between you and the two of them, though the gossips at Wakebryght Castle haven't been as efficient as they usually are or I'd know all about it."

"It's not of much interest, even to gossips," Elizabeth said. "And I'd be happy never to see Thomas of Wakebryght again."

"Indeed," Joanna said in an approving voice. "Thomas is pretty enough in a pleasant manner, but he's nowhere near the man your prince is. I don't blame you for choosing danger over safety."

"I didn't make any choices! And he's not my prince!" Elizabeth said again, too loudly, ready to weep.

"But you'd like him to be, would you not? I know men, and I know women, and I think you'd gladly toss your habit to the four winds for him."

Elizabeth managed a rusty laugh. "You're mad. You've never even seen the two of us together."

Joanna pushed open a door set deep in the wall, holding it for Elizabeth to precede her. "I don't need to. I've seen him, and I've seen your reaction every time his name is mentioned. You'd quite happily bed the dark prince, wouldn't you?" she said.

"Would she?" Prince William asked, clearly curious.

He was seated by the fire in the luxuriously appointed room, and Thomas's uncle Owen was standing near the window. He was a heavyset man, and food stained his overly embellished tunic. He looked at the two of them in the doorway, and there was no missing the possessiveness in his small eyes as they roamed over Dame Joanna.

"Phaugh!" he said. "The two of you look like you've been to a hog butchering. I presume my niece is no longer on this earth. Are you planning to take her place, Lady Elizabeth, as you once longed to?"

If that was the first time the prince had heard of her previous connection to the household, he didn't seem surprised. "Didn't you hear your lady, Owen?" he asked lazily, stretching his long legs out in front of him. "It's me she wants."

Elizabeth was not amused. "Lady Margery was delivered of a healthy son."

"Praise be," Owen muttered piously. "Then maybe this household can get back to normal. If my lord will give me leave, I'll bring the happy word to the rest of the family."

Prince William waved a hand in airy dismissal, and Owen backed out of the room, a model of obsequiousness. He paused at the door, surveying his leman. "Go make yourself presentable," he said—an order, not a request. "I've no great liking to see my woman drenched in the blood of childbed. I'll join you as soon as our guests leave."

Dame Joanna inclined her elegant head. "As you wish, my lord." She bowed low, to both the prince and Elizabeth. "God speed, my lady. Prince William." There was no missing the trace of deviltry in her voice that almost overshadowed the bleakness that had settled over her perfect features once more.

And she left the two of them alone in the small bedroom.

5

"You're a pretty sight," the dark prince observed lazily. "You look almost as bloody as a soldier at the end of a long battle."

"I imagine I feel the same." She was so exhausted she could feel herself begin to sway. Prince William lounged lazily in a chair, and he hadn't asked her to sit. She should stay standing until he said otherwise. It didn't matter—she sat down on the wooden bench opposite him, silently daring him to object.

He smiled at her—totally irritating. "Feeling dangerous, are you, my lady? Is it the blood of Lady Margery? Shall I wish you happiness?"

"What?" She didn't care that she sounded stupid—her wits seemed to have vanished.

"Lady Margery took your place in this household, sending you back to the tender care of your father, according to the gossips. Your appearance here set their tongues free—until now I think you were fairly well forgotten. With Thomas's wife dead you can assume your rightful place and marry him."

"People have been far too busy informing you of my past." Her voice was cool and measured. "I would think you had more interesting ways of passing the time.''

"Not particularly. This household seems unreasonably devoid of attractive women apart from Dame Joanna, and besides, as you doubtless haven't forgotten, I'm on a journey of penance. Such occasions are not suited to lechery."

"You strike me as someone always suited to lechery." Again her unruly tongue betrayed her. "I beg pardon," she added swiftly.

"Oh, don't apologize," he said airily. "I find your candor quite refreshing. I'll miss it on the rest of the journey."

"Why do you keep assuming I'm staying here? Lady Margery has delivered a healthy baby boy, and she herself is strong and recovering rapidly. I don't doubt she'll go on to present Thomas with a dozen offspring before she's done."

"That shouldn't please you."

"Why not?" She stared down at her bloodstained gown. She was a mess, and she had brought no other clothes with her. Once she reached Saint Anne's she'd be wearing the clothes of the holy order, and there was no need to waste good cloth, her father had said. Her cast-off dresses would do for the servants. "I don't know what they told you—if it was Thomas's mother then she was doubtless unkind. She never liked me, and was well rid of me when Thomas changed his mind. In the end, it's all for the best. I am better suited for the convent."

He snorted with laughter. "I've yet to meet a lady

less suited to the convent, unless it's perhaps your new friend Dame Joanna. But you're right, it's for the best. The insipid Thomas would have bored you to tears in a matter of months, and I suspect you know it.''

She didn't bother to argue—one didn't argue with even a bastard prince of England. ''I expect to be very happy and useful in the convent. I hardly have Dame Joanna's…'' She struggled for the right phrase, unwilling to say anything unkind about the woman who'd worked so tirelessly by her side. ''I don't have… Dame Joanna is a very…''

''Dame Joanna is a leman,'' he said bluntly. ''A woman who survives on her back. She's also a woman who survives on her wits, and despite your attempts to prove otherwise, I do believe you're a very clever woman. Dangerously so.''

She leaned back against the wall, the cold stone reaching into her bones through the thin gown, but she was too weary to move.

''I don't feel particularly clever right now,'' she said. ''When do we leave this place?''

''When will you be ready?''

She glanced at him. ''I cannot believe it will be my choice. But if it were up to me, the sooner I'm gone from here the better.''

He nodded. ''You'll want to wash up and change those rags of yours.''

''I have no other rags to wear, my lord,'' she said.

''Then we'll find you some. I'm not traveling with a woman smelling of childbed blood. It could draw wild boars to our caravan, and we have enough danger to contend with without the added complication of marauding animals.''

''And what if I were…'' She stopped, horrified at what she'd almost said. If she weren't so tired she would never have brought up such a blunt subject.

''If you were having your monthly courses?'' he finished for her, unmoved. ''We'd find ways to deal with it. I believe you are blushing, Lady Elizabeth. You seem so matter-of-fact and practical—I'm surprised that a natural bodily function would leave you tongue-tied.''

''It's not something discussed with men,'' she said sharply. ''And I'm not! That is, the time isn't right….'' she added.

''You're snappish enough that you might be. I know more of women's bodies than you'd expect, my lady. I have an interest in medicine.''

She closed her eyes, settling against the cool stone. ''I have no doubt you're completely conversant with women's bodies, my lord William. I find the medical interest to be less likely.''

''Are you accusing your prince of lying?'' His voice was so mild she was forced to open her eyes, to ascertain whether or not she'd finally gone too far. If she'd said half the things to her father that she'd said to a bastard prince of England, she'd be whipped.

But Prince William looked unperturbed. ''There are a great many things about me that would surprise you.''

In for a penny, in for a pound, she thought. "I prefer not to discover them."

His smile was faint. "You really should watch your tongue, my lady. Most men are not so forbearing as I am, and I would hate to see you run afoul of someone inclined to brutality."

"As opposed to you?" The words were out before she could stop them, but she had the sense to quickly apologize. "I beg pardon, my lord. I'm too tired to realize what I'm saying."

"You're too tired to stop from speaking your mind, my lady. You still know exactly what you're saying. Shall we have Lady Isobel attend you, bring you one of her dresses?"

"No! She's half a foot shorter and a great deal rounder than I am. And she hates me—she'd probably drown me as I tried to wash myself. Any servant girl with reasonable height will do. She could probably get the blood out of my dress and use it for her own, and while worn, the cloth is quite fine. I oversaw the weaving of it."

"You have all sorts of hidden talents, my lady," he said. "But I think I won't travel with a lass dressed like a serving wench. It would be bad for my reputation. And no, you needn't point out that my reputation is beyond saving. Dame Joanna is of a fair height, though not so lanky as you, and while her hips are more generous than yours, you both seem equally well-equipped in the chest. Her clothes should do, and be more suitable."

She was beyond objecting at this casual appraisal

of her physical attributes. After a moment all she could manage was a faint protest. "Lord Owen ordered her to wait for him."

"I had the impression that Dame Joanna would be just as happy to be excused from whatever Owen of Wakebryght has in mind." He rose, looming over her, and a belated sense of propriety forced her to try to scramble to her feet.

It was a waste of time. He put one big, strong hand on her shoulder and pushed her back down on the bench. In the two days she had known him he had touched her more than any other man. His hand lingered on her shoulder for a moment, and she must have imagined the slight squeeze that was almost a surreptitious caress.

"Behave yourself, Lady Elizabeth. Prince William is not known for his patience. Watch your tongue when others are around, or you'll force me to do something I'd rather not do."

And what would that be? she thought, but she managed to keep silent. "Good girl," he murmured in an approving voice. And to her utter astonishment he leaned down and gave her a soft kiss on her lips. He was gone before she had time to react.

She touched her mouth. No one had kissed her mouth since Thomas had experimented, and she hadn't found his passionate attempts to be particularly stirring. Whereas Prince William's chaste salute...

No, his kiss was anything but chaste, despite its brevity and softness. For such a brief, offhand kiss it carried with it a wealth of suggestion, and Elizabeth could feel an odd tightness in her stomach. Lack of food, she told herself firmly. And if Prince William had no interest in the women of Wakebryght Castle, then he'd hardly deign to waste his energies on a sharp-tongued woman on her way to becoming a nun.

Still, it would have been reassuring if there'd been at least one other woman traveling to Saint Anne's with them. Someone to bear her company and keep her out of the prince's clutches. His interest in her made no sense—it was simply lack of anything else to occupy his mind, when in truth he should be thinking about the error of his ways. Perhaps Thomas's mother would be so overjoyed that she both had a grandson and that Elizabeth was leaving forever that she might spare a serving woman to accompany them.

She leaned back again and closed her eyes. She could still feel his hand on her shoulder. Still feel his mouth brushing against hers. Sweet Jesus, the sooner she was locked away in the chaste safety of the convent the happier she'd be.

She must have fallen asleep. The next thing she knew it was full daylight, her entire body was cold and stiff, and Dame Joanna had returned, freshly washed and coiffed herself, carrying an armload of rich clothing. "I've had them fill a bath for you, my lady," she said. "Your prince requested I bring you something to wear, but most of my garments are unsuitable for an innocent such as yourself. Neither are they particularly useful for long journeys on horseback, but I've done what I can." She tossed the armload of clothes onto the table, then turned to face Elizabeth.

Once more Elizabeth was stunned by her beauty. Dame Joanna was possibly a full ten years older than she was, with a mature, elegant body and a sad, wise smile that didn't quite reach her beautiful blue eyes. Her hair was a golden blond, rippling down her back beneath her simple headdress, and her cheeks and lips were touched with a color at odds with her pale, unblemished skin. She smiled, and even her teeth were perfect. "You look half asleep," she observed. "The prince wishes to leave by midday, and the monks are already grumbling about the delay. That gives you an hour. If it's not enough, I can tell them you're unwell."

"And then they'd leave without me. Abandon me here with Lady Isobel." Elizabeth couldn't control her shudder. "She hates me."

"She's never been overly fond of me, either. Lucky for her I'm to accompany you to Saint Anne's."

Elizabeth jerked her head so abruptly that she slammed it against the hard stone wall. She rose, rubbing her scalp. "You are?"

"Prince William decided you needed another female along to keep you company. I'm to spend two months at the convent, repenting of my sins, and then return to start sinning once more." She shrugged, seemingly untouched by it all. "I'm just as happy to get away from Owen for a bit. He's fast and rough and far too demanding. A brief respite from the needs of men would be a blessing."

For a moment Elizabeth was unsure what she should say. The company of another woman was a gift she hadn't dared hope for, and from the moment she met Dame Joanna she'd felt an odd kinship with her. Nevertheless, she couldn't subject anyone to the dangers of the notorious Dark Prince. At least Owen of Wakebryght had never killed a woman. "Are you certain there would be no...new demands from our escort?" she asked.

Joanna moved behind her and began helping her pull off the bloodstained gown. "I confess it was my first thought, and warming Prince William's bed would be less of a chore than most, despite the danger. He's a very handsome man."

"He's killed two women. At least."

Joanna shrugged. "There are worse ways to die," she said philosophically. "But in truth, Prince William has no interest in me as a lover, nor is he bringing me for the other men, if I am to believe what he said. And oddly enough, I do. I'm there for your sake and nothing else."

"I find that difficult to believe," Elizabeth muttered as she pulled off the plain worsted dress that was little better than a servant's garb. "I've yet to meet anyone who cared about my well-being. Besides, I've been doing my best to keep out of his way. He's the one who keeps appearing wherever I am."

Dame Joanna laughed softly. "I think it makes perfect sense. You're very young, aren't you? You'll understand when you're older. Though if you're immured in a convent perhaps you might never need to learn.''

She helped slip the gown off Elizabeth's shoulders, so that she stood there only in her plain linen chemise. ''Your father did dress you like a serving maid, didn't he?'' she said. ''I think you'll find my chemise a little more to your liking. The fabrics are very fine.''

''I shouldn't be taking your clothes,'' she protested as Joanna herded her toward an adjoining room and the tub filled with steaming, scented water.

''I have more than I need, and I can easily acquire anything I want. Besides, in truth I have little need of clothing in my chosen profession. Don't blush, little one,'' she added in amusement, stripping the shift over her head so that she stood naked by the tub. ''It's the way of the world.''

Growing up in a household of brothers, Elizabeth was unused to having people see her nude body. She practically leapt into the tub, splashing water onto the floor and the hem of Joanna's dress as she quickly sank up to her shoulders in the blessed warmth. ''You can't call me little one,'' she said after a minute. ''I'm taller than you are.''

''You're taller than everyone.'' The words were matter-of-fact, devoid of insult. ''But in many ways you're still a child.''

Elizabeth resisted the impulse to argue. The warmth of the water was too soothing to her aching muscles, and she liked Joanna. ''Older and wiser than you think,'' she said, ducking her head under water and letting her long, thick hair swirl around her.

"So very old and wise," Joanna said softly when she emerged. "Fortunately you'll be out of harm's way soon enough, so I won't have to enlighten you as to the true nature of most men. And in the meantime Prince William has made certain that you'll have the best possible protection."

"Prince William has no interest in protecting me. No interest in me at all," she protested. There were dried rose petals floating in the water, perfuming the air.

"And we'll keep you believing that as long as possible," Joanna said. "Would you like a serving girl to help you with your hair?"

Elizabeth remembered the contemptuous maids of Wakebryght Castle far too well. They'd clearly deemed her unworthy of their lord, and in the end he'd agreed. No, she didn't want any of them coming around her, mocking her.

"I'm used to dealing with it myself," she said. "I prefer privacy."

"In that case I'll await you in the other room. The maids are busy enough packing clothes for my journey. I suspect when I return some of my favorite pieces will be missing. It will give Owen the perfect chance to buy me more."

"He likes spending money on you?" Elizabeth asked. Her father had always bemoaned even a farthing spent on his wives or lemans.

"When he spends money on me he knows he can expect something in return. It gives him a way to win my gratitude, and he always takes full advantage of it.''

"I don't understand. Aren't you obliged to do what he tells you to do, anyway?'' she asked, unable to hide her curiosity. It was one of her besetting sins— one she would no longer be able to indulge in a convent.

"Up to a point. But there are certain things a man like Owen of Wakebryght enjoys that I can refuse. I'm a courtesan, not a whore. If he wants to do something painful or degrading he has to pay for it.'' ·

"But wouldn't that make you a whore?'' Elizabeth said, confused. And then realized the severity of what she'd said. "I beg your pardon, I shouldn't have…''

"Out of the mouths of babes,'' Joanna murmured. "You're right. In the end that's what I am. I simply have more say in whom I bed and what acts I perform. And I do it on linen sheets, not in a stableyard.''

Elizabeth cursed her unruly tongue. "I'm sorry.''

"Don't be. You'll be spared such an existence. And it's not without its benefits. I dress well, eat well, sleep well when I'm left alone. It's better than being locked in a convent.''

"I think I'd prefer being locked in a dungeon to spending time in Owen of Wakebryght's bed,'' she said with a shudder.

"Then be glad you're spared. You only have a few short days before you're locked behind those safe walls, and if we can keep you away from the prince all should be well.''

"The prince has no designs on me!'' Elizabeth protested for what seemed the hundredth time. "He just wants to finish his pilgrimage, get rid of me and the monks, and go back to his life of debauchery."

"If you say so, my lady," Joanna said softly. And she closed the door behind her.

6

It took Elizabeth longer to dress in the unfamiliar clothes than she had ever taken in her entire life, something she attributed to lack of sleep and physical exhaustion. She'd spent the previous day bouncing around on a horse, the previous night wrestling for Lady Margery's life, and she was facing another day of grueling travel. It was no wonder she stood and stared at herself in the wavering reflection of the looking glass, too dazed to decide what to do about Dame Joanna's dress.

It was made of rich green cloth, and brought the green out in her eyes. Her flame-red hair looked blessedly dark when wet, and she'd plaited it in two tight braids, then had to loosen them as the pain in her head increased. The second time she simply twined the damp hair into one thick braid and tossed it over her shoulder. It hung past her waist—in the convent they would cut it off, wouldn't they? She'd always hated it—it would be a blessing to be shorn.

But even with the demon hair darkened by water and tamed behind her back, there was still the problem of Dame Joanna's dress. It was a bit too snug in the chest, a fact that Elizabeth found deeply disturbing, since Dame Joanna's bountiful breasts were far too noticeable. If Elizabeth were even more generously endowed, it could garner the wrong sort of attention.

The fine cloth swirled around her long legs. The soft linen undergarments caressed her skin, and for a brief moment she stared at her reflection and imagined what it would be like to be a beauty. To spend her nights in the bed of a man who worshipped her.

She shook her head, her long plait whipping around, and common sense returned. All the fine clothes in the world wouldn't make her anything but what she was. A plain young woman unsuited for the world. Too smart, too outspoken, too impatient, too tall for the likes of men.

The dress exposed far too much of her chest, but her lack of hips made it hang down enough to cover her long legs. That was another failing, of course, as her father had often told her. Women needed broad hips for childbearing. But Elizabeth would be bearing no children, and after a night spent listening to Margery's full-throated screams she could only bless that fact. No matter that the arrival of Thomas's red-faced, squalling heir had brought her to unexpected tears. The arrival of a child always affected her that way— a bittersweet joy that was more powerful than anything else she'd ever experienced.

That was one reason she'd become proficient in serving at childbed, learning from the midwives at Bredon Castle. If she couldn't have children herself, and she was illogically fond of them no matter how annoying they could be, then she could at least assist in their delivery. Besides, she had little interest in easing the suffering of mankind—most of their ills were well deserved. But women needed all the help they could get.

After all, the child had come from an act that only men enjoyed. And while the mother would find joy and pleasure in the love of her children, in the meantime she had to put up with some huge, sweaty man invading her body, then months of discomfort as she grew larger and larger, followed by excruciating pain and more often than not, a bloody death. All for the sake of a man's pleasure.

There were ways to avoid conception, of course. She'd learned that from the midwives as well, secrets passed among women. If the church knew of such things it would be to court eternal damnation.

But the church was run by men. And if the good sisters at Saint Anne's were ignorant of such precautions then it made no difference.

Perhaps she'd still find ways to put her healing talents to work once she joined the holy sisters. Most orders divided their time in meditation and good works, and Saint Anne's was bound to include healers. With luck Elizabeth could continue on as before, bringing children into the world, without having to answer to her father or any overbearing man. And no man would ever have the right to force himself upon her in the name of marriage or any other excuse.

Bedding Thomas of Wakebryght wouldn't have been so horrible. He was handsome, kind and gentle, and so lacking in imagination that the act would be over quickly. And in the end there'd be children.

But that was no longer her lot in life, and if she had any sense she'd rejoice in the release from such carnal duty, rather than bemoan the loss of home and children.

Though if Thomas saw her in this green dress he might start to regret his rash decision. Lady Margery was none too pretty at the moment, with her swollen eyes and pale face. And Thomas had always had a weakness for pretty women.

She turned away from her troubling reflection. There was no question that she looked the best she ever had, despite lack of sleep. Perhaps if her father had seen fit to clothe her decently she might have found a husband. Be married to some coarse baron who spent his passion on her body and then left her in peace.

No, that wasn't what she wanted. She was happy with her future, and even the rest of the journey seemed less daunting with Dame Joanna for company. No one would look twice at her with the sublime Joanna at her side. Not even the dark prince with his deep, brooding eyes.

She glanced around the room for her cloak, but she'd left it in Lady Margery's bower. She would go fetch it herself, rather than send a servant. It would set her mind at ease to check on Lady Margery one last time, and to ensure the babe was thriving. And if she ran into Thomas at the same time, and he looked at her in her inappropriate, beautiful dress and found himself regretting his rash decision three years ago, then so much the better.

She glanced out the window before she left the room. The men gathered in the courtyard were her recent companions—she could see the angelic Brother Matthew among them, sitting on his fine horse a few paces away from everyone else. His head was down, and she couldn't see his expression, but she could well imagine it. The sweetness of his smile, at odds with Prince William's faint mockery. The gentleness in his soft hands as he held the reins.

Elizabeth gave herself a little shake as she turned away. Leaving her father's house had surely addled her wits. She was a woman who knew what she wanted in life to make her happy, and to be distracted by memories of Thomas and new thoughts of saintly Brother Matthew was not part of her plan.

Though both were preferable to the memory of Prince William's mouth brushing against hers.

He'd kissed her twice in as many days. The first on her brow, the second on her lips. If things continued as they had been, she'd be horrified to see where his next kiss landed. Or whether it would be nearly as chaste as the first two.

And she was making a fuss over nothing. Prince William was a devil—he'd only kissed her to disturb her, and he'd succeeded full well in doing so. In the future, though, he'd doubtless find distraction with Dame Joanna far more appealing, even if he truly planned to spend the journey in celibate penitence. After this morning, he would barely notice Elizabeth of Bredon, and she could breathe a sigh of relief. Surely she could.

She had to ask for directions back to Lady Margery—when Joanna had first brought her away she'd been too tired to pay attention to her path. The door was closed to keep in the heat, and she pushed it open without knocking, secure in the knowledge that Lady Margery had no secrets from her erstwhile midwife.

She stopped just inside the room, in shock. Thomas of Wakebryght lay curled up beside Lady Margery, holding her hand, looking at her pale, bloated face with such unquestioning adoration that it was painful to see. The wet nurse sat in the corner with the young heir, coaxing him into feeding, but Thomas had no eyes for anyone but his decidedly unpretty wife, and all Elizabeth could do was stare in astonishment.

He must have felt her eyes on them, for he looked up, and a beatific smile swept across his handsome face, a face she'd once thought she'd die for. Now she realized that his chin was a bit weak, his nose too pretty, and his brow without resolution. She would have led him a merry dance if he hadn't abandoned her for his wife.

He jumped off the bed and rushed over to her, and she braced herself, not sure what she was expecting. Certainly not his powerful embrace.

"Bless you, Bethy," he said in her ear, his voice thick with unshed tears. "You've given me my life."

She pushed him away, gently, and if he saw the pretty dress that hugged her curves he didn't take notice. He was already looking back at Lady Margery's peacefully sleeping body. So much for Thomas's regrets, she thought ruefully.

"You're a lucky man, Thomas," she said in a calm voice. "She fought well for you and your child. You chose wisely."

He didn't even seem to understand her reference. He simply smiled at her in an absent fashion before moving back to the bed. "My whole family blesses you, Bethy," he said.

"Even your mother?" she asked rashly.

"Even my mother," Thomas said, climbing back on the high bed, moving so carefully he didn't disturb his sleeping wife. "It was nothing personal, you realize. She just knew she'd have a hard time keeping you in order. Margery is a great deal more docile, and we let Mother do as she pleases."

"No one could have ever said I was docile," Elizabeth conceded. Looking at the entwined couple should have pained her, but instead she merely felt resigned. At that moment the baby cried, and she moved toward it, looking at his red little face. Reaching out a finger to touch the tiny little hand.

"I hope you do well at Saint Anne's," Thomas said doubtfully. "I expect you'll learn to be properly demure once you're there."

It sounded like a sentence of death. "I expect so," she said absently, then turned away from the baby who should have been hers, away from the couple entwined on the bed. Her cloak lay draped across the table by the window, and she picked it up, pulling it around her shoulders and hiding her newfound curves.

She was more herself now, plain, tall Elizabeth, on her way to her new life. "God keep you all," she said in a steady voice.

"And you," Thomas said, but he'd already dismissed her from his mind. And she closed the door silently behind her.

Dame Joanna stepped out into the morning-bright courtyard, breathing in the fresh air. When she was a child she'd loved being outside—it was all her nurse could do to keep her charge in bed at night. It wasn't that Joanna of Kimbrough had been a headstrong or willful child. She'd been a loving, dutiful daughter, a good sister, and had viewed her future as a good wife and mother with calm pleasure.

But the woods called to her, at all hours, and for some reason she could never resist their silent lure. No matter how hard her nurse beat her, no matter how her mother wept, no matter how determined she was to ignore its siren call. Each time she stepped outside, she disappeared into the peace and stillness of the dark woods.

They'd married her off as soon as they could—a child of thirteen with no more knowledge of men than she had of alchemy. Her first husband was much older, and gentle with his child bride. He'd been more interested in companionship than sex, and when he died she'd truly grieved. Not knowing what was in store for her.

Her second husband was a brute. Cruel enough to make even Owen of Wakebryght seem like a thoughtful lover. Harald was rough, hurtful, and had no interest in the begetting of heirs—he had innumerable sons, and he was far more interested in habits he'd picked up while on Crusade in the Holy Lands. Joanna had never met a man less suited to Christian acts—he took pleasure from inflicting pain, and he enjoyed sharing his wife and watching as other men used her.

She sometimes thought that if he hadn't died she might have killed him herself.

Twice she'd been a second wife without issue, and therefore had taken nothing from the marriages, not even security. Her parents were long dead, their estate passing to distant kin. Since then she'd moved from man to man, though there'd been no more marriages. She had been unable to give either husband children, therefore she was of no use as a wife. As a leman, however, she was compliant, warm and an object of physical beauty, or so men always insisted. There were worse ways to survive in this world, she always told herself. Better than the streets.

But she would cherish the next few weeks of privacy and solitude. If the Sisters of Saint Anne were kindly enough, she might decide to join, as well. She had enough money secreted away to pay her dowry, and she truly liked Elizabeth of Bredon. At least there'd be someone she could talk to, unlike the household at Castle Wakebryght. Even Thomas was no more than a pretty dullard, and Owen had recently grown more demanding.

No, a period of rest and reflection would do wonders for her peace of mind. And if Owen found celibacy not to his liking and decided to replace her, then so be it. The thought of a life without men pawing at her seemed like heaven on earth.

No one in the household seemed interested in seeing her off. She'd left Owen naked and snoring, a happy man for at least the time being. At the last minute she'd taken all of her meager jewelry and wrapped it in a linen fold and tucked it in the embroidered bag that hung from the waist of her gown. That way there would be no need to return if she didn't want to. The proceeds from the paltry gems wouldn't last her long—her lovers were not inclined to be that generous—but it would give her time to think. And perhaps the abbess of Saint Anne had a tender heart for a fallen woman.

She could see Lady Elizabeth at the far end of the courtyard, as alone as she was. She had her plain brown cloak pulled tightly around her, but Joanna could see the rich green of her own dress beneath the hem. Joanna had chosen it on purpose, wondering what the girl would look like if she were decently dressed. Lady Elizabeth had beautiful eyes, wickedly lustrous hair, and the kind of mouth that made a man think of sin. She'd managed to avoid that kind of attention so far, by the grace of God, and Joanna would be doing her no favors by lending her pretty dresses and showing her how to wear her wicked hair. She was headed for a convent, and the only alternative seemed to be the wandering eye of the dangerous prince of England.

And he was a dangerous man, Joanna had no doubt about that. A man who had killed before, and would kill again.

But for some reason the prince didn't strike her as a despoiler of innocents, or the murderer of young girls, no matter what she'd been told. Despite the rumors, he struck her as someone who knew how to love a woman. How to give pleasure in an act that wasn't designed for a woman's joy, if such a thing were even possible.

She wanted to do what she could to keep Elizabeth safe. But Joanna had survived on her wits and on her back, and for the next week she would be in the company of a man who wielded a great deal of power in England. He had no interest in her—Joanna could tell such things with absolute certainty, just as she could see his hidden fascination with Elizabeth of Bredon. If she had any sense at all she would throw them together, no matter what the cost. If she were to deliver a much desired innocent to the bed of the only son of Britain's monarch, gratitude would follow, and the gratitude of a wealthy and powerful man was not something to be tossed aside. It would be a boon to have a friend at court.

The idea of delivering Elizabeth up to the hungry beast was intrinsically abhorrent. A life lived entirely without sex was not a bad thing, and in the few hours she'd spent with Elizabeth she'd found much to like and respect. She'd fought hard for the life of a woman who'd supplanted her, and triumphed.

But there was no changing the way the world

worked. Joanna had had to put up with it—there was no reason why the cherished daughter of a baron should be able to escape. Sex was a woman's burden and a man's pleasure, and it was only a few lucky women who could escape it. And the possible rewards of handing Elizabeth over were too great to dismiss.

The convent would still take her, once the prince was finished with her. They might demand recompense for damaged goods, but that would be no problem. From what she had heard, it was clear that Prince William was constantly being delivered from the results of his lechery by a doting father and the treasury of England. It was only when he'd gone so far as to kill someone that he'd had to inconvenience himself long enough to pay penance.

No, someone would be around to pay off the good sisters and quiet any complaints Elizabeth of Bredon might make.

And in the meantime, Joanna would have gained something in power.

She would do what she had to do. Or at least she would try. Despite the rumors, she had no doubt that the prince was not the savage lover he was deemed to be. And perhaps life didn't have to be as bleak for everyone.

She would wait and see. In truth, despite her worst, most selfish intentions, she probably wouldn't be able to go through with such a ruthless plan. Most likely she could no more sacrifice an innocent for her own gain than she could become innocent herself once more. She might not even try. And with any luck

Lady Elizabeth would reach the shrine in as pure a state as she set out.

The wind was cool and damp, swirling around her heavy cloak, and Elizabeth pulled it tighter about her, cursing the gown she wore beneath it. She'd had little choice, but at that moment she was regretting not putting up more of a fuss. Surely Lady Margery would have had a plain gown that would have been more suitable to a future nun. Granted, Margery was a tiny little thing, but in retrospect it was far preferable to expose too much leg than too much breast. Particularly since her overlong legs were a major contributor to her general plainness.

The courtyard was filled with activity—Prince William's knightly escort was already mounted, and the monks were in a huddle, all but Brother Matthew. The gentle monk stood off to one side, head bowed low. She could see his lips moving in silent prayer, and her instinctive start toward him was halted. She wasn't sure why she thought he'd be any particular protection against the prince—she wasn't sure why she thought anyone would be much help. She could see Dame Joanna across the courtyard, her shoulders thrown back, her rich blond hair tumbling down her back, wearing her bright colors without shame. In the cold light of day Elizabeth was no longer so certain Joanna's companionship would do any good, either. She drew the eyes of every man present, with the exception of the devout Brother Matthew, and if Elizabeth were to stay by her side, that attention could possibly spill over onto her own narrow shoulders.

She looked around for her mount. There was no way she would ride with Prince William again—she'd die before she'd admit weariness, she'd throw herself off a cliff rather than have him put his hands on her. Not that his hands had been cruel, or even demanding. Nevertheless they disturbed her so deeply that the very thought of coming in reach again was more than she could bear.

And then Brother Adrian appeared, and she could have wept with gratitude. He was accompanied by a covered cart, pulled by four strong horses. The cart would be bouncy and uncomfortable, but she didn't care if her bones rattled apart. At least she wouldn't have to climb back onto a horse. Or have Prince William hold her against his strong body.

By the time Adrian had reached her Joanna had joined her. "That's the most miserably uncomfortable cart," she observed calmly. "I've ridden in it before. I'm not surprised Thomas was willing to part with it. It's an instrument of torture after a few hours. We'd be better off on horseback."

Before Elizabeth could protest Brother Adrian spoke. "His Highness prefers you both use the cart." He kept his gaze on the ground.

"Why?" Joanna asked. "It will slow you down."

The very question Elizabeth had wanted to ask but didn't dare, for fear they'd change their minds and put her back on a horse.

"Prince William is on a journey of penance, and

the sight of women could be dangerous to his immortal soul,'' Brother Adrian replied, staring at his
feet. ''It's better if you ride behind the curtains.''

''I think his immortal soul has already been com-
promised,'' Elizabeth murmured. ''If someone wants
to transport me, who am I to complain? We'll distract
each other, Dame Joanna, from our aches and pains.
We can share our life stories.''

Brother Adrian made a choking noise, and his head
jerked up to look at Dame Joanna. ''Don't worry,
Brother,'' Elizabeth said with a soft laugh. ''I imagine
she'll skip all the good parts.''

Brother Adrian didn't move, didn't even seem to
be listening. He simply stared into Dame Joanna's
calm blue eyes. And then he turned and left them
without another word, practically tripping over his
robes in his haste to escape.

''She shouldn't be here,'' Adrian said flatly.

Peter turned to look at him. They were well ahead
of the caravan, which was moving with agonizing
slowness now that they'd added a carriage to their
group, and no one could overhear them. ''Why not?''
he said, knowing full well that Adrian was right.
Adrian saw things far too clearly, and Peter was humble enough to listen.

''It's too dangerous. She's temptation itself, and
you can't deny it. A man has only to look at her and
think of carnal pleasure. It's going to make our task
that much harder.''

Peter sighed. ''You're right, of course. Though I'm

surprised you noticed. I thought saintly Brother Adrian was above temptation.''

''I'm only saintly Brother Adrian until we reach the shrine, and then I'm back to being a simple knight. Saint Paul himself would not be above temptation with her,'' he said gloomily. ''I'm surprised you're immune. Her mouth is…bewitching, and you know it.''

Peter closed his eyes for a brief moment, remembering the taste of that mouth. He'd never tasted such innocence. Such warmth. ''Indeed.'' He cast a glance at his young companion, aware of a strange emotion. One might almost call it jealousy. Foolish, of course. Adrian had every right to fancy a young girl—his vow of celibacy was all part of their masquerade. ''We'll be rid of her within the week, Adrian. And while she's quite lovely, she's not likely to do anything about it.''

''That's what you think,'' he said in a morose voice.

The spark of jealousy began to sizzle. ''You must have imagined it. She has no interest in you or any poor monk.''

''I know. Which makes it even more ridiculous. I suppose I could always tell her the truth….''

''You've given your oath, Adrian. No one is to know who the three of us are, or this sham will all be in vain. You wouldn't want to break your vow, would you? Beautiful green eyes are not worth the risk.''

"Her eyes are blue," Adrian said glumly. "Lady Elizabeth's eyes are green."

Peter turned to look at him. "Are you talking about Dame Joanna?"

"Of course. Who else? Lady Elizabeth is hardly the kind of woman to lure a man from his holy vows. She's well-suited to the convent."

"You think so?" Peter murmured. He glanced back at the carriage as it lumbered through the woods at a snail's pace. The curtains swayed, but there was no sign of the women. Adrian's temptress was safely out of sight. As was Peter's far-less-likely one.

But out of sight was not good enough. He could still see the startled expression on her pale face when he'd kissed her lips, and it had taken all his iron determination not to pull her against him, bloody gown and all, and show her what a real kiss was.

She didn't need to know. He didn't need to remember. All he needed to remember was his duty, and what might lay at the end of it. Mortal sin, committed for the sake of the innocent. A fitting price for a man such as he to pay, and it would make no difference. All the penitence in the world wouldn't keep him from the fires of hell. They'd even followed his footsteps on earth.

The sin of murder would make little difference to his eventual fate.

But what would the sin of fornication do? Make the flames hotter? Send him there sooner?

Or simply make his time on earth more unbearable, as he'd know he'd destroyed one more innocent's life?

Death was his destiny. Murder, not love. And he would follow the path laid out for him with single-minded devotion. If the sight of Lady Elizabeth added to his pain, then it was nothing less than he deserved. He would keep her safe. He would kill Prince William if he must, once he was out of his protection.

And then he would take his own life, before he could destroy anyone else.

7

Elizabeth woke with a start. She'd been dreaming, a terrible dream that the earth was falling apart, splitting into crevasses, and she was falling, falling into the darkness, into the steep black night. A hand was reaching out to her, not from the top to pull her back to safety, but out of the pitch black, luring her downward into destruction. She kicked out, trying to escape, and was rewarded with a muffled oath.

It was dark, warm, scented with a rich, spicy scent, and for a brief moment her panic increased, until Joanna's steady voice calmed her. "Are you all right, my lady?"

"Did I kick you? I'm sorry. How long have I slept?" Elizabeth asked.

"The entire day. Fortunately I slept most of the time, as well—we had a busy night with Lady Margery. We stopped to eat but I couldn't rouse you, and the prince told me to let you be. He seems very concerned with your welfare."

Elizabeth resisted the urge to snort. The last thing she wanted was another occasion of falling into the prince's arms, so she moved carefully, sticking her long legs out from the curtains and sliding down on the ground, holding the carriage securely so her legs wouldn't buckle. It was near dusk, though the night was warm, and the caravan had separated. The armed guard in one group, building fires, dealing with their horses, and the monks in another, doing nothing much at all. And Prince William was nowhere to be seen.

Her eyes fell on Brother Matthew, and she started toward him. He could provide protection, spiritual comfort, and the undeniable pleasure of his sweet smile, and he'd keep danger far away. She walked slowly, relieved to find her legs steady enough beneath her, despite her stiffness.

Brother Matthew was sitting on the ground, off a ways from the other monks as they worked, his head bowed in prayer. Elizabeth hesitated, loath to interrupt, when he raised his head and looked directly at her, almost as if he'd known of her approach, and his half smile was welcoming as he climbed to his feet.

"You do me honor, my lady," he said softly, taking her hand in his soft, cold one.

"I don't want to disturb you," she protested. She wasn't used to people touching her, and she wanted to pull her hand free. Silly, because the one man who did touch her was Bredon's priest, Father Bennett, and she'd always felt quite comfortable when he would hold her hand.

But Father Bennett was old, and saintly, while Brother Matthew was young. Saintly, too, perhaps, but she pulled her hand away nevertheless, and he let her go with only a faint reluctance.

"You're no disturbance at all," he said. "I'd just

finished my devotions. I wish I could offer you a suitable seat...."

"Sweet Mary, I don't want to sit!" Elizabeth moaned, then realized her choice of words was not the best. "I've been sitting all day," she added.

"Then will you walk with me? It's not yet dark and it will be a while before we eat."

Elizabeth cast a nervous glance over her shoulder. The prince was nowhere in sight, but Dame Joanna was standing by the carriage, alone, looking at her with a troubled frown.

"Perhaps Dame Joanna would like to accompany us," Elizabeth suggested, suddenly guilty at abandoning her.

"Dame Joanna is no fit company for a child such as you, my lady," Brother Matthew said in a low voice. "It grieves me to say so, but you're better off in my company than in hers. She's a Magdalene, born of sin." He didn't take her hand again, but somehow she felt herself guided away from the others.

"But didn't Mary Magdalene repent of her sins and become a saint? Didn't our lord and savior love her more than the tax collector?" Elizabeth argued, as she often had with Father Bennett.

Matthew smiled. "You're a learned young woman. But the whore who travels with us hasn't repented. And even if she has, our Lord is not here to absolve her of her sins, and I would not dare to. She's a dangerous influence, Lady Elizabeth. You are much safer with me."

That was the second time he'd insisted he was

harmless, and Elizabeth glanced at him curiously. It seemed such an obvious thing—why would he bother mentioning it? What possible harm could a gentle monk do her?

She'd lived her life around men, and she trusted her instincts. Those instincts told her that the dark prince was a far greater threat to her peace of mind than this passive brother could ever be, despite his pretty face, and she was foolish to even think twice about it.

They'd wandered away from the others, down a narrow pathway into the woods. The voices of the men, the sounds of the horses faded into the distance, and she glanced back to watch the plume of smoke from the cooking fire. It would be at least an hour before they ate, and she was with Brother Matthew. She smiled at her companion.

"Indeed, I feel very safe," she said. "I'm so glad you're with the party watching over the prince's penance."

"I trust the prince has done nothing to disturb you. Brother Adrian has particular care of him, though I have grave doubts about the wisdom of that decision. Prince William would have no more hesitation in seducing a man than a young woman, and Brother Adrian seems a bit too young."

His simple suggestion managed to shock Elizabeth, who'd always thought herself unshockable. "I've seen no sign of anything—"

"He's very sly," Matthew said. "He fools everyone he meets, but his appetites are twisted and insatiable. He may even come after you.''

For some reason Elizabeth felt faintly offended at the thought that she would be the last choice, when in fact it had seemed as if she were the first. "He already has," she said glumly.

The monk beside her tripped, then caught himself, as they moved deeper into the forest. "He's forced himself on you, my lady?" he asked in a quiet voice.

"No. Just kissed me," Elizabeth confessed. "Twice." The moment the words were out of her mouth she regretted them. There was no reason why she shouldn't tell Brother Matthew—he was part of the company in charge of the prince's penance, and he had every right to know. But she still wished she could call the words back. She shook her head. "You must be right, though. I'm not the kind of woman to entice men. He must be deviant indeed to want me."

"There is no imagining the depths of Prince William's depravity," Matthew said gravely.

Brother Matthew was totally oblivious. Clearly he'd spent no time around women or he wouldn't be so quick to agree with her disparaging self-assessment. The subject needed changing before she used her sharp tongue on the gentle monk.

She could hear the sound of running water, and the thought of something cool to drink was intoxicating. "This path must lead to a stream."

"I believe so. We can sit by the edge and talk."

But she'd already moved ahead, away from him, feeling suddenly oppressed. If it were midsummer, and if she were ten years old, and if no one was around, she'd strip off her clothes and plunge into the water, letting it flow around her. She'd always loved water, and even though she'd just taken a full bath, the idea of cool, clear water was unbearably seductive.

She ran ahead, following the winding path that must have been made by animals, leaving Matthew to follow behind at a more leisurely pace. He was out of sight, and she was alone, blessedly alone, when she reached the wide stream that ran over rocks with merry abandon.

Brother Matthew was far behind her. She could take off her slippers, just for a moment, and dip her feet into the water. Perhaps she could even convince Brother Matthew to go back without her. Or she could even do the unthinkable, and simply leap into the water, dress and all, and pretend she'd slipped.

Ah, but Dame Joanna's dress was already too tight across the chest, and damp clothes had a habit of clinging far too closely. And if Joanna were willing to lend her dry clothes, they might very well be even more revealing than the soft wool dress. Still, as she stared down into the roiling water, she was fiercely tempted.

"It's quite cold."

The sound of his voice was such a shock that she jerked, almost precipitating an unplanned descent into the waters. At the last minute she regained her footing, to look up into the dark eyes of the missing prince.

She could see where he'd been. He was dressed, though only in breeches and an undertunic, and his hair was wet. He must have been bathing, and thank the good Lord that she hadn't arrived even sooner to find him without clothes. The very thought was horrifying. Interesting, but horrifying.

"I had no intention of going in," she lied. "One could get very sick, exposing your body like that."

"I haven't exposed my body to anyone but the forest at this point," the prince said in his cool, slightly mocking voice. "And I developed a taste for frequent baths during my time in the Holy Lands. I'm willing to put up with a bit of cold water in return for the pleasure."

"You went on crusade?" she asked, astonished. The self-indulgent prince seemed unlikely to risk sacrificing himself, either for the sake of others or his immortal soul.

"In truth I went looking for adventure, clothed behind a veil of piety."

"And what did you find?"

The look on his face was brief, swiftly gone, and so bleak it clutched at Elizabeth's heart. "You have no need to hear such stories, Lady Elizabeth. I prefer you to stay innocent of just how evil man can be."

At that moment Brother Matthew appeared through the brush, slightly out of breath. He stopped short at the sight of Prince William, and Elizabeth could feel the tension in the air.

"We had no notion you were here, Prince William,'' Brother Matthew said in a cool, disapproving voice. "Did I interrupt something?"

"A discussion of evil. I was about to explain to Lady Elizabeth that it lies everywhere, even in the most innocent of guises. And that she'd be better off staying in a group at all times."

"I am capable of protecting my lady from anything that threatens her," he said in a frosty voice.

"I'm sure you are, Brother," he said. "The question is, what threat are you? And who, in fact, could stop you?"

They were no longer talking about her, Elizabeth thought. There was something else between the two men, both of them so very different. The one a gentle monk, the other a prince of such degeneracy that even his less-than-exemplary father had been revolted. It was a battle between good and evil, a gauntlet thrown down between them. And Elizabeth had the unpleasant notion that she was that very gauntlet.

"A good question indeed. I'm a simple monk and therefore quite harmless. One might almost say... impotent. The prince of England, on the other hand, has been called a monster, incapable of knowing right from wrong, heedless of human compassion, rapacious, murderous and vicious. So wherein lies Lady Elizabeth's danger?"

But neither of them looked at her. "I believe you know the prince very well," the taller man said. "But such darkness lives in all mankind, even the best of us. Lady Elizabeth would do well to heed that."

"Perhaps she wants a taste of darkness before she's shut away forever," Matthew suggested.

"The taste you have in mind could choke her to death."

Matthew smiled. "You're uncommonly wise for a king's son, Prince William. I'll remember not to underestimate you. We'll both watch over Lady Elizabeth, shall we? We can see which one of us will keep her safe."

"Merciful Jesu!" Elizabeth broke in, having had enough. "What is wrong with the two of you? Arguing over me, when I'm standing right here, and when neither of you could actually be interested except that for some reason you want to spite the other. I refuse to be fought over like two dogs with a bone that has no meat or value to it. Fight over Dame Joanna if you must, but leave me in peace. Both of you," she said sternly, glaring at Brother Matthew. "I'm going back and find something to eat. I'm famished. And if either of you come anywhere near me I'll push you into the fire."

She'd managed to shock and horrify Brother Matthew. But the prince simply laughed, perhaps because he knew there was nothing she could really do. "You'll lead the nuns a merry chase, lady," he said. "Don't you know you're supposed to be humble and obedient?"

"I'll obey the rule of the holy sisters. I just have no intention of listening to you." Without another word she turned away from them, covering ground as fast as her long legs would take her, till the quiet, deceptively polite sound of their voices faded into the spring air.

"Touch her and I'll kill you," Peter said, pushing his damp hair back from his face. His heart was still racing—he'd heard the voices of Elizabeth and the supposed monk from far off, and had dressed in record time. His sword lay on the ground, not far away, and he had a knife strapped to his ankle within his reach. If need be. "It matters not if you're the son of a king or a butcher," he continued, looking at his charge. "If you hurt her I'll cut out your heart."

William's too-pretty face curved in the angelic smile he'd perfected over the years. "You seem overfond of such a maypole. You're the one who's taken holy orders, despite the game we're playing. She's beyond the reach of a celibate monk, but not beyond mine. It's always possible I've seen the errors of my ways, fallen in love for the first time. Perhaps I'll marry Lady Elizabeth and become a good man."

"And perhaps hens will talk and pigs will fly," Peter replied, his voice as cool as his still-damp skin. "Until that time, keep your distance."

"I think you're the real danger to her, Brother Peter. How long have you been celibate? Seven years since you came back from crusade and decided to immure yourself in a monastery. You've been at my father's court—it mystifies me that you've been steadfast in the presence of some of the most beautiful women in England, and yet fall prey to a girl like

Elizabeth of Bredon. She's no longer young, she's too tall, too thin, too strong-minded, too intelligent, too freckled, and her hair is the color of the Devil. I expect even Brother Adrian would tell you you're mad to even be tempted.''

''Then I would expect you would have no interest in her, either. You prefer to inflict pain on unwilling children.''

''I share my esteemed father's tastes. Have you met his new bride? She was twelve years old when he married her. And I gather my own mother was barely thirteen when she died.''

''Thereby saving her the heartache of watching her son grow into such a monster.''

William laughed, a light, eerie sound. ''You tempt fate, Brother Peter. You are in charge of my spiritual and physical safety until we reach the Shrine of Saint Anne, but once I'm done my penance and have been shriven then we are back in our rightful places. You, a guilt-ridden monk who's taken a vow of chastity, poverty and obedience, trying to expiate sins that will never be cleansed, and me, the only son of the king of England. We already had an old score to settle. The more time I spend with you the less likely I am to forget.''

''I tremble in fear,'' Peter said. ''I repeat—touch her and I'll kill you.''

William shook his head in mock sorrow. ''Be careful—your immortal soul is in danger. It must be the Devil tempting you with that red hair of hers—surely there's nothing else to make you forswear your vows.''

"I'm not forswearing any vows. And I suggest you worry about your own immortal soul, not mine. You're on a journey of repentance. If you arrive at Saint Anne's with no fresh sin on your conscience you will be shriven and be able to lead a new life."

"I'll have no sin on my conscience," William said in a silky voice. "I sin without guilt. You, on the other hand, have guilt without sin. So which one of us is the madman?"

"Do you have any doubt?" He could kill him now. Cut his throat and put an end to it, and no one need ever know. He could say an assassin had found them, killed the prince and then escaped before Peter could stop him. It would be simple enough.

He'd killed, so many times he'd lost count of it. The Holy Lands were nothing more than a sea of blood in his memory, and he'd spent seven years trying to atone for that. It mattered not that his heart and motives had been pure, that he'd believed he was on Christ's business. At night he could still hear the screams of the dying. Not just soldiers. Women and children, as well, in a sea of flames. He swore never to kill again, unless in defense of innocence, and he'd held to that vow.

This would be one man who was beyond deserving it. The journey of penance was nothing more than a sham, a sop thrown to a furious, grieving father. Once William was done with it he'd be back to his old ways, and if he hadn't hurt Elizabeth of Bredon beforehand then nothing would stop him then.

Peter blamed himself. If he'd been less ready to

protect the lady the prince would have doubtless dismissed her as unworthy. The prince was just as likely to turn his wiles on one of the younger knights, and he'd already put his hands on a shocked Adrian. At least the men had the supposed advantage of making a choice.

He could always tell Lady Elizabeth, break yet another vow. He'd sworn that he would protect the prince's identity, and not even the household at Wakebryght had realized the switch. The only ones who knew were the three of them—Adrian, the prince and himself. It was far safer that way.

William laughed then, a soft sound meant to be reassuring. "You worry too much, Brother Peter. I have no interest in the lady—surely you realize that? I prefer ripe flesh and great beauty in the women I bed. She will be perfectly safe, and we will reach the Shrine of Saint Anne in good order, and all will be well."

Peter looked at him, not fooled. "As you say, my lord. But you should have no objections if I keep Lady Elizabeth away from you. 'Tis true, she is no great beauty, but when no one else is around one might fall into temptation, and your absolution depends on your arriving in a shriven state, just as you left London. Surely you wouldn't want to jeopardize that?"

"Surely I wouldn't," William agreed tightly. "A few days more or less will make no difference. She wouldn't do well in a convent, you know. She's too outspoken."

Peter said nothing. He had taken a vow, to the father abbot, to his king, to his God, that he would protect the dissolute prince and help bring him back to a state of grace. He wouldn't break those vows, and cut out William's heart.

Until he had to.

8

"You look as if you've seen a ghost, Lady Elizabeth," Dame Joanna greeted her as she stormed back to the campsite.

"Do I?" Unconsciously she pushed her wild hair back from her face and tried to school her expression into one of serene unconcern. She expected it was a dismal failure, and that Dame Joanna, with her sad eyes, could see through her attempt at composure much too well. "As far as I can tell, the biggest danger comes from the living, not the dead."

"In truth, you're probably right. Where were you? I was going to see if you'd accompany me for a walk. A day spent cramped in that poor excuse for a carriage is enough to make anyone ache."

Guilt was not a familiar emotion, and Elizabeth found she didn't like it. "I should have asked you first. I went for a walk with Brother Matthew, down to the stream. We met Prince William down there, and I left the two of them arguing. I'm certain I would have had a much more pleasant time in your company than in theirs."

Joanna raised an eyebrow. "The prince and the

monk? That must have been a pretty sight. What did they argue about? You?"

"What possible reason would they have?" Elizabeth demanded. "No, don't answer that. I assure you that neither man has the slightest bit of interest in me."

"I imagine the convent will cure you of your talent for prevarication," Dame Joanna observed in a tranquil voice.

Indeed, Elizabeth knew it was a lie. What she couldn't even begin to fathom was why? Why a notorious and dangerous lecher, a man of power and undeniable physical beauty, would even look her way? It wasn't as if she were the only possible choice. Dame Joanna was now among them, and her beauty was breathtaking. Prince William was also known not to confine his sexual proclivities to the opposite sex, and their small caravan was made up of a surprisingly large percentage of good-looking men. Not to mention Brother Matthew, whose classic beauty rivaled Dame Joanna's...

That was it. Pure and simple. She was a pawn between the two men, as she'd always been a pawn in her father's household. She had not the faintest idea why they would be using her, but she had no doubt that they were. Neither of them wanted her—they simply didn't want the other one to have her.

It was a depressing thought, and Elizabeth's reaction was immediate. "I'm starving," she announced. "What's cooking?"

"Rabbit. Have you spent much time outdoors, my

lady? There's nothing better than fresh game cooked over an open fire.''

"I'll take your word for it,'' Elizabeth said doubtfully. "I've never spent the night anywhere but my father's house and Wakebryght Castle. This will be a new experience for me. Where are we expected to sleep?''

"On the ground, my lady. Wrapped in our cloaks and the blankets from the carriage.''

Elizabeth looked at her in dismay. "You sound as if you look forward to the prospect.''

"I do. I love being outdoors. The fresh air and night sky make up for the hardness of the bed.''

"And bathing in cold streams is preferable to hot baths?'' she said in a doubting voice, as unbidden, the image of the dark prince came back to her, his hair wet and long, his shirt clinging to his still-damp chest. His breeches…

"It can be very refreshing.''

Elizabeth shook herself. "You astonish me, Dame Joanna. I would have thought you were a hothouse creature, unused to harsh conditions, and yet you seem to revel in them.''

"It's the only freedom I've ever had,'' she said simply. And then she smiled brightly, the smile not reaching her eyes. "Pay me no mind, my lady. This reminds me of my youth, when as a young girl I was allowed to run free. We all long for the halcyon days of our childhood, don't we?''

Elizabeth considered it for a moment. Her father's ready temper and readier fists, her teasing brothers, the loneliness as her father's wives died, one after the other, and then she was left, the only woman in the household, to cater to a group of spoiled men. "I think my new life will have far more joy than my old," she said.

"Perhaps."

Elizabeth looked across the clearing. Their caravan had divided into strict groups—the handful of knights surrounding one fire, the enticing scent of roast rabbit wafting from the pit. At a distance, the six monks worked in quiet concert, though the odors wafting from their cooking pot were not nearly as enticing. Monks were known for their culinary excesses, but these seemed more intent on mortifying the flesh with something that smelled like boiled weeds.

Brother Matthew stood to one side, watching. He seemed to have some position of power in the small group—he seldom seemed to be doing any of the actual labor, but merely looked on. He must have felt her eyes on him, for he looked up, meeting her gaze across the distance, and the sweetness of his smile would have melted the wariest of hearts.

"I'd be careful if I were you, Lady Elizabeth," Joanna murmured in her ear.

"Careful of a holy brother?" she responded, aghast. "I cannot imagine anyone who would be safer."

"Men are not what they seem. Ever," she added in an uncompromising voice. "Be they knight or monk or prince of the land."

"And women? Are they what they seem?"

Joanna had the sorrowful smile of a Madonna, an odd thing in a woman of dubious virtue. "You have only to look at me. I appear to be a whore, and in fact, I am one. Doomed to be passed from man to man until I am too old and ugly to please, and then I'll end my life on the streets, begging."

For a moment Elizabeth said nothing. And then she shook her head. "Nonsense," she said briskly. "If you don't like your life, change it. I am certain the Sisters of Saint Anne would welcome you gratefully...."

"Your certainty is misplaced."

"Well, perhaps if you come with a big enough dowry," she amended. "I'm not totally innocent in the ways of the world, Dame Joanna. I know that one must buy one's way into God's grace—my father complained loud and long at the price he must pay to get rid of me and my interfering ways. You have jewels—surely they would be enough to secure your entrance. If you really wanted it."

Dame Joanna touched the small cloth bag at her waist, as if to make certain it was still there. "I would come with a heavy burden of sin on my soul, and I doubt the unimpressive contents of my purse would be enough to lift it."

"Then as a lay sister?"

"You have much to learn, little one. Lay sisters are no more than unpaid servants, doomed to perform the most menial tasks with little benefit."

"But isn't that what a holy sister should do? Devote herself to good works without reward?"

"And such saintlike aspirations are what inspire you, Sister Elizabeth? I would have thought you had too much intelligence and too much ambition to long for a life of pure self-sacrifice."

"Well, I should long for a life of self-sacrifice," she admitted. "But you're right—I'm far too selfish and conceited to want to waste my talents mucking out stables in the name of Christ. But it's wicked of me. I should welcome even the most degrading of chores."

"Why? Everyone has their own gifts, and there are countless people on this earth who could best be occupied cleaning stables. No doubt most people think I'm one of them, but given my choice, I'd rather live in sin, in a warm bed with a full belly, than live in rags in a state of grace."

"Even if that warm bed contains someone like Owen of Wakebryght?"

Joanna's pretty mouth curved in a mirthless smile. "The price one has to pay. You should have learned that by now—nothing is ever given to you. You've made your own bargain—the chance of power and using your brain in return for your freedom. The loss of children as a price for the blessed loss of men."

"You have no children?" Elizabeth asked, momentarily distracted.

"My body was not made to bear children."

"Well, neither was mine," Elizabeth said.

"Why do you say that? I would have thought you were untouched."

"Of course I am! You forget—I have assisted at a

great many births. The women I helped have always told me my hips are too narrow for childbearing. The discussion is moot, since I have no intention of ever letting a man beneath my skirts, if anyone is unlikely enough to want me.''

Joanna shook her head. "For such a clever young woman you really are quite blind, aren't you?"

"I think I see things very clearly."

Elizabeth heard the nervous throat-clearing from behind her, and she turned. Brother Adrian stood there, as tall as she was, his head bowed slightly so that he didn't have to look either of them in the eye. But bless him, he brought food. Roast rabbit.

"Brother Adrian, you are an answer to a maiden's prayer!" she cried, reaching out for the tin platter.

He made an odd noise, almost dropping the food, but Joanna moved swiftly, taking it from him, and her hands brushed his. He pulled back as if burned, but still kept his head lowered. The moment his hands were free he pulled his hood up, covering himself, and without a word he backed away, tripping over the hem of his robe as he went, moving as swiftly as if pursued by the Devil.

Joanna turned back to Elizabeth. She was watching the monk's rapid disappearance with a thoughtful expression on her face. "I wonder what he's so terrified of?" she murmured. "He must think women are the spawn of Satan."

"He wasn't afraid of me."

"No? Then clearly it's fallen women who offend his holy sensibilities, not future nuns," Joanna said lightly. "Either that, or his chaste vocation is not as secure as he would like it to be."

"That's a terrible thing to say! He's such a sweet boy!"

"Is he? I've met very few sweet boys in my life, and whether they wear monk's robes or crowns, they all seem interested in one thing. And sooner or later, they all act on it. Just remember that, when you think you're safe in your convent."

"I'm not likely to entice men into forgetting their vows."

Joanna looked at her, a slow, measuring look, then took a bite of her rabbit haunch. "We shall see" was all she said, seating herself on the ground, ummindful of her rich dress.

By the time Elizabeth had devoured the generous portion of roasted rabbit she was feeling much livelier. Unfortunately Dame Joanna wasn't similarly inclined—she simply wrapped herself in her cloak and stretched out on the ground beneath the tree, clearly ready and able to sleep.

The rest of the caravan had settled down, as well. The sound of the monks chanting evensong floated in the night air, and Elizabeth leaned back against the trunk of the tree and closed her eyes. There was a soft evening breeze blowing, tangling her hair, and she wondered if it would make life simpler if she took a knife and hacked it off ahead of time. It would be shorn once she reached the convent, and if the flaming color wasn't bad enough, the sheer, bold abundance of it only compounded the matter. She would make a better impression on the mother abbess if she arrived as a shorn lamb.

Dame Joanna had a small, ornamental dagger at her waist, but she was already asleep, and Elizabeth was loath to wake her. Besides, Joanna would probably refuse to help her. She had such odd ideas about Elizabeth's appearance, including the unlikely notion that she wasn't as unappealing as her father had always insisted. And while Elizabeth could easily dismiss Joanna's words as kindness, the behavior of Prince William and Brother Matthew almost made her begin to doubt what she'd always known was true.

The monks were silent now, stretched out around their meager fire. It was a warm night—they hardly needed the heat, but it provided a comforting beacon in the night. She glanced over at the prince's company. They were still awake, the rough male voices muted, and she wondered idly which of the silhouetted figures was the prince himself. He was the tallest of the men on this journey, and easily distinguishable....

Maybe that was it. Elizabeth let out a small gasp, as realization hit her. It was that simple, that obvious. Her troubling reaction to the dangerous prince, what might almost, in another girl, be called attraction, was a simple matter of mathematics. He was the tallest man she had ever seen, apart from elderly Father Bennett. She was simply reacting to the unusual sensation of looking up at a man.

And knowing that, she should find it easy to ignore her unlikely feelings. Because it made no sense, none at all, to be drawn to a man both dangerous and cruel, one who would have no place in her future. No man would have a place in her future, and she was glad of it, she told herself.

She could see him now, apart from the knights just as Brother Matthew seemed apart from the monks. No one had bothered to erect any kind of shelter for the king's first bastard, and she could only suppose that was part of his pilgrimage. She could tell by the angle of his head that he was looking up at the sky, and she followed his gaze. The moon was half full, lending a silvery light to the scene, and a few errant clouds were scudding past on the night wind. Tomorrow would be a fine spring day for travel, though she almost wished she might ride, rather than be cooped up behind the curtains once more.

She should stay where she was. She could sleep sitting up—she'd done it often enough during mass, and had her knuckles soundly thwapped for it. All she had to do was close her eyes and relax, shut out the night and the questions that plagued her mind, and think of nothing but a peaceful future among the holy sisters....

And unbidden came the vision of the prince, clothes clinging to his damp body, looking down at her in the forest as Brother Matthew rushed to follow her.

She opened her eyes swiftly, to banish the picture, and instead focused on the prince himself, watching her in the moonlight.

She knew he was, even though the shadows made

it impossible to prove. She could feel the very heat from his gaze, warming her better than a fire. It prickled beneath her skin, in the pit of her stomach, between her bound breasts, that still, steady gaze that seemed to touch every part of her.

She was mad. It was dark—he couldn't even see her. He was probably lost in thought, thinking about what new atrocity to commit, what new innocent to despoil....

Except that she was the only innocent around, and she certainly didn't want him thinking about her.

He hadn't moved, and there was no way she could be certain if he was watching her. No way she could sleep if she thought he was.

She pushed against the tree, rising to her full height. Dame Joanna slept on, and the prince didn't move. Were his eyes on her? Or had the long days managed to rattle her brain? Had Joanna's suggestions brought her to a state of complete chaos?

But it hadn't been Joanna's suggestions that had caused him to kiss her mouth. Or to argue with Brother Matthew down by the stream.

She started toward him across the rough ground. No one seemed even remotely aware of either of them. The monks and Dame Joanna slept, the knights were drinking and talking, oblivious to their charge. And he was watching her, she knew it. If she had any sense she'd take a sudden quick turn and dive for the bushes, pretending she'd been heeding a call from nature.

She was heeding a call from nature, but an altogether different sort. The closer she got to him the more clearly she could see him, and he didn't move to meet her halfway. He simply stood in the shadows of one of the towering trees, watching her, waiting for her.

Like a hunter with a baited trap, waiting for a foolish rabbit to wander into the snare. And she could no more resist than she could fly.

Adrian lay on his side, watching, afraid to move, afraid not to. Brother Peter had given him his charge, and he never questioned him. He was to lie next to the false Brother Matthew and watch him at all times, not even daring to sleep. It was far too dangerous to turn your back on the true bastard prince of England, far too dangerous to even close your eyes. Not when there were women around.

Women, he thought with a silent groan. All this would be so much easier if there were no women. He could see Lady Elizabeth walking quietly toward the man she thought was a dangerous murderer, walking into peril without a second thought. God preserve him from a clever woman who thought she was impervious!

And God preserve him from a wise and beautiful woman who lay sleeping far too close to him, a Madonna and a Magdalene rolled into one. Every time he thought of Dame Joanna's sorrowing smile or the scent of her hair his body reacted in a predictable manner. The way she moved, the soft swell of her breasts...

He knew his duty—why was he letting himself be distracted by a beautiful woman? Even worse, why was Brother Peter allowing himself to be distracted by a flame-haired maypole?

Lady Elizabeth was walking toward Peter, her skirts flowing with her long-legged stride, and he was making no effort to turn away. The moonlight was bright, and no one was watching, and danger was thick in the air. *Move away from her,* Adrian thought. *She is a greater danger than you realize.*

Peter would laugh at him. Peter would declare himself immune. But he'd seen the hunger in Peter's eyes, and he knew the same hunger in his heart when he looked at Dame Joanna.

And he knew they were all doomed.

9

Peter stood very still as the girl approached him. And she was a girl, despite being past the age many women would have married and become mothers. She had an unblinking innocence that absolutely terrified him. She would stumble into danger without thinking, just as she was striding toward him on those long legs of hers, the flow of her gown moving with her, and if he had any sense at all he'd dive into the bushes to avoid her.

But he was just as foolish as she was, and if danger was going to come to him on a quiet, moonlit night, then he was going to stand and wait for it.

It wasn't supposed to be easy. And he hadn't thought it was. He'd always been a man of strong sensual appetites, and he'd chosen the strictest order he could find. Not for him the well-fed monks of the Cistercian Order. He'd devoted himself to the strictest rule he could find, a life with unceasing toil, constant penance and the most Spartan of living conditions.

But he had just returned from crusade, and the living conditions couldn't have been worse. The penance was deserved and endless, and the work kept him from going mad with it.

He'd even spent time in King John's household, surrounded by the sight and the scent of beautiful women. Women who found the notion of bedding a monk to be a challenge. The kind of woman he'd taken in the past, gladly and well, leaving them as breathless and pleasured as he had been.

And he hadn't touched them. He'd let them flirt, and smile, and put their soft hands on his arm, and he'd been steadfast and resolute. So why should a long-legged, flame-haired colt of a girl suddenly break through his fierce abstinence?

Sin was easier to resist if you avoided it altogether, and Peter never took the easy way out. It was his only just deserts, to suffer being around Lady Elizabeth, to think of her mouth, to think of the innocence in her eyes and what he could make her do....

He'd been leaning against a tree, watching her approach, but at that thought he stood up straight, half-tempted to bolt. Perhaps he couldn't resist her after all. Perhaps the vapid beauties were the easy ones. The heartbreakingly innocent ones almost impossible to deny. Except that he'd never met a woman that touched him the way Elizabeth of Bredon did.

"You're an idiot," he said in a companionable voice when she was within a few feet of him.

She halted, momentarily confused. Her wicked hair had come loose from her braid, and it was blowing softly around her like a veil. He wanted to wrap himself in her long, sumptuous hair. He didn't move.

"I beg your pardon, my lord?" she said, slightly

breathless. So she must know as well as he did just how dangerous her midnight foray was.

"Go back to bed. You shouldn't be out wandering alone in the forest. There are wild beasts. And there are dangerous men."

Her eyes were so clear and unflinching in the moonlight. He wasn't used to looking directly into a woman's eyes. It wasn't that she was tall enough to meet his gaze. It was that she was open and honest enough. Just the sort of thing to lead her into complete disaster.

"You're the only dangerous man I'm aware of," she said.

"As I said, you're an idiot. Or have you the bizarre notion of becoming a sainted martyr? Trust me, if I rape and kill you you wouldn't become a martyr, you'd simply be buried and forgotten. Find some other way to reach holiness."

"You wouldn't rape and murder me," she said with a calm assurance he found annoying.

"Why not?"

"I'm not the kind of woman who inflames men into dangerous, murderous passions."

"I will say it a third time—you're an idiot. And trust me, you're annoying enough to bring out murderous tendencies in the most gentle of souls."

"I don't bring out murderous tendencies in Brother Matthew," she said.

Peter glanced upward in exasperation. He'd asked to be tested, to be punished, and God seemed willing to be doing just that. "How old are you, Lady Elizabeth?"

"Seventeen."

"Then you should be old enough to know that men are not always what they seem."

"I've lived my life surrounded by men. They seem to me to be very simple, obvious creatures, and I'm a very good judge of character."

"Are you indeed? Then why are you standing alone in the moonlight, talking to a man who's known to have killed women? That seems to show a particular lack of insight on your part. Unless you think the world is mistaken about me, that I'm really a gentle, harmless soul and all those stories are wicked lies."

A mistake. She took another step closer, and he couldn't back away. She had absolutely no idea she was playing with fire, and she looked up into his eyes with her steady, observing gaze. He didn't bother putting up the usual mask that he wore to keep people from seeing his inner torment. He let her look her fill, into the very depths of his heart, so she could know what a monster he truly was.

She shook her head, and a silky strand of flame-colored hair settled on her shoulder. "I can see darkness," she said. "Terrible things, terrible pain." She sounded dazed by the knowledge, but she didn't move away from him. Instead she reached out and put her hand on his arm, almost instinctively, and he wanted to groan.

"Then run away, lady," he said. "Keep your distance from dangerous creatures, be they bastard prince or lowly monk. None of us are safe.''

''Are you warning me against Brother Matthew?''

He wanted to curse her acuity. He knew women well enough—to tell her to keep away would merely convince her to move closer. ''I'm warning you against everyone,'' he said in a tense voice.

''You think Brother Adrian hides a lecherous nature?''

''Don't worry about Brother Adrian—he is a man who keeps his vows no matter what they be.''

''And Brother Matthew is not? I looked into his eyes as well, my lord, and I can see the pure goodness shining through. There are no shadows of guilt and remorse there—he has a guiltless soul.''

''But is he guiltless because he has committed no sin, or because he refuses to take responsibility for it? The Devil himself would be unlikely to be plagued with guilt.''

''And now you're telling me that Brother Matthew is the Devil himself?''

He wanted to take her by her slender shoulders and shake some sense into her. He had no doubt she could look into his eyes and see the darkness there, but it galled him that she could be so blind to the real Prince William's madness.

He wanted to tell her. He wanted to tell her exactly who and what he was, and what her saintly Brother Matthew had done to Baron Neville's daughter, the atrocities he'd committed with no remorse whatsoever.

But he couldn't say a word. All he could do was to keep her safe until they arrived at Saint Anne's.

"What do you want from me, Lady Elizabeth?" he said in a weary voice, looking pointedly down at the hand that still rested on his arm. She wore no jewels on her hands. Even the mother abbess at Saint Anne's sported heavy rings. "Were you looking for a taste of danger before you seclude yourself in the convent? There are any number of men here who are far safer than me." And who would know better than to go anywhere near her. The monks and the knights had full knowledge of who headed this pilgrimage, even if they didn't know his true identity, and no one would dare question his decisions.

"That's what Brother Matthew is. A man far safer than you are, my lord. Can you deny it?"

At that moment, standing so close to him that he could smell the scent of flowers in her hair, she was in far more danger than from a sleeping monk with a bodyguard. No one was watching. He'd put his mouth on her skin twice—once on her forehead, once on her lips. He wanted to kiss her again, all over her body, he wanted her mouth, her thighs, her breasts, her very soul.

He put his hand over hers and removed it from the sleeve of his tunic, releasing it without the slightest show of reluctance. "What do you want, Lady Elizabeth?" he asked in a bored tone. "Surely you must have some reason for traipsing over here in the middle of the night, and it can't be to talk about Brother Matthew."

"I did want to talk about Brother Matthew," she insisted. "I don't understand why you're so harsh with him, and I want you to stop it."

He just looked at her. "You want me to stop it?" he echoed in disbelief.

"You're on a pilgrimage to cleanse your soul of your sins, my lord. Arrogance and bullying won't help."

He hadn't been called arrogant in a long time. Arrogance had always been a besetting sin, one he'd worked hard to cleanse himself of. Apparently he'd failed.

He wasn't sure if he wanted to beat her or kiss her. He would do neither, of course. He was beginning to develop an even stronger devotion to the monastic life, free of maddening creatures like Elizabeth of Bredon.

"If all you want is to defend saintly Brother Matthew, then consider me properly chastised. And consider this—if you go off alone with him again I'll have you bound and gagged for the rest of the journey."

The expression of shock on her face was almost worth it. "You wouldn't dare!"

"You think not? Who are you talking to? Am I a man who carries through with my threats?" She said nothing, as he expected. "And now, if you're finished, go back to lie with Dame Joanna and stay out of the way of the men."

"I'm not finished." She didn't move, and he had to admire her tenacity, if nothing else. Though in fact he admired her courage, her brains, her innocence, her mouth, the sweep of her long neck...

"Continue." His voice was cold.

"I need a knife."

She'd managed to surprise him after all. "Don't you have one? How do you cut your meat?"

"I didn't bring one with me. One of my brothers claimed the jewel-handled dagger belonging to my mother. He said I'd simply have to surrender it when I enter the convent. I didn't think I'd need one until we arrive."

"And you find you do? It's a wise idea to be armed when you're on the road, though somehow I can't see you stabbing anyone."

She gave him a slow, measuring look. "You never can tell," she murmured.

Sweet Jesu, she made him want to laugh. She was absolutely unstoppable, and no warnings, no threats would make her cower like the helpless virgin she, in truth, was.

He had a small blade tucked inside his tunic, next to his skin. Without hesitation he reached for it, offering it to her, handle first.

And then he realized his mistake. Even a bastard prince would only carry heavily jeweled weapons. His knife was plain and ordinary, the knife of a holy brother sworn to poverty.

She didn't say a word, simply took it, tucking it into her long sleeve. "I need it to cut my hair," she said.

He almost grabbed it back. "Why?"

"Need you ask? It's a sign of the Devil, it garners far too much attention, and it gets in my way. They'll cut if off once I reach Saint Anne's, and if I arrive already shorn I'll make a better impression."

"You don't strike me as a woman who worries unduly about what sort of impression she makes."

"That was the least of my concerns," she pointed out. "For seventeen years this hair has been a plague and a curse. I want to cut if off."

"If you've survived seventeen years then you'll survive another three days to the convent," Peter said. "Let the mother abbess see to your fleecing. She's a fierce creature—she won't hesitate to hack it off and burn it."

"You know the mother abbess at Saint Anne's?"

Trust Elizabeth to fasten on the one mistake he'd made. She was far too clever for her own good. There was no reason for Prince William to be acquainted with the abbess of a small shrine in the south of England, and he couldn't even begin to come up with an explanation.

"You are not to cut your own hair," he simply said in a voice that brooked no opposition. "The knife is too sharp, and you would probably end up slicing your wrists and bleeding to death, and then everyone would blame me. No, thank you. You may keep the knife. That way you can scare away any man foolish enough to get too close, though I suspect your tongue is a far sharper weapon. But you will leave your hair alone."

Of course she'd still argue. She was as much a

curse and a plague as her unwanted hair. "It's like a beacon in the woods!" she protested. "It could draw the attention of bandits...."

"Then wear a hood, for Christ's sake!" he snapped. "Now, go back to bed and leave me alone. Unless you'd rather bed with me."

It was the right thing to say, of course. It was what a lecherous princeling would say. Though the real William probably wouldn't ask, he'd simply take.

But the problem was, it wasn't William asking, and it wasn't the decoy taking his place. It was Peter asking, Peter wanting, Peter sinning.

"Madness runs in the Angevin blood, does it?" she responded. "Or does this tendency toward strange delusions herald from your mother?"

"The world will be a far better place with you safely immured in a convent," he replied. "Can you never still your saucy tongue? I could have it cut out."

"I doubt it. And it will be silent soon enough, once we reach Saint Anne's. Didn't you tell me it was a contemplative order, founded on prayer and meditation? Though how you would know any such thing continues to puzzle me. I wouldn't have thought you had much traffic with convents."

Another, earlier slip that he hadn't even noticed. Though he'd lied, just to bait her. The sisters at Saint Anne were as talkative as all women—on that account sweet Elizabeth would fit right in. She was like a small terrier shaking a rat, determined not to let go.

And he was tired of being baited, when there was

nothing he could do, when what he wanted most of all was to silence her mouth with his. "One last time, Lady Elizabeth. Go back to your bed near Dame Joanna, or come back into the woods and lift your skirts for me."

He'd managed to shock her into silence for a brief, blessed moment. "No!"

"If you'd prefer to do it right here I'm entirely game," he said, reaching for his belt. "I have no objection to an audience."

She slapped him. The sound was loud enough in the still night air to draw the attention of those around. Even the monks stirred from their slumber to search for the source of the noise.

They would have no idea who had slapped whom. No woman would get away with hitting a man, much less a prince. They would probably assume he was the one who had hit her—it was only in keeping with his reputation. Except that if he had hit her she'd be on her butt on the ground, and he damned well might have her skirts over her head.

She was looking properly horrified. "I beg pardon!" she said in a thoroughly anguished voice. "I don't know why I did that. I've never hit another person in my life."

"I'm particularly trying," he said calmly. She'd packed quite a force with her blow—his skin tingled. "So what do you suggest I do to you in return? One can't get away with assaulting the son of a king."

She was looking pale, even frightened in the moonlight. He should have felt regret, but her silence was such a blessed relief that he allowed her fear to linger. "You could beat me," she said in a small voice.

He shook his head. "I derive little pleasure out of beating women." Another lie that he hoped she'd be too afraid to pick up on. Not that he enjoyed beating women. But the real prince had a habit of doing just that, as Elizabeth should well know.

She did know, and she opened her mouth to say something of the sort, when she shut it again, finally realizing she'd gone too far.

"Very wise," he murmured. "This is a dangerous game you're playing, and one should never underestimate the enemy."

"Are you the enemy?" Her voice was so low and quiet that he almost doubted the words. Or the plaintive note in them. He stared down at her, unable to look away. Her eyes were no longer defiant, her mouth was soft and vulnerable, and, sweet God, if he didn't get away from her he wouldn't answer for his immortal soul.

Then again, his immortal soul had been thrashed long ago, and spending the rest of his life in penance would not be long enough to wash it clean. What difference would another kiss make?

They were still watching. He didn't care. It would horrify Adrian, amuse the knights, worry the monks. And enrage the false monk who was watching them out of flat blue eyes.

He didn't care. He slid his arm around her waist and pulled her up against him, her breasts soft and voluptuous against his chest, even through the layers of clothing. He put his other hand under her chin, drawing her face up to his, his long fingers cupping her face, his thumb gently brushing her bottom lip.

He heard the gasp of horror, and whether it came from Adrian, or Elizabeth, or his own tortured conscience, it didn't matter. He put his mouth against hers.

10

He was kissing her. This time he was really kissing her, his body pressed up against hers so that she could feel him, the strength, the muscle, the heat of him all along hers. His hand cupped her chin, and she wasn't quite sure how it happened but she opened her mouth for him, letting him taste her, and the strange, clenching need in her stomach blossomed and swelled, and she moved closer to him, wanting to be absorbed into his very skin.

She slid her hands up his chest, to push him away, but instead they moved around his neck, pulling him against her, and she'd closed her eyes long ago, closed her brain just as she'd opened her mouth for him. Just as she'd open her legs for him if he wanted her to.

He lifted his head, looking down into her upturned face, and he appeared to be as dazed as she felt. He put his hands on her shoulders and set her back from him, and she was suddenly cold on such a mild night, and she needed to feel him against her once more.

She didn't move. She swayed slightly in the night air, but she didn't move, didn't dare. Waiting for him to say something. Waiting for Brother Adrian or

Brother Matthew to come rescue her, waiting for the dark prince to laugh at her and tell her he didn't really want her, he was just teasing her, waiting for her own common sense to reappear.

He took her hand, connecting them once more, and a pulse of heat went through them, instantly strengthening her. He turned and pulled her after him, away from the light and the heat, into the darkness of the forest beyond. And she went, without question, without thinking.

The towering trees shut out the moonlight, so that all was shadows, and he pushed her up against the thick trunk of an old oak tree, his hands braced on either side of her, imprisoning her there. And he kissed her again, and again, and when she reached up her hands to touch him, to push him away this time perhaps, he caught her wrists and drew her hands downward, to press against him through the leather of his clothing.

She tried to yank her hands away, shocked, but he was far stronger than she was. She knew what she was feeling, even through the thick leather. For all that she was still innocent, she'd led a far-from-sheltered life, and she had eyes and brains and curiosity. And she knew the significance of that hard flesh, knew that he lusted after her. And the notion was a shocking delight, that he would want her. Want her enough to make this kind of change in his big, hard body, a body that was warm and strong and enveloping, pushing her up against the tree.

He was pulling her skirt up, and she could feel his

rough, warm hand on her leg, on her thigh, her bare skin, and she made a choking sound beneath his mouth at his burning touch. Because she wanted more.

She was mortified with shame, she was terrified, she was so hungry she wanted to touch him, as well. His leather overtunic shielded him too well, and she wanted to reach under it, but he was holding her hand against him, and she couldn't.

He released her mouth, reaching for the fastenings of her cloak, and she took a deep, shaky breath. "Are you going to rape me?"

The words were no more than a whisper, but they stopped him cold, his long fingers still enmeshed in the cloth ties to her warm cloak, his other hand still pressing her hard against his erection. She must have imagined the expression of shock on his face, for a moment later he simply closed his eyes and rested his forehead against hers, blotting out the light.

She could hear the deep, shuddering breaths he was taking as he brought himself back under control. He released her hand, and she no longer had any reason to touch him. Touch his cock, she thought, using the word she'd heard others use. She withdrew her hands, ignoring her strange reluctance, and placed them up against his shoulders. Not pushing, not holding. Just touching him.

She didn't need to push—he stepped back of his own accord, releasing her, and she was glad she had the tree to support her as her skirts dropped back down around her legs.

She couldn't see his face, to know whether there was guilt or boredom or regret. Or any lingering trace of passion. All she knew was that he'd changed his mind, and she should be thanking God at her narrow escape, instead of shivering in the darkness, still hot with need.

"Why did you do that?" She could barely recognize her own voice. Or the next words. "Why did you stop?"

"Because you're an innocent. And I don't hurt innocents." His own voice was a mere thread of sound.

"Since when?"

He took another step back away from her, and a shaft of moonlight came through the trees, bringing light to his dark face. To the unfathomable eyes and shadowed mouth. And then he seemed to collect himself, as if remembering who and what he really was.

"Since I went on pilgrimage," he said in a cooler voice. "I'm trading a few weeks of penance for a lifetime of sin, both in the past and in the future. I've decided it was a good trade. If I need relief I'll avail myself of Dame Joanna. She wouldn't like it much, but at least she's used to it. Whereas you would be far more trouble than you're worth."

"So I've always been told," she said, still watching him. He was breathing deeply, as if he was having trouble, and it was probably only her own racing heart that suggested he was similarly afflicted.

She felt…distraught. There was no other word for it. She could still feel the touch of his hand on her thigh, his tongue in her mouth, and if the rough bark of the tree beneath her hands couldn't bring her back to reality then nothing could.

They heard the crashing through the bushes at the same time, and when Brother Adrian stumbled into the clearing she'd managed to school her features into calm curiosity. One didn't look different after being kissed like that, did one? It felt as if anyone who looked at her could tell what she'd just been on the verge of doing, feeling, but the night was dark, and there would be no physical trace. Just to be certain she touched her mouth, and the prince's eyes immediately followed her fingers, lingering for a brief, pained moment.

"My lord!" Adrian said breathlessly as he came to an abrupt halt. "You cannot…" And then he stopped, clearly confused.

"Cannot what, Brother Adrian?" the prince said in his cool voice. "Neither Lady Elizabeth nor I could sleep, and we thought a walk in the moonlight would help tire us. There is nothing to worry about."

Brother Adrian looked far guiltier than he should have, given the prince's reputation. "I crave pardon, my…lord. I was afraid…"

"Afraid I would betray my vows? When so much depends on what I do? Have faith, Brother. I would not break my pledge no matter how tempted."

Elizabeth looked between the two men. She had the oddest feeling that they were talking about something else entirely. It was not to be wondered at. She could hardly be at the center of such a confrontation. Prince William must have had a fit of momentary insanity, but it had passed, and with Brother Adrian to look out for her she would be safe.

"Accompany Lady Elizabeth back to Dame Joanna," the prince said, not looking at her. "I'll stay in the woods a bit longer."

Adrian looked doubtful. "Aye, my lord. I'll keep Lady Elizabeth out of harm's way. No one will touch her." Again that hidden undertone.

But there was no mistaking the relief in the prince's voice. "I am counting on you for that, Brother. No one." He turned away from them without another word, moving deeper into the woods, heading back toward the free-flowing river.

Would he bathe again, wash the heat from his body? And what would happen if she escaped Brother Adrian and followed him? Stripped off her clothes and…?

Sweet Jesu, she was mad! She looked into Brother Adrian's face and summoned a shaky smile. "You are very kind to be so concerned, Brother," she said. "Perhaps you should go with the prince and I'll find my way back on my own. There can be no danger when there are so many of us."

"I think the prince is best left alone to contemplate his sins," Adrian said in a grim voice at odds with his youthful face. "My lady?" He held out an arm, waiting for her.

She took it, moving forward. And only at the last minute did she glance back into the dark, impenetrable woods, where the prince had disappeared.

The clearing was still and quiet when she and

Brother Adrian reached it. Surely it hadn't been that long since the prince had taken her hand and pulled her into the woods? Not nearly long enough.

She wrapped herself in her cloak and lay on the ground near Dame Joanna's sleeping figure. The ground was hard beneath her, but in truth she was too tired to care, and so deeply troubled that all she wanted to do was blot out everything. The memory of him. The feel of his hands on her, the taste of his mouth. The insistent push of his hard flesh against her hands.

"That wasn't very wise of you, Lady Elizabeth." Dame Joanna's voice was no more than a whisper, and she didn't open her eyes. "If you play with fire you're likely to get burned."

For half a moment she considered pretending to be asleep. But Dame Joanna wouldn't believe it, and she had always had a fierce hatred of liars and lying. "I wanted his knife."

"To stab him?"

"To cut my hair."

"You could have asked me."

"Would you?"

"No." Joanna opened her eyes. "We have a number of days before we reach the convent, a number of days for things to change. I'm not certain you're destined to be a holy sister, Lady Elizabeth."

"What other choice do I have?"

Joanna smiled, closing her eyes again. "I am no seer, my lady. But if you wish to arrive at the convent in the same chaste state you set out in, you'd best keep away from Prince William. Or are you still trying to convince me that he doesn't want you?''

She would have liked to try. But not with the feel of his mouth on hers, his long fingers touching her. "I suspect he probably wants every woman," she said lightly.

"He doesn't appear to want me, thank God."

"'Thank God'?" Elizabeth echoed, confused. "But why? Wouldn't he be a far better protector than Owen of Wakebryght?"

"Right now I don't want anyone to want me," Joanna whispered. "I just want to reach Saint Anne's and cleanse myself of my sins. There'll be time enough to decide where I'll go next. Back to Owen. On to someone else. Or stay at the convent. In any case, Prince William is not for the likes of me."

"I still don't understand. He's strong, he's wealthy, powerful, and he's quite…" Words failed her.

"Beautiful, in his own way. Yes, he is. But he appears to like innocents, and I'll never be innocent again." She rolled over, turning her back on Elizabeth, wrapping her cloak more firmly about her. "And glad I am of it. Innocence only gets your heart broken. Beware, my lady. Once broken, a heart never mends."

"What man broke your heart?"

For a moment she thought Joanna wouldn't answer. And then the words came, soft and tired. "No man. Life, my lady. I would hate to see the same thing happen to you."

The silence of the forest settled around them. Elizabeth closed her eyes, and she could hear the faint call of the night birds, the sound of the leaves as the wind danced through them, even the distant sound of the nearby stream.

It must have been hours later when she heard him return to the clearing. She had no doubt it was the prince—during the intervening hours several of the men had risen, stumbled into the woods to relieve themselves, and she never made the mistake of thinking they were Prince William. She knew his step, his presence, his shadow with an almost unholy awareness.

She almost thought she could feel his eyes on her in the darkness. But that was foolish—she was wrapped up tight in her cloak, and it would be impossible to tell one sleeping form from another in the inky darkness. The moon had set, the fires had died down, and after a moment she heard his footsteps move farther away, the sound of his leather garments as he stretched out on the hard ground. The soft leather she had put her hands on. And wanted to slide her hands under.

At least half the men were snoring now, but the sound was oddly reassuring as the long night stretched toward dawn. The growling noise of slumber was like a wall protecting her from the forest, and she closed her eyes and slept. Dreaming of sweet, black sin.

The attack came at dawn.

The sky was barely light, all was peaceful and still

as Elizabeth opened her eyes, wondering what had roused her. All was silent. Even the morning larks were quieted. And then hell descended.

It was all noise and terror—the crash of steel blade against steel, the shriek of the horses as they thundered through the clearing, the screams of pain. Elizabeth scrambled to her feet, but all was chaos, as horses charged among the struggling knights and monks, and blood was everywhere. She cried out for Dame Joanna, but she was nowhere to be seen, and it seemed as if the marauders were everywhere, slashing, stabbing, intent on destruction.

Elizabeth picked up her skirts and ran, blindly, away from the battle. She had just enough presence of mind to know these were no bandits—they were too well mounted, well armed, to be anything but professional soldiers. Not looking for spoils or wealth, looking for vengeance.

She paused for a moment, searching in vain for the prince. He would have been the first they slaughtered—he'd already be lying on the blood-red ground. They shouldn't be wanting anyone else, but she watched in horror as one of the monks' throat was slashed, and she realized they wanted no witnesses to their savagery. And she scooped up her skirts and ran again, toward the woods, as she heard horses bearing down on her.

If she made it into the forest they might not be able to follow her, at least not mounted, and it might give her just enough time to find cover. She was past thinking, but her legs were long, and she covered the ground fast, her red hair flaming out behind her.

''Get the witch!'' she heard someone order, and she had little doubt they were talking about her. Were the others all dead, and she the only one left? And were they planning on cutting her throat as they had the poor, elderly monk and probably everyone else, or did they have even worse in mind for her?

It didn't matter, all that mattered was escape. She stumbled, going down hard on the rough ground, and when she looked up she saw Prince William, still alive, slashing and hacking with his sword as he worked his way toward the struggling monks that still remained.

She could see Brother Matthew, in the distance, untouched, oddly calm in the midst of the turmoil. The prince was moving toward him, and Elizabeth froze, shocked. William and Matthew hated each other, and yet the prince was risking his life to come to Matthew's aid.

She didn't even hear the horse approach in the chaos, didn't feel the presence of the marauder until he grabbed her long hair in his fist and pulled her toward him.

She screamed in pain, thrashing at him, but the grizzled, bloody knight paid no mind, hauling her over the front of his saddle and holding her there.

She could smell the blood, the horse, the stench of the man who had grabbed her. She struggled, and the horse panicked. The man hit her, hard, but it wasn't enough to stop her thrashing and kicking. She looked up, but Brother Matthew had disappeared, and there was no sign of the prince, who had tried to rescue him.

The sound was first—a gurgling sound, followed by a wash of hot liquid splashing over her. Blood. She knew by the smell and the feel of it, and the man holding her went slack as strong hands hauled her from the horse.

She had just long enough to look into William's bloody, fierce face. "Run!" he said.

For a moment she didn't move, too numb with shock and horror. The carnage was everywhere. "Joanna…" she said, but he simply caught her shoulder and shoved her, hard. "It's too late. Run, damn you!" he said again, and she stumbled forward, into the forest, running as fast as she could.

She didn't dare stop when she reached the river, but it was too rough and wide to cross, so she simply followed it, deeper and deeper into the woods, until she could run no more, and she sank down beside the water, gasping for breath.

By the time her heart slowed and her breath returned to normal, the silence of the forest was complete. She had no idea whether she'd run far enough from the battle to outdistance the noise, or whether it was over. Had they killed everyone, Prince William and Joanna and the others? Brother Matthew had disappeared, presumably fallen, and there'd been no sign of Brother Adrian. The prince had been in the thick of things, fighting like a madman. He would have gone down fighting, she thought, numb.

She managed to pull herself into a sitting position. She shouldn't stay here long—they might be looking for her. The marauders seemed intent on killing everyone, leaving no witness behind, and they may or may not have known of her escape. As soon as she gathered her strength she would need to move, deeper into the forest, until she could go for help.

She had seen death before, countless times. Death was a part of life, and she was well versed in it, both in childbed and with old age, with disease or accident. But she'd never seen violent death. Joanna had been right—she was truly an innocent, more sheltered than she had ever realized. And in a few short minutes all that had changed.

She could smell the stench of blood coming from her clothes. It must have been a killing blow—otherwise Joanna's green wool dress would not be streaked with deep red. And she could no more travel with the smell of it than she could curl up and hide.

The river was there, and she didn't hesitate. She took off her leather slippers and jumped in.

The shock of the cold water almost knocked the wind from her. It was deeper than she realized, and the current was strong, catching her water-soaked skirts and pulling her along. She struggled, but it was too powerful for her, and she felt herself be borne away, the icy stream splashing over her. Maybe it would be better this way, she thought, going under. Drowning was an easy death, they said. Better than at the hands of men.

She surfaced, choking, and kicked out. Drowning

might be easy, but she had never been one to take the easy way out. She tried to swim, but the weight of her clothes dragged her down again, and the water closed over her head. Three times and you went under for good, she'd heard, fighting her way to the surface, breaking free into the blessed air for a brief moment. And then she went down again, and she knew that this time she wouldn't be coming up again, as she sank down, her body caught in the swirling current, pulling her deeper. She would die, and she knew it, and it would be her choice to pick what her last thought would be.

And without hesitation she thought of William's hands on her body, strong and powerful, and she gave in.

11

It had been years since Joanna had been free to run in the forest. It didn't matter that she was running for her very life—a strange exhilaration filled her as she raced through the thick morning air. The noise of the pitched battle faded as she ran, and she closed her ears to the cries of pain and the clash of metal.

When she was young she would run for the sheer joy of it, racing through the countryside for hours on end. There should be no joy in her escape today, with the dead and dying left behind, but the sense of strength and freedom coursed through her body and spurred her onward. She ran until she could run no more, then she collapsed in exhaustion, curling up in a ball and hiding beneath the bushes.

Were they all dead? What bandits would attack such a large party, composed of monks and knights? There would be little of value in the party—scarcely worth such a full-scale attack. She knew that Prince William had many enemies, but who would dare try to kill the only son of the king of England? Who would be fool enough?

She doubted anyone else could have escaped. The marauders had approached silently enough, but they must have made noise enough to rouse her. She woke in the predawn light to stare around her at the sleeping forms. Lady Elizabeth slept wrapped up tight, and the sounds of snoring from the knights filled the air with soft cacophony. Even the knight posted as sentry dozed as he leaned against a tree.

She'd struggled to her feet, heading into the bushes to relieve herself, and she'd just been about to return when the attack came. She didn't hesitate. Too late to warn them, too late to save them. She could only save herself.

Slowly her breathing came back to normal. Her heart had been slamming against her chest so hard that it was painful, but as daylight spread over the forest, calm returned, and she thought of poor Lady Elizabeth. She could only hope she'd died quickly. Men could be very brutal indeed, and even the marriage bed was an unpleasant experience. Rape and murder at the hands of outlaws would be unspeakable horror.

She rose, brushing the leaves from her cloak, brushing the tears from her face. What was done was done—there was nothing she could do to change it. If she had any sense at all she would keep going the way she was heading. She could tell by the position of the sun that she'd been running due west, and if she continued on that way she would reach the sea sooner or later.

She still had her paltry jewels in the sack at her side. As a precaution she pulled the tiny pouch from her waistband and hung it around her neck, tucking it between her breasts. If a man got his hands there she'd be past help, anyway.

Strange to think of them all dead back there. The tall prince didn't seem the kind of man to die easily, though Joanna knew that death was swift and impartial. And Lady Elizabeth had been so young, so naive, so determined.

For some reason the image of Brother Adrian flashed before her, with his downcast eyes. He had the wrong mouth for a celibate, she thought. Even though he'd tried to hide it, he had the mouth of a sensualist. A mouth made for kissing, and he would never kiss. It shouldn't have saddened her, but it did. She'd always had a weakness for kissing, a weakness not shared by the men in her life. It was only what came afterward that was unpleasant and unsatisfying.

She looked west, toward the sea, toward eventual help, then back into the murky depths of the forest. Were they all dead? Had the marauders abandoned their bodies without making certain that some of them could still be helped?

If she had any sense at all she would continue onward, accepting the fate of her fellow travelers as she accepted most things.

But at that moment she seemed particularly lacking in sense. She knew she was going back, at least partway, close enough to see whether or not there was anything she could do. Close enough to know that in truth, they were all dead, and she had no choice but to move on.

Her pace was slow, circumspect, as she retraced her

mad dash through the forest. What had seemed to take her mere moments was now taking her hours. Part of her dreaded what she would find, and her pace slowed accordingly. There would be nothing she could do but pray over them and depart.

The smell of blood and death reached her, and she stopped, clutching her stomach to keep her reflexive gagging from overtaking her. The sun must have hit the bodies. Before long the animals would come, and the thought of Lady Elizabeth's poor body being savaged by wild boars was somehow unbearable. If she could do nothing else she'd somehow manage to bury Lady Elizabeth. It was too cruel a death for one so young and preternaturally brave.

The scene of carnage came as a shock. She was closer than she'd realized, and she almost fell over the outstretched body of one of the monks. He'd been running, and he lay dead in a pool of blood, his tonsured head smashed by a mace.

They lay all around like scattered bits of kindling. Monks and knights, they were all dead. She moved forward, picking her way through the bodies, a sense of strong foreboding filling her. There was no woman here. No swath of flame-red hair, no length of green fabric. No sign of Elizabeth at all.

Which left one of two choices. Either she'd escaped, or they'd taken her, and God have mercy on her soul.

Logic told Joanna that it could only be the latter. That Elizabeth, if she wasn't dead yet, would be praying for it soon enough. And Joanna could only add her own prayers that her end would be swift and merciful.

But there was always the possibility she had escaped. She had long legs that would carry her far and fast, and a bright, inventive mind that would aid her. There was always hope.

There were too many bodies to be certain, but she couldn't identify the prince. There was no way she could, of course—some of the wounds inflicted by the bandits had been savage and disfiguring, and blood turned the clothing black. She went to each one, touching them briefly, saying a quiet prayer, closing the eyes of one poor soul, but she couldn't bring herself to turn them over to check their identity. In the end, what did it matter?

She went to the fallen monks, following the same pattern, a soft prayer for their souls and a brief touch, until she came to the last one who lay facedown in his own blood. He was off away from the rest, as if he'd been running for his life, and yet there was no wound on his back. He couldn't have been struck down as he fled.

She touched his shoulder with gentle hands, but it was warm and pliant, not stiff and cold like the others. And he groaned.

She jumped back, startled. And then she fell to her knees beside him, turning him over carefully.

It was Brother Adrian. She gazed down at him in wonder. His eyes were closed, his chest was red with blood, but he lived. As she'd somehow known he would, when she made the insane decision to turn around and come back to this place of death, instead of seeing to her own safety.

She put her hand against his heart, and it was beating strongly. His color was good, as well—the loss of blood was not as bad as it seemed. "Brother Adrian," she said in an urgent voice. "Can you hear me?"

His eyes fluttered open for a brief moment, staring up at her, trying to focus. "The prince..." he whispered.

"The prince is dead. We have to get away from this place—they may come back. Do you think you could walk if I helped you?"

"No," he said. But he put his hand on her shoulder, pulling himself to his feet, almost toppling her in the effort.

He swayed, and she immediately put her arm around his waist to support him. He tried to pull away, but he hadn't the strength. "Stop fighting, boy," she snapped, nettled. "Save your strength for getting away from here."

"I'm not...a boy..." he managed to say.

"Be quiet!" She moved forward, guiding him, terrified he'd collapse again and she'd be unable to lift him, but he somehow managed to move forward.

It was slow, painful going, one stumbling step after another. Joanna didn't stop to think how heavy his body was, how her own ached, how empty her stomach or how warm the day was becoming. They simply walked, step by step, farther and farther away from the scene of carnage.

It must have been hours later when Adrian stopped to lean against a tree. "I need to rest," he gasped.

"If we stop I may never get you moving again," Joanna said. She felt like an anxious mother with a hurt child.

"I'm not certain I can move anymore. You should go on, see to yourself," he said. "Either someone will come and find me, or I'll die. It's God's will. I have failed in my task. I was to watch him, make certain he didn't harm anyone else…"

"Who?"

"The prince," he muttered. "I tried to stop him. When the marauders came I went after him. Better he should die at their hands than escape. But he was too strong, and he had a knife."

"You're saying the prince hurt you?" She couldn't believe him.

"He hoped to kill me. He may have succeeded," Adrian said, closing his eyes. "Go on without me."

"No," she said. "I was well away from here when something stopped me and sent me back to find you. It could only be the will of God, and I am not about to contravene it. Neither should you, Brother Adrian, if you have any sense. There's no guarantee you won't die, but you shouldn't die defying God's will."

"Who says it wasn't the Devil who sent you back after me?" he whispered.

"I don't take orders from the Devil," Joanna said firmly. "We can argue about that later. In the meantime we need to keep moving. I promise you, as soon as we find some sort of shelter we'll stop and I'll see what I can do about your wound.''

"No!" he said, sounding very young. "You shouldn't touch me...."

"I'm already touching you, Brother," she said, feeling oddly maternal. "And if you don't step forward I may very well kick your arse, as well. Move! With luck we'll find a monastery to aid us, but otherwise you're stuck with me. And stop arguing. I told you to save your strength."

She wasn't sure what else she could do. He was almost at the end of his endurance, and she had no notion of how far she could push him. He walked for another hour, and then collapsed, unconscious, at her feet.

She fell to her knees beside him, terrified that he was dead, but his heart was still beating strongly, though his skin was warm to the touch. Too warm. She had to get his wound cleaned and dressed; he had to rest and regain his strength, or the fever would overtake him and she'd have no choice but to sit and watch him die.

They couldn't stay there. She tried tugging at his shoulders, but he groaned at the pressure on his wound, and he was too heavy. In a moment of inspiration she pulled off her cloak and lay it on the hard ground, then managed to roll him onto it. Taking the hem of it, she began to pull, and slowly his body began to move.

It seemed like hours later when she saw the tiny cottage, and she felt a sudden surge of hope. Dropping the edge of her cloak, she ran forward, calling out for help.

It was long abandoned. Part of the roof was gone, and it was not much better than a shed. But a cool stream ran nearby, and the place would provide shelter and time to let Brother Adrian rest. A few hours would make all the difference.

The last few moments of the journey were the hardest. He seemed to have doubled in weight for such a slight young man, and Joanna was so weary she wanted to sit on the ground and weep with it. But he was growing weaker, and now wasn't the time to give in.

By the time she managed to half push, half drag him into the hovel she was ready to collapse herself. The bed was covered with straw, and she could only hope it wasn't infested with vermin. At that moment all she could do was get his heavy body up onto it. And then she fell into the narrow space behind him, closing her eyes.

For a moment Elizabeth thought it was sheer force of will, the hand that reached down through the water for her. The hand of God, plucking her up into heaven? She surged upward, back into the blessed air, but it wasn't God's face she looked into, it was the Devil's. The prince wasn't dead, he was treading water beside her, hauling her toward the shore.

"Fight me and I'll let you drown," he said, but she was past the point of resistance. He was a much stronger swimmer than she was, and he wasn't hampered by long, heavy skirts. He reached the shore, keeping a manacle grip on her wrist, pulled himself up and dragged her after him, dropping onto the ground. Since he hadn't let go of her she had no choice but to collapse next to him, and no will to do anything else. She lay on her back, winded, staring up at the towering trees overhead, listening to the sounds of the forest. The river was running wildly nearby—why hadn't she noticed it was no gentle stream? Birds were making a racket overhead, a good sign. It meant no predators were trying to sneak up on them. She could hear the man next to her struggle to catch his breath, and she turned her face to look at him, now that her own breathing had returned to normal.

He still hadn't released her wrist, a fact she was uncomfortably aware of. He may not have even realized he was still touching her. He simply lay there, his eyes closed, as rivulets of water streamed down his face from his wet hair.

He must have felt her eyes on him. He turned to look at her, a blank expression on his face.

"Where did you come from?" she asked. Her voice was hoarse from the water she'd swallowed and then coughed up, and she cleared her throat.

"The same place you did," he replied. "Don't you remember?"

"The last time I saw you, you were battling the bandits. What made you turn and run?"

Not the most tactful way to put it, but he didn't even blink. He simply shrugged. "Perhaps I saw it was going to end badly and decided to escape while I still could.''

"They were after you, weren't they? They weren't ordinary bandits—their horses were too fine, their clothes too good. They were sent by the man whose daughter you killed."

"I have more than one enemy," he said, seemingly unconcerned. "He's just one of many who'd like to see me dead."

"So instead everyone else died."

"You didn't," he pointed out.

"Because I ran."

"Because I told you to run. Perhaps you should have picked up a sword and fought them yourself."

"I don't know how to use a sword."

"Ah, yes. Well, you'll need a knife and a sword where we're going. I'll teach you how to use one."

She sat up. She was chilled, soaked to the bone, and a breeze had picked up, sending tendrils of ice down her spine. She tugged at her wrist, but he didn't release her.

"Where are we going?" she said.

"To the Shrine of Saint Anne, of course. You to join the holy sisters, me to perform an act of contrition. Perhaps I'll travel the last few miles on my knees to show my repentance."

"Like your grandfather."

"What?"

"Everyone knows your grandfather made a pilgrimage on his knees after he had Saint Thomas à

Becket killed. You come from murderous blood, don't you?''

"Ah, yes. My grandfather. I'm not so good on family history—I prefer to live in the present.'' He sat up, shaking his head like a wet dog so that the water sprayed everywhere, including into her eyes. "You run too fast. I had the devil of a time catching up with you. I was almost too late. What happened—did you slip on the bank of the river?''

"I jumped in.''

He was silent for a moment. "Suicide is a mortal sin.''

"I wasn't trying to kill myself. I was covered in blood—I couldn't stand it anymore. I thought if I just jumped in it might wash the worst of it away.''

"And instead you almost drowned. I thought you were smarter than that. You don't jump into a river without testing the depth and the current.''

"I'm not in the habit of jumping into rivers at all. I've spent most of my life in my father's household, protected from danger.''

"And now you have the horror of discovering how dangerous life can really be. Much more terrifying than a bullying father, I expect. You must be shaking in your shoes.''

"I left my shoes on the riverbank when I jumped in,'' she said, glancing up the swift-flowing stream. "If I'm shaking, it's because I'm cold. And I'd rather be dead than spend the rest of my life trapped in my father's household.''

"And the danger?''

She knew what her answer should be. But there was something about the prince that cut to the heart of the matter. She said things to him that she never said out loud to other people, only thought.

"I liked it."

"You what?"

She'd managed to astonish him. "I liked the danger. Oh, I didn't like people being hurt, people dying. But there's something…invigorating in running for your life, isn't there? I imagine it would be just as stimulating to fight." She turned to him eagerly. "Would you really teach me how to use a sword? I imagine I could stab anyone easily enough with a knife, but a sword seems a great deal more complicated."

He stared at her for a long, perplexed moment. "You never fail to astonish me, my lady," he said. "You should be weak and fainting with horror."

"Then you'd have to carry me, and I'd just as soon you didn't touch me." She looked down at her wrist pointedly. His long fingers still encircled it, and he made no effort to release her.

"We would all like a great many things that we'll never receive. And let me assure you, knife fighting is far more complicated than you might imagine, and requires brute strength. The only way you'd succeed is if you depended on the element of surprise."

"That should be easy enough. Who would expect a gentle young lady like me to stab them?"

"Anyone who'd spent much time with you," he

muttered. "How far back did you decide to go for your little swim?"

"I don't know. It seems as if I was in the water for hours."

He finally released her hand, rising to his full height. She didn't move—if she stood she'd be too close to him, too easy for him to touch. "You stay here. I'll follow the river back and see if I can find your slippers. We've got a long walk ahead of us and your feet are going to need some kind of protection."

For some reason she didn't like the notion of being abandoned, even for a short while. "I can come with you...."

"You can stay right here. I can only assume they were Baron Neville's men, intent on vengeance. I have no idea whether they followed us or not, but I'd have a much easier time dealing with them if I didn't have to worry about you. Sit in the sun and dry yourself out—I'll be back as quickly as I can. And don't make the mistake of thinking you could go on without me. I'll drown you myself if you try it."

She'd been thinking that very thing. For all that she didn't want to be left alone, the thought of spending even one hour alone with the dangerous man who'd pulled her from the river was unnerving, and the thought of nights along the way to the shrine was absolutely terrifying.

"You wouldn't drown me," she said, wondering if she believed it.

"Maybe not. But I'd beat you, and I think you've already mentioned you want me to keep my hands off you. Don't anger me, then, or you definitely wouldn't like the consequences.''

''I've been beaten before,'' she shot back.

''You wouldn't like what came afterward.''

She closed her mouth. She could just imagine what he might have in mind after he beat her, and she had no doubt he'd follow through. The bastard prince of England was not known for his self-restraint, and anger could release a lot of other, dangerous emotions.

''I'll do what you tell me to,'' she said, only faintly sullen.

''Yes, you will,'' he agreed. ''Because you have no choice in the matter.''

She stared up at him. He towered over her, and she was half tempted to scramble to her feet so that she didn't feel so small and helpless. She wasn't used to that odd sensation, and she wanted to fight back.

But he'd already made it clear that fighting back was not a wise idea.

The sun had moved past the trees, shining down on her, and steam began to rise from her soaked gown. ''I'll wait for you,'' she said, stretching out on the ground again, trying to look at ease.

He stood over her for another moment, looking down at her, an odd expression in his eyes.

And then he turned and left her, without another word.

12

William's triumph, such as it was, was short-lived. He had no notion whether he'd managed to kill Sir Adrian, his father's appointed bodyguard, and Gervaise had been in too great a hurry to allow him enough time to find out. It wasn't as if it mattered—everyone was dead. There would be no witnesses to testify that the murderous attack by outlaws was no such thing.

They were days late as it was—he'd been counting on his prearranged rescue before they'd reached Castle Bredon. Each day spent in the scratchy, shapeless robes of a humble brother was an affront. He would make someone pay for the delay, most likely Gervaise himself. Except that Gervaise, his lieutenant and the closest thing he had to a friend, had a taste for pain, and any punishment short of death would be received quite gratefully. And William still had need of his services and his talents, which were unique and varied.

The girl had escaped, as well. Gervaise had sent men after her, but they hadn't returned, and he could only assume she'd escaped and they'd been too frightened to return to their prince as failures, knowing the inevitable consequences.

The very notion that he would acquiesce to a degrading pilgrimage such as this one was ludicrous, but his royal father, too besotted with his infant whore, had for once been paying attention, and William hadn't dared to defy a flat-out decree. He thought he'd arranged it cleverly enough. Within two days of setting off on his penitential journey the small caravan was to be attacked by robbers, with everyone left dead. His escape and eventual arrival on his own at the holy shrine would be viewed as something akin to a miracle, ensuring he be left alone for a goodly length of time with no one interfering with his pleasures.

He hadn't actually meant to kill Neville's daughter. He was much too smart for a mistake like that— daughters of the nobility couldn't simply disappear as other, lesser souls could. But he'd misjudged her capacity, and she'd ended up dead, and there hadn't been time to dispose of her. Too many people had seen her with him, too many people who held a grudge. He'd been well and truly caught, but he had no intention of paying the price for his playful misdeeds.

But there was something to be gained from every disaster, and it had been simple enough to arrange for the renowned Brother Peter to head the expedition. His father had doubtless thought it was a boon, to place an old acquaintance in charge of his son's penance. Not knowing that he'd presented a perfect opportunity for William's long-delayed revenge. Brother Peter, the former Sir Peter de Montselm, would end up gutted in the forest, dead along with everyone else who might bring back tales.

But Gervaise was late for the planned ambush that would kill Brother Peter and liberate the prince. William had been silently fuming by the time they'd arrived at Bredon Castle. None of their party had known his real identity apart from Brother Peter and Adrian of Longacre. The knights and soldiers had come from the north, and their orders were to protect the so-called prince and the monks with their very lives.

The prince. William sneered at the notion of that tonsured monk trying to pass himself off as royal blood. Peter had always been above himself, convincing their fellow crusaders to follow him instead of the king's son. He carried himself royally, even as a lowly monk trying to expiate his pathetic little sins. Once he doffed his monk's robes it had been a simple matter. Everyone had believed him, treated him with more innate deference than they'd ever shown their real prince.

It had taken seven years, but vengeance was finally at hand. Peter had been a legend of the Crusades, bearing William's sainted uncle company, cutting a bloody swath through the Holy Lands. And in the end, in the face of triumph, what had the fool done? Left the spoils of war behind, returned to his native land a pauper, and joined the most austere order he could find in a futile attempt to cleanse his soul.

Guilt was a wasted emotion, William had always

believed. Its only use was in blackmailing others. Brother Peter was riddled by it, making him easy prey for William's taunts. If he'd been sent on pilgrimage he should have been accompanied by an archbishop, no less. Not a simple monk with a taste for self-flagellation. And Peter had no notion his presence was no accident. During the long years since they'd returned from the Holy Lands, he'd forgotten just how devious the king's son could be. Though Peter could hardly have forgotten what William had done to him. The scarred flesh lay beneath William's robes, but Peter could not have forgotten.

Adrian of Longacre was almost as bad. A member of his father's court, he'd been sent along to watch over William and make certain no one else was harmed. It was only fitting that he'd be the first to die.

But there was no certainty of that fact, though the blow William struck had been a deep one. And if by any chance Adrian survived, he could contradict William's story of an outlaw attack and a miraculous escape.

It wasn't worth worrying about. If Adrian survived, it wouldn't take much to silence him. And it wasn't his blood William wanted.

It was the saintly Peter, who played the prince better than the real one did, who owed him a debt so great that only eternal torment could repay it, who concerned him. He'd survived the attack—William had seen him charging into the woods after that red-haired girl.

It didn't surprise him. Brother Peter was ripe for disaster, and William knew just how to effect his revenge. Through the innocent affections of Elizabeth of Bredon.

If she lived, it wouldn't be for long. He would use her to get to Peter. And then, in the end, he'd finish them both, by his own hands, rather than trust such important work to an underling like Gervaise.

All the while he would revel in his new status as a living miracle. Who knows, in the end he might even become a holy man.

His mouth curled in pleasure. It was somehow fitting that an innocent like Elizabeth of Bredon and a conscience-ridden monk die in a welter of pain and blood.

William would become a modern-day saint. And eventually king, because he had every intention of making sure his adolescent stepmother never gave birth to a living son.

Even now she might be pregnant, with him too far away to do anything about it. It was all Gervaise's fault.

It would take two more days to make it to the shrine, and then he could return to his life of pleasure.

Knowing that the greatest gift was yet to come. The throne of England. Bathed in his father's blood.

Elizabeth must have dozed off. When she awoke the sun had disappeared behind the towering trees, her clothes were cold and clammy, clinging to her body, and she was shivering. The mixed blessing was that she was no longer alone.

The prince stood over her, a bundle of brown fabric in his arms, looking down at her outstretched body with an enigmatic expression on his face.

She scrambled to her feet, well out of reach, and shoved her still-damp hair behind her face. She'd lost the silver circlet that had held it in place, and it covered her shoulders like an icy cape. "How long were you staring at me?"

He laughed. "Oh, for hours! I stood staring down at you, totally besotted, too shy to wake you, waiting for you to rouse—"

"Never mind," she snapped. She was trying to control her shivering, but the words came out in a slight stutter, anyway.

"We have more important things to concentrate on than my insatiable lust for your body. Such as surviving the next few days when we're being hunted through the south of England."

The faint drawl in his offhand words made her blush, a tiny bit of warmth to her chilled body. "We're being hunted?"

"Whoever attacked us isn't going to stop until every one of us is dead. They'll keep searching, and we won't be safe until we reach the shrine."

"We? What reason would they have to kill me?"

"You're a witness. If they had no qualms about butchering monks, then they would be unlikely to hesitate in slaughtering a mere woman."

"Then it seems as if I'd be much safer if we parted company."

"You think you'd be better off alone in these woods? Feel free to go, then. Far be it from me to restrain you. I tend not to have altruistic motives, anyway, and I'd move faster without you holding me back. Godspeed, lady. If I make it to the shrine and you don't, I'll make sure the good sisters pray for your soul."

She would have given almost anything to turn and walk away from him, into the woods, never to see him again. Almost anything, except her life, and unfortunately he had the truth of it. If she struck out on her own there was a very good chance she'd never arrive at her destination.

He was waiting for her response. "I can see why people want to kill you," she said. "You're very annoying."

"So, dear lady, are you. We're agreed on that, as well as the need to stay together. Any more arguments?"

She wanted to kick him. "No."

"'No, my lord William,'" he prompted.

"No, my sainted bastard prince," she said through gritted teeth. The moment the intemperate words were out she regretted them.

Another man would have hit her. She almost flinched, but then, she had never flinched from any blow, even her father's.

To her astonishment he threw back his head and

laughed. "I find it in my heart to have pity for the mother abbess if she has to deal with you, lady. Take off your clothes."

"What?"

"You heard me. Take off those wet clothes before you catch an ague. I can't be bothered having a sick woman on my hands, and a well-dressed lady wandering through the forest would cause too much attention, even if she doesn't look a bit bedraggled. Take off your clothes or I'll cut them off you."

She was learning, slowly but surely. "And what will I be wearing instead?"

He tossed a bundle of brown fabric at her. It smelled like herbs and sunshine. "This."

"You jest." It was a monk's robe, similar to the ones worn by the friars who'd accompanied them on the first part of their journey.

He had already begun stripping off his leather tunic. "I cannot think of a better disguise."

She remembered touching the soft leather, touching the hard flesh beneath it, and the heat that filled her fought against the cold encasing her body. "Where did you get these?"

"We're not that far from where we spent the night. When I couldn't find your shoes I went back the rest of the way. The ones left behind won't be needing these."

She crossed herself quickly. "Did you bury them?"

"It took me all this time to get there and back, lady. And there were too many for one man to bury."

His words were light, unemotional. She must have imagined the bleak darkness in his eyes, the banked rage.

"Were they all…did they all…?"

"There was no sign of Dame Joanna. Nor of Brother Adrian or Brother Matthew. The rest were dead."

She crossed herself again. "And all for your sake, my lord. They must have been trying to kill you— probably the family of that poor girl you killed. I only hope you prove yourself worthy of other people's sacrifice."

His smile was slow and mocking. "Oh, I have. Countless times over. Too bad I wasn't left with Dame Joanna instead of an asp-tongued virgin. Take off your clothes, lady, and stop arguing, or I won't share the food I brought."

The mention of food was enough to make her move. "I'd like a bit of privacy," she said, picking up the robe. He'd stripped the leather jerkin over his head and the undershirt followed, leaving his chest bare in the dappled sunlight. She froze for a moment, momentarily distracted.

She was used to big, burly men, covered with hair, laden with muscle and fat. The prince was none of those things.

His skin was smooth, a deep golden color stretched over his elegant bones. She knew for a fact that he was very strong, but the sinew and muscle beneath that beautiful skin was only subtly defined. He was lean—almost too much so, as if he hadn't eaten as much as he should have. Too busy ravishing women instead of letting them feed him, she thought absently.

"Have you looked your fill, lady? Or do you want to see everything?" He was reaching for his hose, and she let out a squeal, scampering into the bushes.

Dame Joanna's ruined green dress was fastened with lacing up the back. The ties were soaked, knotted and impossible to budge with her chilled fingers. The more she tugged, the worse the knots became, until she was ready to weep with frustration. She had no choice—she was going to have to ask for help from the prince. Help in undressing—the fates could not have been more unkind.

Enough time had elapsed that he'd be decently covered, and she reemerged from the bushes, carrying the robe with her. He was standing by the stream, staring into the forest with an abstracted expression on his face.

He wore the rough brown habit with elegance, as she would have expected. "I've never seen someone who looked less like a monk," she said.

He turned to look at her, his eyes narrowed. "I thought I looked quite pious. And you look even less like a monk than I do. Why haven't you changed?"

"I need to borrow your knife."

"What happened to the one I gave you?"

"I lost it. If you might remember, I left in a hurry."

"So you can protect yourself from my rapacious ways?"

"So I can cut the lacing that holds this dress on.

It's too knotted for me to unfasten and the dress is ruined, anyway.''

''If anyone's cutting your clothes off you, then I claim the honor,'' he said, coming toward her at a lazy pace. ''But first, let me see if I can untangle the strings. You may not need this gown anymore, but there are peasants who could still make good use of the fabric.''

''And you're so concerned with peasants? I had no notion that Prince William had the welfare of the poor in mind.''

''I doubt he does,'' he muttered. ''Turn around. Unless you want me to reach around you and do it blind.''

She spun around, quickly, before he could put his arms around her. She had little doubt he would do just that, and the thought of him touching her was even more disturbing now that he wore the deceptively sober garb of a monk.

She jumped when his hands touched her back. ''Hold still,'' he muttered. ''The more you squirm, the longer this will take. I brought bread and cheese and apples with me, and I imagine you're quite hungry by now. So behave yourself.''

''Behave myself?'' she echoed, incensed. ''I'm not the one who needs to worry about bad behavior.''

''Oh, are you not?'' He caught her heavy sheaf of wet hair and tossed it over her shoulder. ''Calling me a sainted bastard prince isn't a polite form of address by most standards.''

''I was goaded.''

"Indeed." His fingers brushed the bare skin above the neck of the dress, and she shivered. Still cold, she told herself, ignoring the heat in her belly. "And I will admit I'm better at arousing intemperate behavior in women than most."

She felt a tug, and the dress suddenly loosened around her. She caught it before it descended in a wet heap, holding it around her. "Thank you," she said grudgingly, heading back toward the privacy of the bushes.

She half expected him to try to stop her, but he said nothing. This time when she glanced back he was simply standing there, staring after her.

God help him, he'd almost kissed her, Peter thought. Kissed the smooth white skin of her shoulder. When he'd moved her long, damp hair out of the way he'd exposed the nape of her neck, and found himself instantly, violently aroused. He hadn't seen the nape of a woman's neck in years—he'd forgotten how intensely erotic the sight was. He would have given his immortal soul to have put his mouth against the soft, tender skin at the base of Elizabeth's neck.

And that was exactly what it would have cost him. His immortal soul. He was on shaky ground already, and a lifetime of penance and self-denial might make the difference. If not in the matter of heaven and hell, at least in his ability to live in peace for the rest of his days. To willingly commit even one more grievous sin would make the guilt unendurable.

But the ties had unfastened beneath his nimble fingers sooner than he would have wanted, and she moved away, out of his reach, before he could let the madness take over.

At least she would be covered, head to toe, in drab brown cloth. He would no longer be distracted by her flaming hair, her saucy mouth or her defiant eyes. No longer distracted by her beautiful long legs that he could just imagine wrapped around his hips as he…

He cursed beneath his breath. There was no way he could punish the need out of his body—she would never believe that the bastard prince had a repentant bone in his body. And it was greater punishment to simply have to bear the need and do nothing about it. Far worse pain than self-flagellation or a hair shirt. Looking at Elizabeth's ripe mouth and not being able to do anything about it was the true definition of torment.

Of course, he'd already done something about it. The taste he'd had of her had only made things worse. He'd made it through seven years of celibacy, and it had never been easy, but he'd managed to resist some of the most beautiful women in England during his time at court. Why would a long-limbed, flame-haired termagant manage to undermine his vows when no one else had done more than tempt him?

He could always tell her the truth, now that things had fallen in such disarray. He had impersonated Prince William to keep him safe, for all the good it had done. He had no idea whether or not the prince still lived, though he expected he did. Evil wasn't easily diminished, and Peter knew full well the extent of William's cruelty. A monster lived inside him, one that wouldn't die easily.

Was Adrian with him, watching over him? Or had he been killed as well? And what of Dame Joanna? He should have stayed, fought till the end.

But he'd looked up from fighting his way toward the prince and seen Elizabeth, and everything else had fallen away but the need to save her. She'd run, and three men had gone after her, and in the end it had been no choice. Three more men on his conscience, their blood staining his soul. It didn't matter that they were hired killers, bent on destruction. It didn't matter that he killed them to save an innocent life. Each life he'd taken was part of the debt he owed.

No, he wouldn't tell Lady Elizabeth that he was nothing more than a lowly monk. She despised Prince William, and that was one of his few defenses. As Prince William he could insult and cajole her, tease and annoy her. Brother Peter could do none of those things.

And if they happened to meet anyone on their journey to the shrine, the less she knew the better. He would deliver her up to the mother abbess, safe and sound, and then go in search of the missing prince. With any luck he'd find him in pieces in the forest, or hanging from a tree outside Neville Castle. Peter would have failed in his task, but the world would be a safer, better place without such a monster living in it. He could face the king's wrath and vengeance with equanimity. As long as Elizabeth was safe behind the cloister walls.

Though in truth he'd meant it when he said she was ill-suited for the veil. Her unruly nature would make obedience difficult for her, and obedience to the rule was essential to the cloistered life. She should be married, the mother of many children who'd drive her mad just as she was driving him mad. She'd need a strong husband, not a weakling like Thomas of Wake-bryght, but not a bully, either. In truth, he could think of no man who would be her equal—she would terrify half of them and enrage the other half.

He was thankful that it wasn't his responsibility. She'd chafe at whatever yoke the world put upon her—at least in the convent she'd be able to use her wits.

He heard the bushes rustle, and he quickly schooled his expression into princely hauteur. She emerged, swathed in the rough brown habit, and he wanted to groan. The layers of cloth may have covered her feminine shape effectively, but they did little to hide her natural, coltish grace.

She was carrying the sodden green dress, but he could see no lighter colors in the pile that she set on the ground. "Where are your underclothes? Your chemise?"

"Still wearing it," she replied. "If you think I'm going around in nothing but a monk's robe you are sadly deluded."

"Why not? I am."

She blushed, as he expected she would. Interesting that the thought of his naked body beneath the robes would disturb her.

As for him, it didn't matter what he thought she was wearing beneath the rough wool. If she was dressed in her loose chemise or nothing at all, he was still aroused. One more torment that he richly deserved.

"You were supposed to get out of your wet clothes so you wouldn't catch cold," he said, exhibiting nothing of his thoughts.

"They'll dry well enough. Besides, the cloth is too coarse next to my skin. It's a curse that goes with my devil's hair—my flesh is easily bothered." She raised her head. "What was that noise?"

"A cough," he said, covering his heartfelt groan of dismay at the thought of her pale, bothered flesh. "We need to get as far away from this place as we can—we've wasted too much time already. Put up your hood and we'll make haste."

"You were going to feed me."

This time he didn't let the groan reach his lips. "We need to get away from here first. Unless you're too weak from hunger…"

"I'm not weak," she snapped, straightening her shoulders. She pulled the hood up over her head, drooping it down low so that it hid her face. "How does that look?" She started forward. "Will people truly believe I'm a monk?"

"They would have no reason not to. And despite the fact that you walk with a girlish gait, even that is acceptable. There are any number of young monks who flit around like pretty moths."

She jerked her head back to him so fast the hood

started to slip off her head. He'd come up to her, and he simply reached up and readjusted the thick brown wool, hiding her face. Hiding it from his own hungry eyes. "Don't worry, Lady Elizabeth. Just follow my lead and keep your tongue in your head. We're just a couple of mendicant monks on a pilgrimage, and I, as your elder, would be expected to do the talking. Can you remember that?"

"Of course," she said, affronted.

"And can you keep quiet and do as you're told?"

"Certainly. I'm a female—I've spent my life doing just that."

"Not since you left your father's household, lady," he said. "Never mind. Behave yourself as if your life depended on it. It may very well."

"Yes, my lord."

"Yes, *Brother*. And speak in deeper tones."

"Yes, Brother William," she said in an exaggeratedly bass voice. "Anything you say, Brother William. I am yours to command, Brother William."

"If you say so, Brother Bratling." And he moved past her, down the winding path, without bothering to see whether she'd follow.

13

Joanna dreamed of heat and bright, blessed sunlight. When she awoke, the late afternoon sun was pouring down on her from the broken doorway to the hut, and the man next to her was burning with fever.

She scrambled out of bed in a panic. How could she have been so weak, to fall asleep like that when the young monk was wounded and possibly dying? He was so pale, his dark hair curling against his face, and the blood soaked through his robes.

She glanced around the small hut, looking for something that might hold water. She needed to clean his wound, find him something to eat. A bit of food for herself wouldn't come amiss.

She managed to find a bowl amid the broken crockery, and she headed for the door, casting one last glance at Brother Adrian. He lay so still, he almost looked dead already.

If she had any sense she would leave him, strike out on her own. She could either make her way back to Wakebryght and the tender mercies of Owen's bed, or she could move farther, look for someone a little less brutal, a little less demanding. She could even find her way to Saint Anne's on her own. Even if the sisters wouldn't let her join, they would never turn a pilgrim away. Particularly one who could pay her way with jewels, soiled as they were with their acquisition.

Adrian made a faint noise. A groan, most likely, but it sounded to Joanna's ears like a protest. She couldn't leave him yet. Not until she'd made some effort to see him safe.

The stream running not far from the shack was clear and swift running, and she filled the bowl, washing her hands as best she could in the process. More dirt in Adrian's wounds would hardly improve matters. When she ducked back into the shelter he hadn't moved, his eyes were closed, his ridiculously long lashes resting against his pale cheeks.

She was adept at undressing men, but she'd never undressed a monk before. The rough weave of his habit was stiff with blood, and it stuck to his wound, so that when she tugged at it he groaned again, this time more loudly.

"I'm sorry, my love," she whispered. "But if we leave it like this you'll die of blood poisoning." She poured some of the water on the wound, hoping to loosen it, and he moaned again.

She had little choice. She took the small, jeweled dagger from her waist and carefully cut the robe away, pushing it off his chest. And then, holding her breath, she ripped the rest from his wound.

Adrian's eyes flew open, and he screamed. His hand clamped around her wrist with crushing force as he stared up into her face, trying to sit up. And then he fell back, unconscious, his hand releasing hers.

The wound could have been worse—she'd seen men more grievously hurt and survive. It was deep, but it had bled freely, and it was bleeding afresh.

She washed it carefully, looking for signs of infection, the dark red streaks that would radiate out from the wound and signify probable death. Some had set in—there was no doubt, or his skin wouldn't be so hot to the touch—but it wasn't yet a lost cause. She washed the knife wound clean, and the bleeding slowed. She needed to bandage it and pack it with powdered yarrow, then get some food in him.

She wet his dry lips with some of the water, and bandaged the wound with strips from her chemise, then stepped back.

Leaving him was the only sensible alternative, before it grew too dark to find her way. She would head west, stop at the first village she came to and tell them of Adrian's presence in the hut. Someone would come to his aid, and she could be safely on her away, sure her Christian duty was done.

It was a relatively simple matter to rip the ornamentation off her gown, replace her jeweled girdle with a rough swath of fabric. She stripped off her rings and set one on the bed next to Adrian, as payment for anyone who helped him, and she put the jeweled dagger there as well. She hated to go out without any weapon, but the fancy knife would alert everyone to the fact that she was no ordinary woman.

She had a few silver coins in her bag, as well. Even one would buy her a plain, serviceable knife, a loaf of bread and directions to the nearest city. She would tell them she'd come across Adrian by accident, and then hope his God would protect him.

She brushed a dark curl away from his pale, hot skin. He lay still, deep in a sleep of pain.

"Poor, pretty little boy," she said softly. And she leaned down and put her lips against his for a brief, gentle kiss.

She might have dreamed it, but it seemed for a moment as if his lips clung to hers. And she must have imagined that faint sigh as she pulled away.

"Goodbye, my angel," she whispered. "May God look after you." And she turned her back on him for the last time, heading out into the bright afternoon sunlight to find her way back to comfort and safety.

It was a good thing she had big feet, Elizabeth thought as she struggled to keep up with the prince's long stride. The rough monk's sandals fit her well enough. Indeed, her overall size was, for the first time, a boon. If she were as small as most women the man's robe would drag on the ground, tripping her up, and the sandals would fall off her tiny feet. She'd have to take three running steps to every one of the prince's steady footsteps, instead of one and a half.

Yes, she should definitely be counting her blessings. Her devil's hair was now decently covered by the enveloping hood, and, in fact, if she had to be caught alone in a menacing forest with murderous bandits abounding she probably couldn't have chosen a stronger companion. The prince didn't appear to be particularly powerful—he hadn't the bulk of most of the soldiers she'd seen, but she'd had enough of a glimpse of him in battle to know that he was fearless and powerful.

Which didn't explain why he'd run away from the fight to follow her, if he wasn't afraid for his life.

And then the simple, obvious answer came to her, so plain and unacceptable that she made an inadvertent sound of protest.

He halted abruptly, turning to look at her. He'd pulled his hood up over his head, as well, but he looked like no monk she'd ever seen. "What's wrong?" he demanded.

"Nothing."

"You said 'no.' I heard it distinctly. If you're already mentally rehearsing the battle for your chastity you might as well put it out of your mind. We have more important things to consider than whether or not I'm going to get beneath your skirts. Such as how we're going to stay alive for the next few days."

"I wish you'd stop it," she said crossly, catching up with him. "I have little doubt that overwhelming lust for me is the least of your problems."

He said nothing in response to that. She told herself that was a relief. "Then what was the horrified noise that came from your petal-pink lips, my sweet scold?"

He was deliberately trying to annoy her, as always. Presumably he did so because he could get away with it. Even a bastard prince was relatively above chastising, except by an angry church or a kingly father whose power was threatened by his son's intemperate behavior.

"Why did you leave the battle?"

"Which battle? I've run away from many," he said lightly.

That was a lie, making clear that the other was a lie as well. "Why did you leave when the bandits attacked?"

"I was scared to death. I'm used to having knights and soldiers to protect me, and they were outnumbered. A strategic retreat seemed the wisest thing to do."

"You weren't scared. I saw you—you were enjoying the battle."

"I do like killing. I'm very good at it." There was a strange, almost bitter tone to his voice. The rest had been lies, but this she believed.

"You didn't run because you were afraid," she accused him. "You were coming after me. To save me. Weren't you?"

He put his hands on her shoulders, and his smile was cool and disdainful. "Dear lady, you can't have it both ways. Either I'm quivering with overwhelming desire for you or I'm not. Make up your mind and I'll be happy to act on it."

"You didn't come after me to bed me. You came after me to save my life," she said, stubborn, with the weight of his hands on her shoulders.

The gentle mockery in his smile should have chilled her. "Ah, my secret is out. In truth I have no interest in shallow pleasures, I simply go about the countryside looking for virgins to rescue, wanting no reward but the sharp side of their tongues. Sweet maiden or wicked scold, it makes no difference to me as long as I have the joy of preserving their maidenheads.''

"It doesn't matter how you mock me," she shot back. "I know you came after me to save my life."

"And why would I do that? Why would I care?" He put his hand under her chin, tilting her face up to his, and the hood fell back on her shoulders. "Surely if I were driven by lust I would have been far smarter to have saved Dame Joanna."

"Is she dead?"

"I told you, I didn't see her body, so I can only assume she escaped."

"So then, why did you come after me instead of her?"

"Child," he said, "I came after no one. I ran for my life, and you happened to be in the way."

The lie was so clear, so easily told, and yet she knew without question that a lie it was. She opened her mouth to say as much, then shut it again, for once wise enough to know when silence was a better option. If she insisted he'd followed her out of concern, he might be tempted to show her just how physical that concern might be.

"I'm hungry," she said instead.

"So am I. We wait until we get to our destination before we eat."

"We're not going to eat until we get to Saint

Anne's Shrine?'' Elizabeth shrieked. ''I'll drop dead.''

''I expect you'll manage to survive,'' he said dryly. ''A great many people go longer than a few days without solid food, and they're usually walking when they do so. But, in truth, we'll be stopping for the night in a few hours. You'll have a full belly and a good night's sleep before we head out again.''

A good night's sleep sounded promising—she'd have to be lying alone for that to happen. ''What if the outlaws sneak up on us while we sleep? The forest muffles any noise, and we could have our throats slit before we knew it.''

''If someone slit your throat you probably would be past noticing, anyway. Besides, if anyone's going to kill you it will be me, out of sheer frustration. We're not sleeping in the forest.''

She waited, but he didn't elaborate. ''You're just like my father,'' she said. ''Thinking you don't have to explain a thing, that I'll just do as you say without questioning.''

''I'm a great deal smarter than your father, and I know perfectly well that you wouldn't do anything anyone told you unless you had no choice. Trust me in this matter, lady. There is no choice.''

She opened her mouth to protest, then shut it again. She wouldn't give him the satisfaction of asking again. As a matter of fact, she had no intention of having any more conversation with him at all. She was stuck with him—he knew his way to the shrine, and it was in his best interest to deliver her there. She could make it through the next few days without wasting another word on the wretch.

"No more questions or complaints? Good." He seemed unmoved by her sudden silence. "Then let's keep moving. I don't want to travel much after dark."

He turned and kept walking, not even stopping to see whether she followed or not.

She would have given ten years off her life to let him go on his own. But it would probably be more than that—it would be the rest of her very short life that would be forfeit if she let her pride get in the way of her better judgment.

He was right—she had no choice. She scampered after him, cursing beneath her breath.

He was dying, he knew it. His shoulder was on fire, his body in flames. He was alone in the darkness, the thick, blanketing darkness, and he was dying.

He had no idea how he got there, or even what had happened to him. His last memory was the horsemen descending on them, the noise and blood of a pitched battle. He'd done his duty, gone to protect the prince, only to face the end of a knife from his very hands.

Somewhere in the dream he remembered Joanna, with the sorrowful smile and the cool hands. It felt as if she'd brought him here, but it couldn't be. She wouldn't have been strong enough, or cared enough, to see him safe.

Someone had brought him to this dark, hot place. Perhaps he'd stumbled there on his own, but he was going no farther. His strength had left him, and he was burning up with fever. He would die here, alone in the dark, and there would be no one to mourn him. He would die alone and unshriven, and no one would ever weep for him.

He drifted off, deep into the warm dark place that awaited him. Someone was crying for him after all— he could feel the drops fall on his skin, and he half expected them to sizzle with the heat of his tortured flesh. There was a glow beyond his closed eyelids. Either the night had passed and day had come, or the golden light of heaven was beckoning him. Or the fiery flames of hell.

There were weights on his eyelids, heavy weights, and he couldn't open them. Even though he knew he must. He tried to move, but he was too weak, and he felt cool, strong hands against his flesh. His bare flesh, skin to skin.

"Stay still," a voice whispered.

He could smell the tang of yarrow. The sharp bite of cheese, and something flowery, feminine.

Definitely heaven, not hell. There would be no cheese in hell, and no flowery females.

Not heaven, either, since heaven wouldn't offer his soul such temptation when his body couldn't act upon it. He managed to open his eyes, just a crack, to see Dame Joanna, framed in firelight, leaning over him. Tears on her face.

"You should go," he said. Or at least, that's what he tried to tell her. The words came out in little more than a tangled groan.

"Hush," she said, stroking his forehead. "Hush, love."

Love, Adrian thought, closing his eyes again. Perhaps he might decide to live after all.

14

The bishop had warned him, Peter thought. One of his many sins was his pride, and he'd been so sure he was immune to the blandishments of females. In truth, he was. He just wasn't immune to the charms of a flame-haired Amazon with the prickly nature of a hedgehog.

He slowed his stride imperceptibly. He didn't want her to think he was making any accommodations for her—it might get her to thinking that the dark prince had a heart, or at least a speck of human feeling.

It would make life so much simpler if he could tell her the truth. That he was nothing but a poor, cloistered, celibate monk, and that sweet-faced brother she'd been so protective of was actually the fiend from hell he'd been charged with escorting.

But he'd been disobedient enough. It was another failing—he'd been on his own for so long that submitting to the rule of the order had been a sore trial. One of the reasons he'd sought out the most punitive of monasteries in all of England.

No, this task was not meant to be easy. And, in fact, he should look on the presence of Elizabeth of Bredon as simply a variation on the punishment he deserved. Though he wondered how God could have devised such a cunning, irresistible torment like her.

God, or the Devil.

"I'm going to drop," she announced.

"Then I'll have to carry you." That shut her up, as he knew it would. Putting his hands on her was a much greater threat than abandoning her, and yet he wondered if she had the faintest idea why.

He'd never met anyone quite so innocent, quite so deluded and unknowing, while at the same time so clever. Her knowledge was wide-ranging, outstripping that of most of the monks he knew, and rivaled Brother Michael's, keeper of the library. And yet she was absolutely untutored when it came to the simple facts of life.

She knew how to bring a baby into the world, even the most troublesome of deliveries. She would know how those babies were made, even if she'd never known the touch of a man. But all her wisdom about the nature of human beings and their passions was based on theory, not experience.

She'd been brought up in a household of men, and while Peter knew there'd been stepmothers, they had each died so rapidly that she'd had no time to learn from them. Knowing Elizabeth, she probably hadn't wanted to. Her ignorance was a comfortable one— she'd lived in it all her life—and she wouldn't want her safe world shaken up.

She was no Madonna-like beauty like Dame Joanna. She was no tiny cherub like Margery of Wakebryght. She was no elegant whore of the court nor sweet virgin of the countryside.

She was too tall, too thin, her hair was the color of the Devil, and she had freckles scattered across her nose. And for the last two days he'd wanted to kiss every freckle, and then see if there were more scattered over her long, coltish body. And kiss them, as well.

No, she wasn't pretty by most standards, she was right about that. But to the right man, she was hauntingly beautiful.

To the wrong man, as well, he reminded himself sharply, picking up his pace. She hadn't found the right man, and she was unlikely to do so in the safety of a convent. All that tamped passion would be spent on learning and good works, and she would die a virgin nun, most likely heading straight to heaven with no unfortunate stops on the way.

And he'd be in hell, where he belonged, because no atonement was enough. Not when he continued to sin in his heart, every time he looked at Elizabeth of Bredon.

He glanced back at her through the gathering dusk. There wasn't much to see—the hood was pulled low over her face, the robe was enveloping, and she was struggling with the sandals, tripping over the long hem.

He stopped and turned, but her vision was obstructed by the hood, and she barreled into him, the solid heat of her smaller body bumping against his. He controlled his instinctive reaction.

"The robe is too long," he said as she hurriedly stepped back from him.

"I'm a maypole, not a giant," she replied.

"And you can't see when you wear the hood that way."

"I thought I was supposed to be properly hidden."

"We don't want people to see your face and know you're a woman. That doesn't mean you aren't allowed to see things yourself. I'll show you..." He took a step toward her, but she backed away skittishly.

"I'll be fine," she said.

"Don't annoy me, Brother," he said. Calling her that should have cooled his ardor a bit. After all, that was how he should view her. Woman or man, it should make little difference to a celibate.

"You're easily annoyed."

"Not really." He took another step toward her, catching her shoulder as she tried to escape. "Hold still."

She did as he told her, for once, holding herself rigid. "You can shorten the robe by pulling it up over the rope around your waist." He caught the rough weave and showed her.

His hands were too near her breasts, and he knew it. So, he expected, did she. He concentrated on the loose folds of fabric, arranging it just so. He didn't dare step back to survey the effect—she might not let him get close enough again. "There," he said. "That's the way some of our shorter brothers deal with it."

"I wouldn't have thought I'd be one of the shorter brothers," she muttered.

"You're tall enough for a woman," he allowed, "but there are a great many men taller than you are."

"Like you."

"Like me," he said, reaching for the enveloping hood. Dangerous ground, and he knew it. He was too close to her, and pushing the hood back on her head was curiously intimate, as her eyes and mouth came into view. She was looking up at him, that vulnerable, unhappy expression on her face, and if he kissed her she'd stop frowning. There was no telling what she might do, despite the fact that they'd already kissed. She might hit him, kick him in the shins, scream at him.

Or she might kiss him back.

She'd probably do all of those things, but in the end it would be mouth to mouth, skin to skin, sweet, dark sin that would condemn them both.

He saw the sudden darkening in her eyes, and he knew what brought it, just as he knew why she bit her lip, why her breathing suddenly became labored, as the silence between them stretched and grew, and he leaned forward, to touch her mouth with his, when the sound of a starling's cry broke the stillness of the dusk-laden forest.

He stepped back hastily, almost as if burned by the fires of hell that awaited him if he gave in, and she reached up and defiantly pulled the hood back down around her face.

"Suit yourself, Brother Elizabeth," he said. "Just

keep an eye out and try not to walk into me. That wouldn't be good for either of us.''

She didn't ask him why, a wise thing, because he would have been tempted to show her.

Sweet Jesu, he thought. This had started out as a pilgrimage to cleanse the soul of a hopeless monster, and instead it was turning out to be a pilgrimage of his own. If he survived the hourly pain of being near Elizabeth without touching her again, if he brought her safe to the convent in as virginal a state as she set out, then he might just be redeemed himself. Surely the temptation he was going through right now, and managing to resist, would be worthy of sainthood at the very least. Entrance into heaven wouldn't be too much to ask.

He could hear her stomach rumbling. He was used to fasting, but she wasn't, and he ought to at least hand her a hunk of bread while they walked. But that would be a kindness, opening the door to other kindnesses, and he didn't dare.

They were almost in sight of the Abby of Saint Bartholomew, and safety for the night. A night spent among holy brothers would set him straight, and he and Elizabeth would set out tomorrow anew. He would have the added strength of the brothers' piety, and she would have the added strength of a good night's sleep.

And they'd be one day closer to Saint Anne's.

He could always confess to the abbot who and what he was, and even more important, who Elizabeth was. He needed to discover the fate of the real Prince Wil-

liam, and the sooner he passed Elizabeth off into safe
hands the sooner he could go in search of him.

But his vow of secrecy extended to other clerics,
as well. And the brothers of Saint Bartholomew were
a notoriously rigid bunch—they allowed no women
travelers beneath their roof, and few male travelers,
as well. They would turn them away if he told them
the truth about his companion.

No, he had no choice but to continue with his orig-
inal plan, bluff it through, and move on in the morning with the holy brothers no wiser as to who had
passed the night beneath their vaulted roof.

He could hear the bells of vespers on the evening
air, and he stopped once more. This time Elizabeth
was paying attention, and she halted in time to keep
from slamming into him.

"We're almost there."

"Almost where?"

"The Abbey of Saint Bartholomew. Pay attention,
and for once don't argue with me. We are two traveling monks, on pilgrimage to the Shrine of Saint
Anne."

"Why don't we say we're going somewhere else?"
she interrupted.

"Because Saint Anne's is the logical destination
for this route, and one should never lie when the truth
would serve just as well. Stop arguing. We're two
mendicant monks on pilgrimage. You're merely a
novice, and you've taken a vow of silence. As well
as obedience to your superior."

"But..."

"You may as well start practicing that vow of silence right now. You're Brother Thomas—"

"No! Any name but that."

"Stop arguing. No one likes a scold. I'm Brother Peter." Using his own clerical name was probably a mistake—it was always possible he might find someone who knew of him—but it was a chance he was willing to take. At least if someone called him by name he would be likely to answer.

"Ha! I've never seen someone who looked less like a 'Brother Peter' in my entire life. They won't believe you're a monk. You don't look like one, don't talk like one, don't act like one."

For some reason her words stung. "We'll leave that for the abbot to judge, shall we? In the meantime, keep your hood down and your voice still, and I won't have to tell them you're fasting as well as silent."

"You wouldn't."

"Try me."

"I really hate you."

Music to his ears, he thought. "Come along, little brother. And try not to sway your hips like that. Feminine monks are nothing new, but you carry things a bit too far."

"I'm not feminine!"

He hid his smile. She actually believed that. And it was far from his place to prove her wrong.

"Silence!" he thundered in his most princely voice, moving onward toward the old abbey, leaving her to scramble behind him.

The wisest, kindest, smartest thing to do would be

to find her a good man, instead of letting her throw herself away on a convent. Not that the cloistered life wasn't a blessing, but she was particularly ill suited to it, and besides, she didn't even know what she was giving up. Therefore the sacrifice would be far easier, too easy in fact.

No, she needed a strong man to withstand that wasp tongue, one who could show her what her strong, beautiful body was made for. One who could give her love and babies and everything else she deserved.

And finding that man for her would be such a torment for him that it far outstripped any hair shirt he might find.

He would do it. She would only be a lay sister for the first year—he could find someone and send him to Saint Anne's and let nature take its course.

And spend the rest of his life in torment, thinking he should have been the one.

Elizabeth would have thought a monastery would offer some sort of protection, a haven from the elements and the danger of being alone with the dark prince. After less than an hour she was seriously considering climbing out one of the unshuttered windows and making her way alone.

The brothers of Saint Bartholomew were an unpleasant lot. They weren't fond of bathing, and clearly they'd missed the lesson that cleanliness is next to godliness. How a place so sparsely furnished could be so filthy was beyond Elizabeth's understanding.

She sat at the table next to the unlikely Brother

Peter, eating dried bread and drinking sour wine. She could smell the roast meat from the abbot's place at the head of the table, but apparently it was reserved for members of the order, not travelers.

It was not an order devoted to silence, though Elizabeth decided that it would have been a gift from God if someone could still the old abbot's grating voice. Eating his rich supper didn't slow him down—he talked through his food, through his wine, he probably talked in his sleep. Fortunately Elizabeth would never have any reason to find out.

They'd been welcomed grudgingly, and her enveloping hood made it impossible for her to tell if they'd had any suspicions about her real identity. The prince was astonishingly convincing as a monk—they seemed to accept him at face value.

"Brother Peter!" The abbot's voice thundered down the length of the table.

"Yes, Father Fillion?"

"What do the brothers of Clauvern Abbey think of women? Are they of the same mind as we, or are they weak?"

"The brothers have taken a vow of chastity, as have all monks," he said in his smooth voice.

"I'm talking about more than vile fornication," the abbot said. "Their very presence spawns the seeds of evil."

Do seeds get spawned, Elizabeth thought, not feeling particularly evil herself at the moment. Though her opinion of Abbot Fillion was none too charitable at the moment.

"At Clauvern Abbey we consider women to have their uses," the prince said smoothly. "They are excellent laundresses and scrub women, and while men make the best cooks, women are adept in the kitchen. Surely even the most wretched of God's creatures have something to offer mankind?"

"We do very well without. Better to endure a bit of God's good dirt than risk eternal damnation by contaminating ourselves with the presence of women."

Elizabeth made a choking noise, and the prince kicked her under the table. "Amen, Father," he said piously. "Was there any reason to bring up the subject? I ask because clearly there are no women here, and haven't been for a long long time."

"The last woman to stain these hallowed halls was here more than ten years ago. She was nothing more than a whore, about to give birth to a bastard spawn of Satan. We put her out in the snow."

Elizabeth had just taken a sip of the awful wine, and she choked again, casting a surreptitious glance up at the man presiding over the head of the table from beneath her enveloping hood. He was an ugly little man, with mean eyes and a thin, harsh mouth. His robe, made of much finer stuff than the rest of the monks', was stained with the traces of his excellent meals, and his rounded stomach attested to his appetite.

"I imagine she repented of her sin when faced with the winter air," the prince said smoothly.

"She died. We had the trouble of burying her and

her stillborn brat, and the ground frozen solid. Had I any doubts about the uselessness of women, that convinced me. She actually had the gall to ask for shelter! A household of men, to assist her in the disgraceful business of childbirth.''

"And yet, without that disgraceful business none of us would be here," the prince said smoothly, and Elizabeth suddenly felt more in charity with him than she had in days.

"You are a fool, Brother Peter," the abbot intoned. "You might as well glorify fornication, for without that none of us would be here."

"Ah, fornication," said the man next to her, moving his leg under the table to rest against hers. She jumped, but there was nowhere else to go other than the lap of the unsavory monk sitting next to her. "A dreadful thing, to be sure," he continued, as he slid his foot under her robe. He was wearing sandals as well she, and she could feel his skin against her bare leg. She set the rough chalice down with shaking hands, folding them in her lap as she tried to kick him away. "And yet even our mothers were guilty of it."

"But not the Holy Virgin!"

"No. But then, we're not Christ, even if we wish to be."

The silence in the room was shocking—so complete that she fancied they could hear the sound of his leg rubbing lazily against hers.

"You come from a very lax order, Brother," the abbot said sternly after a long moment. "We do not tolerate laxity here."

Elizabeth held her breath, waiting to hear how the prince might respond. "Indeed, Father, I can see how dangerous such tolerance might be. I rejoice to know that I'm in a place of such strict order, and I hope I may learn from your faultless example."

The irony in his voice would have been clear to a man less steeped in his own ignorant importance, but the abbot merely nodded.

"And train your young novice well. Beat him often, to teach him humility and obedience."

"Oh, I have every intention of doing just that. Brother Thomas has a willful streak that sorely needs taming."

"If you wish, you may send him to me for the night. I've broken many a larger man's selfish spirit. Strip him down and give him a few lashes—that would do the trick." He licked his thin lips, clearly even more interested in that notion than the roast pheasant in front of him.

"I could not allow you to take on my burden," the prince said smoothly. "He is my responsibility—I'll be the one to teach him obedience, as unpleasant a task as that might be."

The abbot nodded, not bothering to hide his disappointment. "God's peace be with you then, Brother. Join us for compline, and then Brother Adolphus will see you to your cell. You will share, of course. The pallets are not large, but the two of you should do well enough."

Elizabeth's instinctive squeal of protest was swallowed by yet another cough. "Even the rudest shelter would be an honor, Reverend Father," the prince said smoothly. And slipping his hand under the table, he calmly stroked her thigh.

15

The boy was getting worse, and there seemed to be nothing Joanna could do about it. No, he wasn't a boy—in the few hours she'd become familiar enough with his body to know that he was fully a man. Men's bodies had never bothered her—they were astonishingly simple machines that responded universally, at least when it came to women, and she'd used her knowledge efficiently.

But Adrian was another matter. She bathed his fevered body in cool water, she dripped more on his parched lips, she coaxed bits of food down his throat, all the time wondering whether insanity had truly taken hold of her usual level head.

She'd meant to leave him. She'd had every intention of doing so, telling herself that she'd stop at the first village she came to and send someone to help him. He might be dead by then, or he might not—it would be God's will and none of her own.

But the tiny village was nearer than she expected, and the people friendlier. Stripped of ornament, she looked only slightly more prosperous than one of the villagers, and they believed her story quite easily— that she was a serving woman separated from her traveling party. And they'd given her bread and wine and herbs in return for the gold ring Owen had given her when she'd first pleasured him with her mouth. She'd been sick for days, and the very sight of it brought back her illness. She had a piece of jewelry for each time she served him thus. Bribery had been better than force, she'd told herself. Knowing what it made her.

When she left the village she'd been fully intending to keep heading west, toward the sea and the next big town. She must have lost her direction in the woods, because the next thing she knew she was back at the tumbledown shack, running across the last bit of field to race inside, terrified that she'd find him dead.

He'd been out of his mind with fever, and she told herself he wouldn't survive the night. Told herself it was a waste of time—she couldn't save him, and it would only make her difficult life harder. And then she rolled up her sleeves and set to work.

It was an endless night—he was alternately burning with fever or shivering from the cold. She packed the wound with the yarrow she'd bartered from the herbalist, bathed his fevered skin, covered him with her cloak when he shivered. He was only a man, but she didn't want him to die. For some reason it had become of the utmost importance that he live.

Near dawn he grew very still, his endless thrashing finally quieted, and she knew that no matter what she did, how hard she prayed, he was out of her hands. Death hovered near.

She knelt by the bed, exhausted, feeling the help-

less tears stream down her face as she brushed the
dark curls away from his high forehead. He seemed
so young, when in fact he was probably not that far
from her own age. Too young to die, that much was
certain.

"Sweet boy," she whispered, "I can't save you
and it's breaking my heart, and I truly thought my
heart had broken long ago." She leaned forward and
kissed him softly on his parched lips. Her tears
dropped on his skin, and she half expected it to sizzle
in the heat of his fever. But he didn't move, still as
death.

She put her head against the side of the bed. He
was going to die, but no one should have to die alone.
And she climbed up onto the bed beside him, pulling
his still, frail body against her own, and slept, holding
him against her breast.

"We're going to what?" Elizabeth demanded in
whispered fury.

"Hush! You've taken a vow of silence," the prince
muttered under his breath as he shepherded her down
the long, dank hall of the abbey. They were following
in the abbot's footsteps, and the monks up ahead were
chanting plainsong. They were off-key—not the finest
voices in the land—and it had been a matter of great
shock when the fake monk beside her had joined in,
his own voice deep and rich. The voice was her first
shock, though it shouldn't have surprised her. After
all, his speaking voice was warm and sinfully beguiling, just one of his many dangerous charms.

But what was far more astonishing was that he knew the chant. The words, the melody. It made no sense at all—he was hardly the kind of man to have spent time in a monastery unless compelled to.

But perhaps he'd grown up in one. It wasn't unheard of to have well-connected bastards raised by the church. It kept them safe and protected and out of sight, and away from mothers who might cause trouble. Doubtless that was how Prince William was raised, but the holy influence had failed to do much good, apart from a knowledge of plainsong.

At least it made his absurd masquerade more believable. And she had to admit that it had been a wise decision to make her a mute penitent. She might have been able to manage the deep voice, but memorization had never been her strong point, and she would have had to fake it with the Latin. She had to do a little skip to catch up with her companion, but fortunately they were at the end of the procession, and no one could see her. It was enlightening being in this household of men, such as they were. For one thing, she realized she wasn't as freakishly tall as she thought she was. There were at least half a dozen of the monks present who were taller than she was. In her father's household she'd been a fluke—the men were short and the women were shorter. Apart from Father Bennett she doubted there was one person taller than she was, with the possible exception of Will, the gatekeeper, and he was so bent over with age it was hard to tell how tall he'd once been.

The man beside her was quite possibly the first man

she'd ever seen who managed to tower over her. Even Thomas had barely reached her own height. It was little wonder that she would react as she did to the dark prince. It was unsettling to finally have to look up at someone. Unsettling to know that she was no longer an overgrown freak—at least by the prince's standards. Little wonder that she...

Where in the name of sweet Jesus was she going with that thought? She skipped again, catching up with him, and she could feel his sideways glance from beneath the enveloping hood. The man was a monster, for all his charm. The fact that she'd actually liked his kisses, the feel of his hands on her body, only proved that, in fact, she was an entirely normal, healthy female, albeit a tall one. Had she been small like the rest of the females of her acquaintance she would be married and a mother by now.

Married off to a dolt of her father's choosing. And perhaps she would have been placid and happy.

Somehow she didn't think so. Somehow she didn't think she would have even been happy with Thomas of Wakebryght, even though he'd been a childhood friend.

She was tired from the endless day, frightened of the future, irritated by the man beside her, disgusted by the monks and their lack of cleanliness, and totally without any kind of security at all. She didn't know if they'd ever make it to Saint Anne's, and she wasn't sure what she'd do once they got there. She could thank the prince for one thing—she'd learned there was a dark, disturbing pleasure to be had between

men and women. Though perhaps it was only someone as dark and wicked as the prince who could summon those reactions.

Lord, she was mad! Too much had happened in the
last few days—birth and death and friendship and
loss. And all she could think of was the man beside
her as they sang their way through the filthy halls of
Saint Bartholomew, and what the night would bring.

The procession stopped at a small doorway, and the
abbot beckoned them forward. "Behave yourself,"
the prince hissed beneath his breath.

She had no choice, though she was sorely tempted
to throw back her hood and expose her wicked hair
and her unacceptable gender. Too bad there wasn't a
snowstorm so they could put her out there as they had
the poor, pregnant woman they'd murdered....

No, perhaps she wasn't suited for a life of cloistered obedience, she thought dismally. She was far
too questioning, far too opinionated. But if she wasn't
to become a nun, and no man wanted her, what was
to become of her?

The prince took her arm with unnecessary rough-
ness and pulled her into the small, cold room, taking
the branch of candles from one of the sour-faced
monks. She could have done without the illumination.
The room was small, with two narrow pallets on the
floor and a narrow window to the outside. It had begun to rain, and a wet wind was blowing through.
There didn't appear to be any way to shutter the window, and it was going to be a cold, chill night. At

least there were two pallets and enough space between them.

It would have been a waste of time to protest. If they weren't there they would have been alone in the woods together. At least in the abbey someone would hear if she screamed. The prince would keep his distance—even he wouldn't break his penance by forcing her under the very dirty but still holy roof of the abbey.

And she didn't fancy sleeping outside in the rain, or anywhere else in this filthy place. The prince would provide some sort of protection.

"We'll see you both at prime," the abbot announced. "May God keep you from dreaming."

She waited until the door closed behind them. Waited until the sound of their chanting faded away in the distance. And then she threw back her hood, stepped away from the false monk, and said, "I'm not sure I'm going to spend the night with you in this tiny room."

"Don't be tiresome, Brother Elizabeth. You know perfectly well you are. It's that, or out in the rain with you. The abbot wouldn't take kindly to being fooled by a sinful, unclean woman, and he might be tempted to retaliate."

"If anything is unclean it's this monastery."

"That's because there are no women to clean it," the prince said cheerfully, tossing back his own hood, as well.

"Men can clean as well as women," she said.

"Perhaps they prefer to spend their days in prayer."

"Perhaps they prefer to spend their days eating," Elizabeth replied. "I've never seen such a corpulent bunch."

"Then you haven't seen many monks. They tend to be well rounded. If they can't indulge in carnal pleasures, they have to make do with other fleshly joys."

"Another reason why you're the least likely monk I've ever seen."

He merely smiled. "Which side of the pallet do you want? Beside the wall or on the outside?"

She froze. "There are two pallets here. One for you and one for me."

"Indeed. And I intend to sleep on that one, with or without you." He nodded toward the pallet on the left.

"Then I'll sleep on the other one."

"With my blessings," he said. "But you'll be sharing it with bugs you won't soon be rid of. I can see them from here. Difficult as it might be for you to admit it, I really am preferable to lice."

She looked at the pallet in horror. She hadn't the best vision in the world, a sore point, but even she could see the movement against the rough weave of the blanket. She shuddered.

"What makes you think that one is any better?" she demanded.

"At least there's nothing crawling on it. And it

smells like cedar—nothing better for discouraging bugs than cedar.''

She stared at him. ''How would you know that? How would you know plainsong? How would you know such things?''

''I have many talents,'' he said smoothly. ''I'd be more than happy to demonstrate them, but I expect you'd rather I swear to keep my hands to myself if we're going to lie down together.''

''We're not going to lie down together!''

''Then you'll sleep standing up.'' He stretched on the pallet, looking altogether too comfortable.

''What makes you think the bugs won't migrate over there?''

''You were the chatelaine of your father's castle— you must know better than I do that they won't come near the cedar, no matter how enticing warm new flesh might be.''

She thought of his skin beneath the rough weave of the monk's robe. Was it warm and enticing? Was such a thing possible?

''Why do you look at me like that?'' he said. ''Have I suddenly grown horns?''

The candlelight wavered as a gust of wet wind blew in the open window. In the shadows he was no longer the dangerous prince, no longer the false monk who did far too good a job of pretense. In the murky light he looked both warm and dangerous, and she didn't know which was the louder call.

''Move over,'' she said in a cross voice. ''I'd feel safer sleeping on the outside.''

"Nearer the bugs."

"The inside," she amended, slipping off her sandals. The rope was still tied tightly around her waist, and she considered loosening it, then thought better of it. It kept the fabric bunched up around her body, which in this case was a wise thing.

He lifted the thin blanket, making a place for her between his body and the wall. Too narrow a space, she thought, but she didn't have any choice.

"I'm leaving the candles burning," she warned him as she stepped over his recumbent body.

"As you wish."

"And if you touch me I'll scream. I don't care if they toss me out into the rain, I won't tolerate you putting your hands on me."

"It's going to be more than my hands. The pallet is too small."

She slid down beside him, trying to make herself as narrow as possible, lying on her side facing him. She would have rather had her back turned to him, rather have faced the wall than his dark, knowing eyes, but she didn't feel safe turning her back on him.

"You swear I can trust you?" she asked in a tight little voice.

He was so close, so big, so warm. Maybe she should scramble out of bed and see if she could sleep sitting up. Maybe she could make friends with the tiny creatures that infested the other pallet. A thousand tiny itches might be better than the deep, incomprehensible need that clawed away at her.

"You can trust me, Brother Scold," he whispered, closing his eyes. "Just as far as you want to."

And she had to make do with that.

The birds woke him. Adrian was usually fond of birdsong, but this time their cheerful singing made a horrendous din, and he wanted to shut the noise, the bright light away, and sink back down into the soft, blessed darkness that had enveloped him.

But the light was prickling at his eyelids, the birds kept up their relentless twittering, and though his shoulder still felt like fire, it was no longer blazing, but merely a sullen glow of pain.

He opened his eyes slowly, grudgingly. A beam of light speared directly onto his face, blinding him, and he shut them quickly again. But not before he'd seen what lay pressing against him far too comfortably.

Joanna. He thought he'd dreamed her. He'd been dying, he was sure of it, and he'd wanted to tell her all sorts of things, but the words wouldn't come past his parched lips, and no matter how often Joanna had pressed a damp rag to them he'd been unable to speak.

But he wasn't dead after all—the sweat covering his body told him that his fever had broken. And Joanna hadn't been a dream, though he still couldn't believe she'd wept over him, kissed him.

But then, she was here, wasn't she? And someone had taken care of him. He realized with a sort of disjointed surprise that beneath the blanket he was naked. At least she lay on top of the blanket, curled up so peacefully by his side.

He opened his eyes again, more cautiously against the blinding sunlight. If he'd had any doubts about her tears, the sight of the salt stains on her pale cheeks convinced him. What was she doing here, taking care of him? How did they even get here? He could remember the horrifying, hungry malice on the real prince's face as he'd sunk the knife into him, and then everything became disjointed.

He shifted, ignoring the pain that shot through the left side of his body, and she stirred, murmuring something. She'd stripped all the ornamentation from her gown, and loosened it to sleep. From his vantage point he could see the rise and fall of her perfect breasts, and he wanted to bury his head against them. He didn't move.

She looked exhausted, and he wondered if she'd slept at all. How long had he been suffering from the effects of the knife wound? How long had he been lying there, doing nothing, when his duty was abandoned? He needed to rouse himself, find his monk's robes and see about getting to Saint Anne's. He had no idea who had survived the massacre, though he had little doubt that the prince had made his escape, pausing only long enough to stab one of his guardians.

Did Brother Peter escape, as well? Surely a man didn't survive the brutal horrors of the Crusades only to be bested by paltry outlaws.

Except that Adrian suspected those were no ordinary outlaws, and there was a reason Prince William hadn't been one of the first to die.

There were two possible answers. One, the most obvious, was that the raiding party had been sent by the vengeful Baron Neville, in retaliation for his daughter's death. He may have insisted the prince be brought before him so he could punish him himself.

But that was romantic and impractical. Most men would simply require justice be done, and any henchman would serve as an instrument of vengeance.

The other, horrifying possibility, was that those were William's men, come to spare him a few days of discomfort in an unwanted penance. And the lives lost were of no account when it came to the prince's pleasure.

The more he thought about it, the more he was sure that hideous possibility was the only one. He couldn't be sure, but he thought he recognized one of Prince William's favorites, a degenerate named Gervaise, among the attackers. Which made it doubly important that he rise from this surprisingly comfortable bed, pull on his tattered robes and take off.

They probably thought he was dead. And he would have been, if it weren't for Joanna. He'd seen no sign of her when the bandits first attacked, and he'd headed toward the prince, hoping she'd be safe. For some reason she must have come back. Must have found him, and brought him away from that place of death and betrayal.

She'd saved his life, maybe several times over, first in getting him away from there, then in watching over him. And for what reason? A woman in her position couldn't afford to be sentimental over a penniless monk.

He lifted his head and looked at her. She was exquisitely beautiful, with her heart-shaped face and soft, tender mouth. She was sleeping so soundly, surely she wouldn't wake if he moved. Just one brief kiss, a reward to himself for surviving. An indulgence, brief and bittersweet, and then he'd forget all about her.

But nothing on this earth could stop him from leaning forward and putting his mouth on hers.

16

Elizabeth wouldn't have thought she'd be able to sleep, but she'd underestimated her capacity for exhaustion. No sooner did she close her eyes than she immediately fell into a deep, heavy slumber, lulled by the quiet and the warmth of the body that lay between her and the outside world, protecting her.

When she awoke, all but one of the candles had burned out, and the final one was sputtering with the last remnants of tallow dripping onto the floor. And she was lying with her head on the prince's shoulder, his arms draped casually around her, his hand on her breast, and she felt warm, drowsy, sleepily aroused. And then reality set in.

She shoved him off the pallet, away from her, kicking at him. "Get away from me!" she cried. "How dare you touch me when you promised…"

He'd been sleeping quite soundly, and it was clear his rude awakening didn't put him in the best of moods. He moved so fast her accusing words were cut off midsentence, as he slammed her body back down on the thin pallet, covering it with his own, larger one, and put his hand over her mouth, silencing her. She tried to kick him, knee him in his privates, but he managed to trap her beneath him so she couldn't move, couldn't throw him off her, couldn't make him budge. She tried to bite the hand that covered her mouth, but his long fingers held her jaw frozen.

He leaned over her, breathing deeply after the brief, fierce struggle, and she could feel tears of impotent rage fill her eyes.

His breathing slowed, but she could still feel the heavy slamming of his heart against hers. It was a strange, almost otherworldly connection, her heart with his, both beating fast. It was almost as if the blood flowed between them, life flowed between them as she lay trapped beneath his body, unable to escape. Not wanting to escape.

"Not the way to wake a man up, lady," he growled. "Not a man who's had more than his share of battles."

She couldn't apologize, not with his hand over her mouth. Not that she would have. He'd been touching her. He was touching her now, heart to heart, breast to breast, hip to hip, and she could feel him. Hard. Aroused.

But men always woke that way, or so she'd been told. It had nothing to do with her.

"I'll move my hand, but if you scream again I'll snap your neck."

He wouldn't, and they both knew it. Whether or not he'd killed other women was not the question. He wouldn't kill her.

He moved his hand slowly, ready to silence her

again if she cried out. She contented herself with glaring at him.

"Get off me, you big oaf!"

His sudden lazy smile was even more disconcerting than his anger. "Is that any way to talk to a prince of England? For shame, my lady. I know you were brought up in a household of barbarians, but I would have thought you'd learned polite address by now."

"Get off me, my lord oaf," she said sweetly.

"I don't think so."

"You promised you wouldn't touch me!"

"I promised no such thing. As a matter of fact, I distinctly remember telling you that this pallet was too narrow to sleep without touching."

"You didn't have to touch my breast!"

She tried to push him off her, but he simply caught her wrists in one hand and held them. Held her. "I was asleep. A man can't be held accountable for what happens when he's asleep. How do I know you didn't put my hand there, trying to seduce me, and then changed your mind?"

She was speechless with rage, and she bucked up against him, trying to throw him off.

"Now, that's a mistake, lady," he murmured. "If a man's lying on top of you he might take that as an invitation."

"It's an invitation to dismount."

He laughed. "We have a small problem here. You go out of your way to be annoying, and the only way I can silence you is to try to seduce you. You keep protesting that you don't want to be seduced, but if you truly did not you'd learn to be quiet and stop goading me. Every time you annoy me I think of more and more inventive ways to stop your mouth. I find you very tempting, but right now I really should try to keep my celibacy intact, at least until we arrive at Saint Anne's. I'm afraid I'm going to have to resist your offer.''

''Offer? The only thing I want to offer you is the sharp end of a sword.''

''No, you don't.''

''You are the most smug, contemptible man...''

''And you want me. Oh, I admit, you probably don't even realize it. All this bickering and goading is just to mask your unrequited passion....''

''You're teasing me.''

''No. I'm flirting with you.''

She stared up at him with awe and shock. ''You are? No one's ever flirted with me before.''

''Now, that's not true. I've been flirting with you every chance I get. I will admit that this is the first time I've ever gotten a woman pinned and then started trying to seduce her, but I am infinitely adaptable.''

''Your notions of seduction are very strange.'' Her voice was a bit wobbly, but maybe he wouldn't notice.

''No, they're not. I just decided you wouldn't respond well to traditional compliments. You're like a hedgehog, all covered with prickles if anyone tries to stroke you.''

''You aren't going to, are you?''

"What?"

"Stroke me."

He smiled slowly. "I thought I'd start with kissing you."

He leaned down and put his mouth against hers. And at that very moment the last candle flame flickered out, plunging them into darkness.

With the light went her common sense. Alone in the darkness, with his mouth pressed against her, she was lost. Elizabeth of Bredon had been left behind somewhere in the forest. The woman lying beneath the prince's strong body was nameless, faceless, beautiful and desirable, and when his fingers touched her face, tugging her mouth open, she let him. Her body softened beneath his, and she was no longer holding her legs tightly together. He moved between them, and she could feel him up against her, the unmistakable shape of his erection, and she knew the soft little moan in the darkness came from her own throat.

This time when his hands touched her breasts she knew it, and God help her, she liked it. His slid his fingers lightly over her hardened nipples, and the sensation was so exquisite she wanted to weep with the joy of it. He seemed to have no trouble at all unfastening the monk's robe, when she herself wasn't quite sure how to do it, and then there was nothing between her body and his hands but the thin chemise she'd clung to.

This was unlike nothing she had ever felt before. She'd had a taste of it the night before, when he'd pulled her into the trees and kissed her, but this was magnified a thousand times. Her skin was hot, her stomach tied in a knot of desire, the fire between her legs surging and unquenchable. And she loved the darkness, his hands, his mouth, touching her, tasting her, making her arch her hips toward his in silent need.

He put his hand between their bodies, touching her, and she couldn't speak as a shiver of something swept over her body. He pressed harder, sliding his fingers up against her, and he buried his face in her shoulder as he stroked her, stroked her as he'd warned her, promised her he would.

And still she wanted more. When he slid his fingers inside her she cried out, and he stilled her voice with his mouth, all the while his touch worked its dark magic.

And then the sound of church bells floated into the room, and he pulled his mouth away, freezing.

"Don't stop," she whispered, to her complete shame. "Please."

But he'd taken his hand from between her legs, rolled away from her, moving as far away as he could, until he was up against the door to the cell, sitting there leaning against it, a dark, terrible look on his face.

It was dawn—the rich darkness of the night vanishing. The cool breeze of morning brushed against her skin, and she realized she lay there almost completely naked, her shift pulled down low over her breasts, rucked up high around her hips.

She pulled the thin linen back around her, with

such force that it ripped, and she frantically reached for the monk's robe, which now lay discarded on the stone floor. She quickly donned it, tying the rope tightly around her waist. He wasn't looking at her. He was sitting on the floor, one knee drawn up, the other leg stretched out in front of him, a look of inexplicable torment on his face.

It was, she admitted, a beautiful face. She should have kissed it while she had the chance, touched him before he'd come to his senses and realized he was trifling with a flame-haired giant whom nobody wanted.

All cats are gray in the dark, they said, and he probably didn't care who and what she was. But the light had come, harsh and illuminating, and she knew he wouldn't make the mistake of touching her again.

"Sweet Jesus," he muttered under his breath. "What the hell did I almost do?"

If he expected an answer, none was forthcoming. He surged to his feet, not meeting her quiet gaze. "Stay where you are. I'll tell the abbot you're not feeling well and we decided to make an early start of it. They'll give us enough food to last for a couple of days—that should get us to Saint Anne's if we don't run into any more trouble."

She didn't answer. He wasn't looking at her, as if he didn't want to be reminded of who she was. "Do as I say for once," he said in a harsh voice. And he closed the door hard behind him.

For a moment Elizabeth didn't move. Shame flooded her body, shame and anger and deep, mortal pain. The pain was the strongest, and she curled up in a ball and pressed her fist to her mouth to keep from sobbing.

It didn't work.

Joanna's eyes fluttered open when his mouth touched hers. Her blue eyes stared up into his brown ones, as he barely brushed her lips. And then she put her hands against his shoulders and gently pushed him away.

"No," she said.

He held himself above her for a moment, staring down into her beautiful face. And then pain shot through him, and he sank back with a groan.

She sat up immediately, fussing over him. "You need to keep quiet," she scolded him. "Last night you were at death's door, today you're ready to start frolicking? I think not. Be still and I'll get you something to eat."

"How…?" His first words came out in a husky voice, and he cleared his throat, watching her as she moved around the tiny hovel. "Where are we?"

"Near a tiny village called Beckham. I managed to get you this far while you were still partly conscious."

He frowned. "I remember a little bit. I remember you left. Why did you come back?"

A faint color stained her pale cheeks. "I have a sentimental streak. And there was a practical aspect to coming back. I have a great many sins to atone for, and saving a holy friar might balance some of them when I die."

Now it was his turn to flush with the guilt of things unsaid. "I don't think you'll be judged that harshly."

She smiled. "Then you don't know men, and God is, after all, a man."

"But his mother wasn't."

"True enough. You think the Holy Mother would have much sympathy for me?"

"The mother of God has compassion for everyone. She knows anyone can be tempted."

"As you just were, Brother Adrian," she pointed out coolly. "Don't let it happen again. I've done enough harm in my life—I wouldn't want to be responsible for the fall of a monk."

He managed to sit up, stifling his groan of pain. He wasn't sure whether it was lessening or he was just getting more adept at enduring it. He only knew that watching Dame Joanna move around the tiny hovel made him forget everything.

Except that she was right, he shouldn't touch her. He owed her his life—the least he could do was respect her wishes.

"Eat this," she said, setting some bread and cheese on the cloth that covered him. He realized belatedly that it was her fine cloak, now torn and stained with blood. Presumably his blood. He looked at his shoulder.

"You did a good job of bandaging," he said. "It looks like it's healing well enough."

"It's too soon to tell."

"I've always been a quick healer. We've got to leave this place as soon as I get dressed."

"It's too soon for you to travel. We're safe enough here. The villagers who sold me the food and wine think I'm long gone, and they don't even know I had someone with me."

"It's not the villagers who concern me," he said, biting into the coarse bread.

"The bandits who attacked our party would have no reason to follow us. Neither of us would seem particularly wealthy—why would they bother?"

He hesitated, considering. There were still lies he had to live, but he owed her at least some of the truth. She'd need it, if they were both going to stay alive.

"To keep us silent," he said. "They would want no witnesses to their treachery. They weren't ordinary bandits, and they weren't after money or jewels. They were after the prince and all who accompanied him. If they suspect anyone survived who could tell the king what happened to his son, they'll do everything they can to silence us."

"We don't know what happened to his son," she said. "Prince William's body wasn't among the fallen. He may have escaped, or they may have taken him prisoner."

Relief flooded him. If she thought the prince had survived it meant that Peter had managed to escape the carnage. There was no way they could have captured him—he would have died fighting. Which meant he got away, just as the real prince had.

"And the others?"

"No sign of Lady Elizabeth. I was not that familiar with the rest of the party to know who was or wasn't there."

"Which makes it even more important that we move from this place. If the prince escaped they'll be hunting for him, and we can't have them finding us instead." He finished the last bite of hard cheese. "Where are my clothes?"

"I had to cut them off you. They're soaked in blood."

"The color is dark—it won't show too badly."

"Won't it look strange for a monk and a woman to be traveling alone?"

"We have no choice." He started to push the cloak away from his nude body, and she turned away.

"You've already seen this body, my lady," he said. "You've suddenly turned shy on me?"

"You were unconscious. It's a great deal easier to deal with a naked man when he's not talking to you."

"If you find me my robe I won't be naked."

"I stole you some clothes." Her voice was so quiet he almost couldn't hear her.

"You did what?"

"I stole some clothes for you. I couldn't very well buy them—I told the people in the village I was traveling alone. But someone had done their washing, and it was easy enough to sneak in and take things off the line. I left them one of my brooches as payment—it was the best I could do."

He stared at her back in wonder. She'd given up her jewelry for him, risked her life for him when she would have been safer far away from this place. She could have expected nothing in return from a poor monk, and yet she'd done it, anyway.

"That was very wise of you, my lady," he said after a moment. "I'll simply look like your servant—"

"I don't look like a fine-enough lady to be traveling with a servant," she said. "More likely brother and sister."

"More likely husband and wife."

Unwillingly she turned. He was sitting up on the bed, still covered from the waist down, but she blushed, anyway, jerking her face back. "I don't think—"

"Where are the clothes?" he interrupted her.

"At the foot of the bed. I put them on top of you for extra warmth."

He dressed as swiftly as he could, ignoring the searing pain. She was incomprehensible—a modest whore, a shy leman.

"Do you need any help?" she asked, her nursely concern overwhelming her reservations.

"I'm dressed, my lady. And we need to go."

She turned and blinked. "You look very different," she said finally.

He glanced down at the rough garb. "Like a good peasant husband?"

"No," she said. "Like a man."

She didn't sound pleased with the notion, and he wasn't sure he could blame her. She probably hadn't had much good from men, if Owen of Wakebryght was anything to judge by.

"I've always been a man, my lady, monk's robes or no."

"It's easier to forget when you're a monk."

"And why should you want to forget? Why should it matter?"

She wouldn't answer him. "Shouldn't you rest a bit before we leave? It's only been light an hour or two."

He shook his head. "The sooner we're out of here the better." He pushed off the bed, rising to his feet. For a moment he felt a wave of dizziness, and then the world righted itself. "Let's be off."

She looked at him for a long moment. And then crossed the room, putting her arm through his, adding her strength. "Where are we going?"

"Where else? The Shrine of Saint Anne."

17

Elizabeth might almost have thought the prince was being solicitous of her during the endless hours of daylight. They walked steadily, without conversation, and she was just as content to stay several feet behind him, watching his tall back carefully to make certain she'd know when he stopped. She wasn't going to make the mistake of keeping too close and running into him. She wasn't going to make the mistake of getting near enough to touch him. Since he'd made it very clear that he had no more interest in touching her.

They would stop to rest, to eat the tasteless bread the abbot had sent with them, along with a stern warning to avoid both sin and women, something he seemed to think were one and the same. They rested without talking, the prince closing his eyes, closing her out, until he decided it was time to move again.

After her first burst of tears she was well past it, she told herself, moving steadily behind him. She had never been one for tears—it gave her annoying brothers too much pleasure to be able to reduce her to such a state. She hadn't even cried over Thomas of Wakebryght.

And she wasn't going to cry over someone as worthless as a degenerate prince who toyed with her only out of malice. She was ashamed that she'd given in for a brief moment, but she told herself it was simply lack of sleep wearing down her reserves of strength.

She glanced up ahead at him, surveying him as coldly as she could. He moved well enough in that rough monk's robe, almost as if he were used to it rather than the heavy robes of a wealthy prince. He was like some wild animal, able to blend into his surroundings.

He had many gifts, she recognized that now. One of those was a wicked ability to lure even the most resistant of women. Those who knew of his reputation, knew the truth of his dark deeds and foul appetites, were drawn to him, anyway, lured by some strange power. As she had been, for a brief moment when she lay beneath him in the monk's cell.

And that, of course, had been what he wanted. Not really her at all, but simply the knowledge that he could have her. Once he had her beneath him, weak, willing, he'd left her, smug in the knowledge that he'd bested her in the most cruel of ways.

He wouldn't do it again. She was unused to the ways of men, at least in matters such as these. She understood belligerent fathers and annoying brothers, she understood stubborn soldiers and worried servants and even weak-willed men like Thomas.

But she had never had a man's touch reach her,

make her melt. And had never had a man use that power to hurt her.

It wouldn't happen again, now that she knew what danger it could be. And, having succeeded in demoralizing her, he would have no need to repeat that action. His only reason in touching her had been to weaken her, hurt her. It should have come as no surprise—he was a man known to find pleasure in hurting women.

At least she'd survived, virginity and life intact. Even a depraved soul like Prince William had no real desire for an overgrown, flame-haired, useless female.

"We'll stop for the night soon," he announced, slowing his steady pace and glancing at her over his shoulder. She nodded, keeping her head down, keeping the hood pulled low. She'd kept it that way since he returned to the cell, just in case her eyes were still red and swollen. He didn't need any more proof that he'd managed to hurt her. She didn't need any more shame to scorch her soul.

He seemed to expect an answer, so she simply said, "Good," waiting for him to turn away.

Instead he halted. It was near dark, though at least the night was warm. If they were to sleep in the woods she wanted no excuse to move close to him— she'd freeze to death before she'd accept even a tiny bit of body warmth.

Not that he was offering. And no one would be freezing to death on such a balmy spring night.

"You've been unnaturally docile all day," he observed. "Aren't you going to ask me where we'll spend the night? Aren't you going to threaten me with dismemberment or at the very least castration if I put my hands on you?''

''No.''

''I think I like you better when you're insulting me,'' he said.

''I think I don't care,'' she replied, goaded. He smiled at that, and she could have cursed. She didn't want to give him anything, even the knowledge that he could make her angry whenever he truly wanted to.

''There's a small farmhouse not far from here. It's empty, but I expect it's still in good-enough shape to provide shelter, and a stream runs nearby.''

''Where are the people who lived there?''

''Dead. They had an outbreak of the fever here some ten years ago, and whole families were wiped out, including the ones who lived in the house.''

''But what makes you think someone else hasn't moved in, brought his family with him? People don't just leave houses abandoned and vacant.''

''They do this one.''

''Why?''

''Ghosts.''

Maybe he thought to scare her into once more making a fool of herself, but she wasn't about to let that happen. She'd happily face a thousand bloodthirsty ghosts than turn to the prince for safety or comfort.

''Good,'' she said. ''I expect I'll prefer the company of the dead.''

She could sense his smile, and she pulled her hood

lower to keep from seeing it. "Are we going to stand here forever? The sooner we arrive the sooner I can retire."

"As you wish, my lady." She couldn't blot out the amusement in his voice. He moved forward, and she followed him, slowly, knowing she had no choice.

She half hoped the farmhouse would be filled with people, just to prove him wrong, but of course it wasn't. It was a small building, neat enough for an abandoned space, and the thatched roof looked to be in good condition. She could hear the sound of rushing water through the row of trees behind the building, and the setting sun cast a warm, benevolent glow on the place. Like the smoldering embers of the flames of hell, Elizabeth thought grimly.

"How did you know of this place?" She hadn't meant to initiate any unnecessary questions, but her curiosity got the better of her.

"The monks told me of it."

"Father Fillion? I'm surprised he hasn't claimed it for his own abbey."

"It's too far away. We've walked a long way today. But it was the monks accompanying the... accompanying me to the shrine who told me of it. It was suggested as one place we might stay on the way to Saint Anne's."

"How far are we from the shrine?"

"On foot, perhaps another day and a half. On horseback, merely a few hours."

"But we don't have any horses, do we?" She didn't wait for an answer. "I'm going to the stream to wash some of this travel dirt from me. Don't come anywhere near me.'' It wasn't a request.

''I'll try to control my insatiable lust,'' he said.

She was not amused. ''And I'll be sleeping in a separate room. I find I prefer crawling vermin to your company.''

''What about ghosts?''

''Come near me and you'll join them.''

''Yes, Brother Elizabeth,'' he said in humble tones, pushing his hood back onto his shoulders.

Elizabeth stared up at the elegant lines of his coolly beautiful face, stonily unmoved, leaving her own hood in place. A day and a half of travel, at the most. Which meant one more night on the road.

He should be happy, William thought as Bishop Martin pronounced his absolution. His confession had been detailed and entirely fictitious, and the good bishop had blessed him and announced him shriven. No one would want to kill him while his soul was unblemished—they would wait until he was caught sinning. With any forethought, he could avoid that, continuing his role as a miraculous survivor of an ambush, and no one would ever know better. That is, if Gervaise did as he was bid and managed to track down the stragglers who had unaccountably managed to escape the butchery of his well-trained men.

He was fairly certain Adrian was dead, and the doxy had run off before the battle even started. She would have nothing to tell, if by any chance she managed to slip through the net his men had drawn about the countryside.

Peter was another matter. He knew the land well—it had once belonged to his family, and he would doubtless know of a dozen hiding places. And he had the girl with him, who'd be slowing him down as well as complaining. In some villages they drowned scolds. If he got his hands on her maybe he'd cut out her tongue.

He wanted to kill Peter himself, have the pleasure of feeling his blood on his hands, but in the end his death was all that mattered. He could always take his frustration out on Gervaise once they were gone from this place. After all, the delivery of pain was a universal pleasure.

All was in place, if they could just make certain the others were dead. He would wait two more days, enjoying the frugal hospitality of the good sisters, listening to Bishop Martin prate on and on, and he'd be sweet and humble. Once his men brought back word that there were no more witnesses, he could take back his life.

He should have asked Gervaise for a souvenir. Peter's head would have held a certain charm, but keeping it hidden might have been too difficult. Perhaps a hand. Or even more fitting, that which he'd deprived his prince of. That which makes a man. Taken while he was still living.

And he would not be there to witness it. William kept his face blissful and innocent as he pouted inwardly. Someone would have to pay for depriving him of his fun. And that someone would have to be Gervaise.

The stream was shielded from the house by a high riverbank and a copse of trees. Which meant that the prince could sneak up on her if he so desired, and she wouldn't be able to see him coming. But he'd have no reason to do so, no reason to try to torment someone he'd already managed to vanquish. And if he appeared when she was bathing, so be it. She didn't expect the sight of her naked body would somehow be more irresistible than it had been in the dark hours of morning when she lay beneath him.

But he wouldn't follow, and she knew it. She needed to wash herself clean, to wash the dust and the dirt of travel from her skin. But more important still, to wash the touch of his hands, his mouth, from her flesh.

She stripped off her clothes and folded them neatly on the riverbank, setting the knife on top of them, before moving down to the water. She climbed out onto a large rock and looked down into the deep, clear pool. Into her reflection.

Her face looked pale, sorrowful, unlike her usual self. The features were still the same—eyes that were large and green and far too direct, a forehead that was too high, a chin too stubborn, a mouth too large, an insignificant nose. All surrounded by a heavy fall of devil's hair.

She couldn't change the mouth, the eyes, the chin

or the nose. She couldn't shorten her long legs, or widen her narrow hips. But she could rid herself of what had drawn taunts and stares and whispered mutterings of witches all her life.

She went back and fetched the knife, then returned to her perch on the rock. Never in her life had she sat around completely nude, and she should have felt shy, uncomfortable, exposed. She reached up for one thick hank of hair and began to saw away at it.

When she was done she sat there for a moment, watching the heavy strands darken and sink in the water, then be carried away with the current. She felt strange, light-headed in the most literal of ways, and she reached a hand up to her shorn head. She'd cut as much off as she could, and what was left was very short, curling above her ears, rough and uneven, shorter even than most men's hair. It was fitting. In this world she was of no use as either a man or a woman, and getting rid of her hateful hair gave her a freedom that she'd never felt before. And watching the heavy strands float down the slow-moving stream, she started crying.

It was almost dark when she climbed the riverbank and made her way back through the copse of trees to the house. She felt numb—the cost of the icy-cold water and too many tears. She'd finally stopped bawling like a babe. She hated her hair, she'd always wanted to get rid of it. What in heaven's name was she doing crying over it? No one was ever going to see her bare head again—she would keep the monk's hood over her head until they reached the shrine, and then she'd be welcomed into holy orders, with a veil and wimple to cover what in other women would be vanity. But the more she tried to stop the more she wept, and it wasn't until she just let go that the tears finally halted.

He was standing outside the door, leaning against the rough building, watching her as she made her way back. She didn't see him for a moment, the heavy weight of the hood blocking her vision, and when she did she almost jumped. In the darkness he looked like neither monk nor prince. Just a tall, silhouetted shape, waiting for her in the shadows.

"I almost came after you, my lady. Surely you weren't that dirty? I was afraid you might have run away."

"Where would I run to? You know the way to Saint Anne's, not I."

"You could always ask directions. Most holy brethren travel in pairs, but it's not unheard of for one to make a lone pilgrimage."

"An excellent point, now that you mention it," she said. Her voice was husky from weeping, but clearing her throat would make it even more noticeable. "I'll meet you at the shrine." She started to turn away from him, but his cool voice stopped her.

"Don't even try it. I said you might be able to make it on your own, I didn't say I'd let you go. I've set out food for you and made up a bed."

"One bed?" There was no way she could avoid the question. The answer would determine which way she would go—to the house or into the woods.

"I intend to keep guard most of the night. When I

need to rest I'll rouse you and let you take over. Does that set your mind at ease?''

"Yes." It had been a foolish question to ask. That too-short tussle on the pallet had been an aberration. He must long to return to court and the women there. Beautiful, wanton women.

"There's no need to keep your hood up," he said. She didn't need an unrestricted view to feel his eyes upon her. "There's no one else around, and I already know you're a woman."

Do you? For one horrified moment she thought she'd said the words aloud, then realized for once she'd kept her tongue silent when it ought to be. "I like it," she said flatly.

"Suit yourself. Eat something and then go to bed. You won't be getting a full night's sleep if we're to take turns keeping watch. You may as well take full advantage of the bed while it's yours."

"And where will you be?"

"Availing myself of the stream, as well. Unless you prefer me travel-stained?"

"I don't prefer you at all." That came out wrong. "I mean, it makes no difference…"

"I know what you meant. When I come back to the house I'll expect to see you sound asleep in bed. Is that understood?"

She managed to wake one last ounce of defiance. "I haven't needed a nurse to tell me what to do since I was six years old."

"You haven't had anyone tell you what to do. That doesn't mean you haven't needed someone."

"I don't need anyone."

There was dead silence, and she was afraid she'd pushed him too far. Instead he simply moved away from the house, passing her without touching. "Eat your dinner and go to bed," he said over his shoulder.

The empty house was surprisingly neat. No animals had made their homes there, no vagrants had moved in. Maybe the ghosts had scared them away.

It hadn't scared people from taking whatever furniture had once been there. All that was left was a rough table, with the meagre offerings they'd brought with them. Bread, cheese, the sour wine of the abbot's, and some dried meat.

She wasn't hungry, but her stomach was growling, and tomorrow would be another day of hard traveling. Fainting was not an option. She ate slowly, forcing herself, and then went in search of the bed.

She found it in the adjoining room. He'd cut cedar branches and laid them down for protection from the hard dirt floor, and the sweet smell hung in the air, reminding her of the monk's cell. Not that she needed any reminding. He'd tossed a blanket over the branches, and it looked comfortable enough. At that point she was so weary she could have slept standing up. But she didn't need to—he'd made his point—he had no more interest in her. She would sleep unmolested until it was time to take over the watch.

She wasn't sure what wearied her more, the hours of walking or the helpless crying. Her chest and throat still hurt from the tears, and she pushed the hood onto her shoulders so that she could feel her shorn head.

She could feel her eyes begin to sting once more, and she pulled the hood back up over her, covering her face.

She lay down on the bed, closing her eyes. Right then a ghost would be a welcome diversion from her own thoughts.

But there were no ghosts. Instead sleep came, and she embraced it gratefully.

He wasn't going to think about her, Peter told himself. He was going to plunge his body into the coldest water he could find, cut himself bloody if he must, anything to drive the devouring monster out of his heart. The devouring monster of lust for an innocent.

His soul was still ravaged by what he had almost done that morning, under the very roof of the monastery, just as prime bells were ringing. He'd run as fast as he could, not from her, but from his own dark needs.

Seven years of celibacy, seven years of never even looking, and now he was brought low by an overgrown colt of a girl with hair the color of autumn leaves, who looked at him as if he were a monster.

Which he was. Both as the deviate prince of England, and the philandering monk who'd thought to attain forgiveness for acts too horrendous to contemplate. He knew now that he was beyond hope, beyond redemption. The very best he could hope for was to keep true to his task. To protect the innocent.

Watching over Prince William had been the antithesis of that vow. A murderous deviate, the prince might already have been cleansed by a miracle, by the grace of Saint Anne.

But Peter wasn't holding out much hope. Some men's evil went so deep that even God couldn't reach it. And rather than let William harm another innocent, Peter was entirely willing to commit cold-blooded murder once more.

Such a noble sacrifice, he mocked himself. Kill the ravager of innocents, while he himself ignored his vows and despoiled a virgin on her way to a nunnery. He was as deluded as the most sinful of creatures.

The icy water did little to cool him. He kept thinking of Elizabeth in that same water, her body pale and beautiful, her breasts surprisingly full, peaked with dark, hard nipples that he'd wanted to suckle....

He wouldn't even wake her. He didn't need sleep—he was impervious to physical needs such as sleep, food and warmth.

The only thing he wasn't impervious to was Elizabeth of Bredon's beautiful green eyes, her soft, damp mouth, and the eternal damnation her sweet body promised.

And he'd take it, gladly embrace an eternity in hell for the price of lying between her long legs.

But he wouldn't take her with him. She'd either go to heaven a virgin nun or a wife and mother. But she wouldn't go to heaven despoiled by a celibate monk with the souls of hundreds on his conscience.

He made his way slowly back up the path to the house. She would be asleep by now, or at least pretending to be. If he'd been more deluded he might almost have thought his pulling away from her had hurt her. Even if she had wanted him for one brief moment, wisdom and disgust had to have set in. It was little wonder she kept her distance, her head down, her voice low. She had gone past dislike for the dark prince to deep, abiding hatred for a seducer, a man who had nearly raped her in a monastery.

His hand had stopped bleeding. He'd slammed it against a broad rock at the edge of the water, hitting out in helpless frustration. A single strand of her long red hair had shone in the moonlight, and the sight of it had him instantly aroused. Only the pain and blood had cooled him, and now he was beginning to curse his foolhardiness. At least he'd had enough sense to strike out with his left hand, not his right. He still needed to be able to fight. To wield a sword if he must.

To kill the prince of England. If he must.

18

Adrian gained strength as he walked. It came as no surprise—he was young and strong and he'd always healed quickly. By noon he'd begun walking on his own, without any assistance from Joanna. It had been a hard choice—the warmth and feel of her by his side had given him a strength far out of proportion to what she'd been able to provide.

But it was a drain on her own reserves, and he slowly weaned himself from it, taking more and more of his weight onto his own body, until he released her arm and walked on his own. At her insistence he used a walking stick, but he didn't need it. The day was sunny and bright, he was getting stronger by the minute, and he had, inexplicably, impractically, fallen in love.

She was older than he was, and by anyone's standards, soiled goods. She'd been married twice, she'd told him, and he hadn't asked how many lovers she'd had. She hadn't volunteered that information.

She fancied herself a Magdalene, a fallen woman, but he saw her more as a sorrowful Madonna. Or perhaps neither—just a woman, real, flesh and blood.

A woman he wanted, not just with his body, but with his heart and soul.

She wasn't ready to hear that yet. She'd been horrified when he'd kissed her, and she doubtless thought he was simply an innocent, smitten monk. And it wasn't his place to tell her otherwise.

His mother would have a fit. Until she got to know Joanna—his mother was strong-minded but ultimately fair and loving, and she would recognize Joanna's goodness. And even if she did not, she'd love Joanna because her son did. Mothers were like that.

"You're smiling, Brother Adrian," Joanna said as they walked down the narrow road. Together they had chosen to take a more public route to the shrine—less chance for ambush, less chance for improprieties.

"You'd best call me Adrian. Or husband," he replied, secretly pleased at the notion. "Someone might hear us."

She glanced around at the wide fields newly planted, but there was not a soul in sight. "I still think we should be brother and sister."

"We don't look alike."

"Many siblings do not."

"I can protect you better as your husband. I know not where we're sleeping, but there would be no reason for a brother to lie with his sister. A husband would be by your side, keeping away strangers."

She opened her mouth, to protest, he was sure, then shut it again. She could hardly argue with the wisdom of his words.

Finally she said, "Do you truly think we're in any

danger? Why should they have been anything but bandits, seeking out any hapless group of travelers?''

"For a number of reasons. Even bandits and outlaws, if they are not religious, are at least superstitious. They avoid attacking holy orders, for fear of their immortal souls. Second, we were not a wealthy caravan. Monks, knights and soldiers, all dressed plainly, with no apparent wealth. Our most prized possession was the prince himself, and he was in disguise.''

"Disguise?"

He was still bound by his oath. "He was dressed much more simply than his usual wont.'' That much, at least, was true. "Add to that, robbers seldom attack such a heavily armed group without good reason. The men who came were well armed, well mounted, and they came to kill, not rob. Which makes me believe that they won't stop until they finish their task. They'll want no witnesses left alive to proclaim the truth as to who and what they are.''

"But I have no idea who they are. I ran, like a coward," she said.

"Like a wise woman. If you'd remained you'd be raped and dead. And I have a very good idea who they are. I recognized one of them.''

"And?"

"It would be safer if I didn't tell you. If by any chance we're set upon, your only chance would be ignorance.''

She halted, turning to look at him with a stern expression that almost reminded him of his mother.

"I've been through a great deal already, and you and I both know that they wouldn't let me go no matter how innocent I proclaim to be. Who do you think attacked the prince's caravan? The family of the girl he murdered, yes?"

"No." There could be no harm in telling her of his suspicions. "The prince's men themselves."

She drew in a hiss of breath. "Why? Why would they kill their master and slaughter the rest of us? It makes no sense. Surely you're mistaken."

"What makes you think the prince is dead? You didn't see his body, nor that of some of the monks, is that not so? I think Prince William had arranged this very thing. He hated having to go on pilgrimage, despised having to live frugally and chastely, even for a fortnight, having to answer to priests for everything. I think he planned to have his men kill us all, and then he'd show up at the shrine on his own a few days later, full of tales of his miraculous escape."

"You have a very wild imagination."

"I know men," he said.

"So do I. Far better than you, I expect."

"I expect," he echoed in a nonjudgmental voice.

"And I looked into Prince William's eyes. He could no more do such a thing than he could fly. To be sure, he is a man of violence. He's killed too many times to make peace with it—that leaves its mark on a man. But he's not the deviant creature people make him out to be, and he could not have planned such a foul betrayal."

He couldn't very well explain the truth of the matter, or that she was wiser than she even imagined. He could only guess at the horrors Brother Peter had lived through, and even committed. But a man like Peter would strike cleanly, in defense of his life. Never a sneak attack on someone pledged to protect him.

And Prince William was most definitely a coward. A coward with a small army, which made him very dangerous indeed.

"Perhaps you're right, my lady," he said. "Even so, I cannot dismiss the feeling that we're still in danger."

"I agree," she said softly, to his amazement. She glanced around her, at the open fields, the narrow road out ahead of them. It had rained the night before, and the road was muddy and rutted beneath their feet, but there was no mistaking the sound of a rough cart headed in their direction.

"Should we hide?" she asked.

He considered it only for a moment. He was much stronger, but they would have had to run for it, and he might not be able to make it. He shook his head. "We've agreed to try it this way. Perhaps we'll be able to find directions to the next village, a decent meal, even a bed for the night."

"Or perhaps we'll find the end of a sword."

"It's a cart and two horses, not a group of armed men," he reassured her. "Have faith."

She looked at him, and he wanted to kiss the doubt from her blue eyes. He kept his own face impassive. "I do," she said after a moment. "In you."

If the cart hadn't appeared over the rise behind them he might have kissed her after all. It was as he expected, a farmer's rough cart.

The driver, a grizzled old man with a friendly smile, pulled to a stop beside them. "You and your woman headed toward Beckham?" he asked. "There's no work there, but you'll at least find a good meal and a bed for the night. Climb on the back of my cart and I'll give you a ride the rest of the way."

Adrian was ready to refuse the offer, politely enough, when he cast a sideways glance at Joanna. As he'd grown stronger she'd grown paler, and he realized she probably hadn't slept much at all during the time she cared for them.

"My wife and I thank you, friend," he replied, using the soft, slurred tones of his southern cousin's farmers. "We're pilgrims, on our way to the Shrine of Saint Anne. We're hoping the holy saint will bless us with a child." He put a possessive hand on Joanna's flat stomach, and she jumped, nervously, then held still, managing a nervous, wifely smile at him.

"That's not the way to make babies, lad," the farmer said with a chuckle. "And so your father should have told you."

"Spare my wife's blushes, good sir," Adrian said smoothly. "We've tried everything."

The farmer shrugged. "Then praying to the saint will do no harm. Lying with her under the moon beneath a rosemary bush on the first day of the month did the trick for one of my sisters. She gave birth to a fine baby boy not nine months later. You might want to look for some rosemary.''

Adrian didn't dare look at Joanna, afraid he might laugh. ''We'll be sure to try it.''

The back of the cart was high off the ground, and he had no choice but to put his hands on Joanna's waist and lift her up. She was light, and her waist was small, and if he moved his fingers just a bit he'd be able to feel the swell of her breasts. He behaved himself, as he knew he must. For now. Playing the part of husband in front of an audience would give him the perfect excuse to touch her, to kiss her.

But it would be a lie, with her thinking him a celibate monk, and it would cause her nothing but pain. He'd touched her, kissed her, as much as he could dare allow himself. From now until they reached the Shrine of Saint Anne he must remember he was truly Brother Adrian, a gentle monk, and not a knight bent on making his way in the world. A knight pretending to be a monk pretending to be a peasant. A man in love pretending to be a celibate monk pretending to be a tender husband.

If they didn't arrive at the shrine soon he might very well go mad. Not with the lies and confusion. But with the wanting of what he must not have.

''We've found no trace of them, my lord,'' Rufus said, eyeing his prince with a wary expression. He had run afoul of the prince's temper before, and lost friends to it.

Prince William pushed the woman off his lap and

rose, fastening his hose. Few people would have dared bring a doxy under the roof of a holy shrine, but the prince was uncaring of such matters. "I'm certain I didn't hear you right, Rufus. We have four people wandering the countryside between the river and Saint Anne's, and you tell me there's been no trace of them? Who were you asking—blind men?"

"M-my lord..." Rufus stammered. "I sent one group of men north, another to the east, but they could find no trace. You said we were to tell no one what we were searching for, so we couldn't very well ask questions of the peasants. Even so, no one mentioned seeing strangers. Gervaise's men are very thorough— I think they must have wounded them so grievously that they went off into the woods to die."

"They're human beings, Rufus, not dumb dogs. They don't run away to lick their wounds, they go for help. And Gervaise's men weren't good enough, were they? Which is why Gervaise is now nailed to a tree back there and you're in charge of the men. For now."

Rufus swallowed. He was a huge man, the kind who put fear into everyone who looked at him, who could snap necks with one meaty hand. The prince caused him to break out in a cold sweat. It wasn't so much he feared death. It was just that Prince William was so inventive about it.

"You'll go out yourself this time, Rufus," the prince said softly.

"I can't be in two places at once, sire," he said, desperation getting the better of him.

"You could if we split you in half. Four ways might be even better—then you could go north, south, east and west in search of those you let slip by."

"Sire…" he said desperately.

"Don't whine at me, Rufus. Find me the holy brothers who managed to escape. I stabbed the young one, but I cannot be sure it was a killing blow, and the man who dared pretend he was me got away unscathed. Taking the woman with him, no doubt. The red-haired witch."

"Wouldn't he have taken the pretty one, my lord?"

"Brother Peter has no sense, and even a fool could see he was ridiculously enamored of the creature. You'll need to kill them both when you find them. And you will find them, Rufus."

"Yes, sire."

"Begone, then."

The sweat was pouring off his broad forehead, this time with relief, and he began to back out of the room when the prince called out to him in a lazy voice.

"Oh, Rufus."

"Yes, my lord."

"When you find them, kill the girl first. But take your time, and make certain he gets to watch. You understand? If I can't get the job done myself I'm counting on you to do it right."

Rufus understood perfectly well. He had long since passed the point of feeling any pity for the helpless, and Elizabeth of Bredon's fate was a foregone conclusion.

But that didn't mean he had to make it hurt. The

prince would never be able to prove that it wasn't a slip of the knife that ended things too quickly. And he wouldn't kill a useful man over something like that. Probably.

"As you wish, my lord," he murmured. And bowed himself out of the room as the young girl next to the prince gave a muffled cry of pain.

Elizabeth lay sleeping facedown on the makeshift pallet. Peter told himself he had to check and make sure she was safe—she was, after all, his responsibility, at least until they reached the convent, where he could place her in the safe hands of the mother abbess.

She slept soundly, on her stomach, still wearing the enveloping cape and hood. Still hiding.

It was just as well. He could look at that sleeping form and tell himself it was just one of his brethren. Unlike others of his order, he felt no desire for his own kind, and he should be able to view the sleeping form on the bed with equanimity.

He couldn't. He still knew what lay beneath the rough weave of the monk's cloth, could still taste the untutored sweetness of her mouth, feel the silken texture of her skin. Why did women have to have such gloriously soft skin? Why did they have to smell so wonderful? And why was he suddenly no longer immune?

He turned away, forcing himself. In truth he doubted anyone needed to keep watch—they'd been circumspect enough that no one would be able to find them. He knew this land better than anyone—if he didn't want to be found he wouldn't be. And if the prince was dead, no one was going to care who was left behind.

If the prince was dead. Somehow he didn't feel it was going to be that simple. That easy.

He stepped outside into the cool night air. It was a waning moon, and the gilt sliver in the sky gave a faint light to the old house. It had belonged to one of his father's tenants, who'd been wiped out in the same fever that had killed his family and a goodly portion of the countryside. While he'd been off in the Holy Lands, oblivious.

If he'd been home he would have probably died from the fever, as well. Which would have been a blessing for all concerned—in his single-minded haste to do God's business he'd done just the opposite.

If any ghosts were to haunt him it wouldn't be the farmers who'd died of a fever, it would be the innocent souls of the murdered who would whisper in his ear. But superstition had no place in the life of a man of faith, his abbot had always said, and Peter agreed. There were no ghosts, there was no lingering sadness from the souls now departed. They had gone in peace, and were doubtless in heaven, not wandering through the countryside, terrorizing anyone who happened to stray near their old home.

Peter sank down on a patch of grass beneath a pear tree just blossoming with the newness of spring. He could sleep anywhere, and intended to. By tomorrow, after a solid night's rest, perhaps some of his temptation might vanish. And Elizabeth would be back to her old, scolding ways.

He dreamed, first of wanton things so powerful that he almost awoke with it. The night shifted and the nightmares came, the screams of the women as they died, trapped, and he could do nothing to save them. And then he realized the scream was not in his dream at all, but coming from the house.

He'd left the door ajar, but he banged against it as he raced into the house, knife drawn, ready to kill if need be. The screams had stopped, as they always did, and perhaps it was already too late.

His eyes grew accustomed to the inky darkness. She was sitting up in the bed, her face in her hands, the hood low around her face. And she was crying.

He didn't stop to think. He put the knife down and went to her, kneeling on the mattress and reaching for her hands. "What happened?" he asked gently.

At his touch she jumped back, but he didn't release her. "A bad dream," she managed to say, her voice still thick with tears. "I dreamed of the ghosts."

"There are no such things as ghosts, Elizabeth."

"I know that," she said with her usual asperity. "My dreams are not as convinced." She raised her head, but he couldn't see her face in the darkness. "You were supposed to wake me up. I should take my turn keeping watch."

"There's no need. No one can find us here."

"Then why did you say otherwise?"

"To make me stay away from you." He shouldn't

have said it, but in the darkness of the room he seemed to have lost any restraint.

She yanked her hands free from his grasp. "Stop it!" she cried. "Stop lying!"

He stared at her cowled head in astonishment. "What are you talking about?"

"Go away. You have no interest in me other than to torment me to a state of surrender, and you've already succeeded in that. What else have you got to gain? Go away and leave me alone."

He sat back, staring at her. "Explain this to me," he said with great patience.

"What explanation is needed? The great lecher of England has no interest in the only female available to him, except to tease her into thinking she's desirable and then abandoning her. Go away."

"You may as well stop telling me to go away, because I have no intention of leaving," he said, still marveling at her.

"Then I will." She tried to rise but he simply caught her and pulled her back, so that she tumbled onto the mattress, the hood of her habit falling onto her shoulders.

Her thick, beautiful veil of hair was gone, replaced by a rough-cut mop that was curling around her face. She looked like a beautiful boy, and he'd never had any interest in boys, but he was afraid he'd reached the point of no return.

"Your hair," he said.

"I cut it off. It's devil's hair, or so everyone has always told me. I'm ugly, anyway, and I hate it, and

I'm glad it's gone and…'' Her voice was getting more and more ragged with tears. "And now I look like an ugly boy and I shouldn't care because I'm going to be a nun because even you don't want me and I'd cut it off again and burn it because I hate it!'' She was running out of breath. "I hate it, I'm glad it's gone.…''

He caught her face, threading his long fingers through the curly strands. "You didn't hate it. It was beautiful and you know it, even if few people had the wit to appreciate it.''

She stared into his face, momentarily silent. Her eyes were swollen, her cheeks stained with tears, and he suspected she had spent longer than the last few minutes crying.

"Don't touch me,'' she whispered. "I'm ugly and you're a monster.''

He was doomed, and he knew it. He could resist the termagant, the saucy tease, the harridan, but he couldn't resist this woebegone creature shorn of her defenses as well as her hair.

"I'm no monster,'' he said, brushing the tears away with his thumb. "And even without your long hair you'll never look like a boy. You're beautiful, even if you don't know it, and I've been trying to do the right thing and leave you alone. It isn't from not wanting you, lady. It's from wanting you too much.''

"Liar,'' she said.

And truly, he had no choice but to kiss her. No choice but to give in to what had been eating him alive. And the Devil take the consequences.

19

Elizabeth should have been frightened. She should have berated herself for her stupidity and her foolish, weak vanity. But when he kissed her she could think of nothing at all but the taste of him, the touch of his body beneath the rough weave of the monk's robe, muscle and sinew and strength. He was known to hurt women, she couldn't deny it. All she knew was he wouldn't hurt her.

He lifted his mouth from hers to stare down into her eyes, a silent question in the unreadable depths. She could stop this at any time, she knew it, and she simply closed her eyes as he brushed his lips against her nose, her cheekbones, the corner of her eyes and the warmth of her temple. He turned her mouth up to his again, using his tongue this time, kissing her so deeply that her entire body seemed to rise to his. Dame Joanna had told her this was rough and tedious, other women had bemoaned the degradation and the rest didn't speak of it at all. But the wonder of his mouth, the answering fire that burned between her breasts, in her belly, between her legs, was so powerful she wondered how anyone could hate it. No matter how awful it became, surely this was worth it.

She was shaking, and she realized that she might be a little bit afraid after all, as one of his hands slid to the shoulder of her robe, unfastening it with blind dexterity that shocked her. It fell away, around her, so that she wore only her chemise.

She started to speak, but her voice seemed to have deserted her, and she had to clear her throat before the words would come out. "You're very adept at unfastening that robe. Have you much experience in undressing monks?" she asked lightly.

He was kissing the side of her jaw, and he stopped for a moment, and she was afraid he wouldn't start again.

"More than my share," he said in a rough voice, sliding his hands under the soft cotton of her chemise. He must have already loosened the ribbon that held it up, for it simply fell away beneath his deft hands to pool around her hips, and she sat there with her breasts exposed in the shadowy darkness.

"You seem to have experience with women's clothes, as well," she said nervously.

"More than my share," he said again. "Have you changed your mind?"

She had. She'd been lying to herself, she was terrified of this, lying naked with this dangerous man, letting him touch her, invade her body. "No," she said.

"Then stop trying to distract me." He kissed her mouth again, as his hands touched her breasts, and she jumped.

"What are you doing?"

"Touching your breasts. I'm going to put my mouth on them in another moment, in case you were wondering."

She shivered in fear and delight. "I don't think you ought to. Shouldn't you just... I mean, I thought we were going to..."

"You're going to lie back, close your eyes and stop asking questions," he said, and there was no missing the faint thread of amusement in his rich voice. "I need to concentrate on doing this properly."

"Don't I have to do anything?"

"Not until you want to. Not until you're ready to. In the meantime, all you have to do is lie back and enjoy it."

"En-enjoy it?" she stammered.

He pushed her back on the bed, gently, and a moment later he'd pulled the chemise the rest of the way off her, so that she lay in front of him, completely naked. It was dark in the room, but she suspected he could see her quite clearly, and she reached her arms up to cover herself, only for him to take her wrists and place them back down beside her body.

"Pretend you're somewhere else," he whispered. "Lying in a field of grass with the sun beating down upon you. Floating on a cloud. You'll come back when you're ready."

And then he did as he warned her, put his mouth on her breast, drawing on it like a babe sucking at his mother.

She did as she was bid, closing her eyes, trying to float away, but the tug of his mouth on her breast was an insistent demand, a fiery line of clenching desire that traveled down between her legs. He cupped her other breast, and the peak was hard and pebbled against his fingers, and she clutched at the rough blanket beneath her as a strange knot began to grow deep inside her.

He released her breast, only to put his mouth on the other one, and she made a strange, involuntary noise as her hands lifted and threaded through his thick hair, cradling him against her breast as he suckled her.

When he pulled away, her breast was wet, cool, and she opened her mouth to say something when he stopped her with his tongue, and his kiss made the knot inside her wind tighter, deeper.

He said he knew what he was doing. She hoped so, because she needed his touch, but she didn't know where, she only knew she was restless and anxious and burning up, and if he didn't do something soon she'd either burst into tears again or explode.

When he put his hands between her legs it shouldn't have been a shock. She tried to tighten her legs against his touch but he was much stronger, and he simply used his own body to wedge her legs apart. When he slid his fingers inside her she should have been expecting it, but she froze, anyway.

"Don't fight me, Elizabeth," he whispered, kissing the soft skin of her belly. "This is for you, not me," and he touched some special place that made her whole body shake in some dark kind of pleasure.

"That's right," he whispered against her skin. "I

want to make you come for me. You'll do that for me, won't you? Give me that much before I have to hurt you.''

She had no idea what he was talking about, and she really didn't care. He was going to hurt her? It didn't matter—she'd go down that road willingly, anything to make this devouring need be filled.

She was having trouble breathing, her breath coming in strangled little whimpers. She needed something but she didn't know what to ask for, as the gnawing ache between her legs grew stronger and stronger.

And then he sat back, taking his hands from inside her, cradling her hips, and she let out a helpless cry of protest and longing. Only to follow it with a shriek as he put his mouth where his hands had been, kissing her there, between her legs, using his tongue on her.

She tried to buck, but his strong hands held her captive. She tried to push at his shoulders but she had no strength. She could only grip the blanket beneath her once more as her legs curled up and her head fell back and her body exploded.

For a moment she thought she was going to die, and she didn't care. Her body had turned into a white-hot, devouring flame, and all she could do was lie there and shiver, as wave after wave of clenching response seemed to pull her under into a world of eternal darkness.

He pulled away then, wiping his mouth on his sleeve, and stripped off his robe with even more dispatch than he'd used with hers. His skin was white gold in the moonlight, and she looked at him, at his scarred, muscled chest, his lean, flat stomach, at the part of him that was hard and much too big to ever fit inside even her body.

She was going to say so, when he took her hand and placed it on him, on the hard, silken length of him. It was like nothing she had ever touched—velvet soft and steel hard, and whether it would fit or not didn't matter. She wanted it.

He cupped her fingers around him. "Do this," he said, moving her hand up and down the length of him. "Not too hard. It'll be better if I come this way. That way I can take you to—" his voice choked as the flesh beneath her hand jerked "—take you to Saint Anne's still a virgin."

She knew what he meant now, when he said *come*. It was what he'd done to her. And he wanted her to make him spill his seed outside her body, a sin, to be sure, but not as great a sin as seducing a virgin destined for a convent.

She pulled her hand away. "No," she said in a rough voice, lying back on the mattress, reaching her hands to his strong shoulders and pulling him with her. "I want it all."

He didn't fight it. "God help me," he said, looming over her. "God help us both." And she felt him between her legs, that solid rod of flesh, sinking into the wetness he'd already prepared with his mouth, moving in deep and hard and then stopping when he reached the final barrier.

"No," he said, starting to pull away.

"Yes," she said, pulling him down on top of her, pulling him deep inside her so that he broke the final veil and thrust deep inside her.

The pain was brief, fleeting, and it took her a moment to catch her breath. "There," she said in a choked voice. "Now you don't have any choice. Finish it."

When he kissed her this time she could taste herself on his mouth. He slid his hands up her thighs to her hips and pulled her up tight against him, wrapping her legs around his narrow hips as he began to move, deep inside her, slow at first, then faster, and he could no longer kiss her. They were both covered in sweat, and he had buried his face against her neck as he thrust, hard and deep, more and more, until he froze, and the sound he made was like a cry from hell as he spilled his seed deep inside her, hot and wet and powerful.

And then he collapsed on top of her, so heavy that he might have crushed a smaller woman. She was trembling, but she slid her hands down his body, to his narrow hips, and pulled him in deeper still, unwilling to let him go.

His face felt wet against her shoulder, but it must have been sweat. She wanted to say something—that strange knot seemed to have reawakened, but it came accompanied by a deep, heavy lassitude. And all she could do was run her hands up his strong, scarred back, press her lips against the side of his neck, and sleep.

* * *

Peter slowly, carefully withdrew from her body. She was already asleep, and deep inside she instinctively tightened around him, unwilling to let him go.

He lay beside her, watching her. Odd, how he should be the one to cry, not her. She had no idea what had just happened between them, apart from the rudimentary knowledge that she'd lost her virginity. She had no idea that with her loss he'd lost all hope for his immortal soul. And that the act had been so powerful, so profound, that his greater sin was that he couldn't regret it.

His sin, not hers. God would know she was blameless in this night's work, even if those on earth did not. Since they wouldn't understand, they didn't need to know.

He hadn't even had the sense to climax outside her body, keeping her safe from pregnancy. When he'd lived in the secular world, as a knight, he'd been noted for his capacity for sexual pleasure, and yet with all his countless partners he'd never made the mistake of leaving them with his seed. And now, the time it mattered the most, he had lost his head and let himself come deep inside her moist, sleek body, and if there was such a thing as double damnation he deserved it.

The moon was shining in the shuttered window, illuminating her perfect body. Perfect to him, at least. Her legs were long and sleek and beautiful, her hips narrow, her stomach flat and her breasts full. She was as beautiful naked as he'd imagined her to be, perhaps even more so. If he'd only been able to keep his imagination in check he might have been able to keep his body under control, as well.

In the last seven years he'd resisted lust and temptation. Even now, though the thought of moving deep inside her body once more sent a shiver of anticipation down his body, he knew he could resist. Could stop himself, force himself to keep away.

The only thing he couldn't stop himself from doing was loving her.

His father had always said he was a stubborn, contrary soul, and so he'd proved him, going off on crusade when he should have been safeguarding the family estate, so that he came back to England with no land, no family, nothing but a guilt so heavy that he might break under it.

He hadn't listened to his father, and he'd paid the price. He'd been appreciatively impervious to the charms of women everywhere, making love to them without loving them.

So why should a redheaded, bad-tempered, long-legged scold like Elizabeth have managed to get past conscience and common sense and snared his heart? A heart promised to his holy order?

It wasn't her fault, it was his. His weakness.

If he dressed swiftly in the darkness, left her, she'd be safe enough for the time being. He could make it to the shrine, see what he could find out about the prince's whereabouts, and send someone after Elizabeth. If he were very careful, if she still clung to her cloistered future, then she might never have to know the truth. She could just believe she'd spent one night lying beneath the bastard prince of England, and never have to know the truth about the liar who'd taken her virginity.

Even better, she could marry, stay in the country and bear many children. And the pain of knowing someone else had her, someone else had the pleasure of listening to her scolding tongue, would be only a small penance of the huge debt he had to pay.

If he left she'd be safe enough. A sin committed once and deeply repented could be absolved. A sin repeated was a sin too stubborn to be eradicated.

And he leaned over and kissed her, anyway.

Once Adrian made up his mind it was simple enough to follow through. He had made up his mind about Dame Joanna with her Madonna eyes, and everything fell into place. They stopped early soon after dusk. His strength was greatly improved, but a good night's rest would only make things better, and the town of Beckham, though poor, was welcoming to a pilgrim and his beleaguered wife. The next best thing than going on pilgrimage was to offer comfort and hospitality to those doing so, thereby gaining some sanctity without having to travel, and the miller had a room with a real bed in it, a good meal and strong ale to strengthen the blood. Everyone offered helpful suggestions as to how they might conceive, some so complicated and detailed that Adrian wanted to laugh, but Joanna didn't seem to share his amusement. He could sense the wariness in her, beneath her calm, wifely demeanor. She didn't trust him, and she was wise not to do so. Years of experience with men had taught her when a man wanted something from her, they usually wanted one thing, giving as little as possible in return. A penniless monk with a vow of chastity would be the furthest thing from a hopeful prospect as any man she might meet.

And yet he knew she was not immune. She looked at him when she thought he wouldn't notice, and there was a strange kind of wonder in her calm blue eyes. As if he were different from the men she had met.

He wasn't, in the most basic of ways. He wanted, longed, ached to lie with her, lose himself in the warm comfort of her woman's body, and if things were only the slightest bit different he would have already had her. He never would have thought celibacy would hit so hard, and until Dame Joanna had joined their party he'd come through relatively unscathed. He'd barely seen her when he met her at Wakebryght Castle, and while his first glimpse was intensely beguiling, he'd been able to avoid temptation simply by staying out of the way.

That had changed once she joined their journey. And every moment he spent with her only made his desire stronger. A desire he had every intention of indulging as soon as he could.

But for this night he lay side by side with her in a narrow room at the miller's house, with barely enough space to move, and he closed his eyes and thought dark thoughts and tried not to think of the woman who lay pressed up against his side, sleeping quietly.

It would have been simple enough to roll on top of her. He might have bled afresh, but he was a quick healer, and once he'd given her pleasure she'd probably forgive him for breaking his promise not to touch her. He was good at pleasuring women—he never took half as much joy in the act of loving if his partner didn't enjoy it, as well.

The more experienced a lover, the easier it was. Women who'd known men knew what they liked, and most of them would tell him, after a little coaxing if they were shy. Once he got Joanna stripped and on her back it would be easy enough. There was a bond between them already, even without the joining of their bodies. He could feel it, and he knew she could, as well, though she'd deny it if asked. It probably scared her.

He needed to concentrate on keeping them safe—there would be time enough for pleasure once they reached the holy shrine. In the meantime he slept with Joanna, like some ancient knight and his lady upon a tomb, chaste and untouching.

With luck, by late tomorrow they'd reach their destination. His shoulder would be one day better, his body would be one day stronger.

And he would take Dame Joanna in a soft bed with warm covers and clean water. Take her under the saint's very nose, take her all night long. And in the morning he would love her again, until he blotted out the memory of any other man who had touched her.

It wasn't that he was jealous, or condemned her for her past. It was simply that he was her future, and the sooner he claimed her body and made it so, the better.

She'd be skittish. Resistant. Then eventually pliant and loving. The minute he left the service of the prince, he'd take her back to Longacre.

If he was really lucky, the prince would be dead. The outlaws were truly just that, or else sent by the father of the girl he'd murdered, and the prince's last act of spite had been to try to kill one of the men set guard over him.

With any luck he was dead, his body discovered and brought back to the shrine for holy burial.

And he'd have nothing more to do but concentrate on loving the woman lying next to him.

Even if the prince still lived, it wouldn't take long to find him. If he didn't repent sincerely, then the rest would be up to his increasingly annoyed father. King John was far more interested in his child bride, and he would probably simply banish him.

Either way, Adrian would be free to return home.

With Joanna by his side.

20

Peter stood by the riverbank, fastening his robe around him as he watched Elizabeth. They'd gone a few feet down the river and found a calm spot where they could bathe peacefully. He'd taken her every way he could think of, until he was certain her body could stand no more, was certain his body wanted no more. And then she put her mouth on him, and he wanted her all over again.

Oddly enough, she was shy when he first woke her, embarrassed at what had passed between them, her asp-tongue momentarily stilled. He'd brought in cool water and bathed her, but somehow his ministering efforts had quickly turned to something else, and this time he coaxed her into climbing on top of him and finding her own pleasure, with him inside her.

It had only made his own response stronger, feeling her body milk his as she cried out in wonder. He had to hold her as he finished it, before he let her collapse like a boneless doll on his sweat-soaked body.

Each time he took her he told himself it would be the last. Each time he found himself hard and wanting her, all she had to do was look at him with that shy, wondrous look and he was gone.

The cool water should have cooled their ardor, and he stretched out on the spring grass while she soaked. Her poor body was unused to such blissful punishment, and it was only her suppressed moan of discomfort that had stopped him from taking her there in the river. She hadn't liked him setting her firmly away from him, but she'd said nothing, turning her back on him and diving under the water.

She could swim—something he wouldn't have suspected when she nearly drowned. He wondered how she'd managed to escape supervision long enough to do so. He sat on the bank and watched her long white body glide through the water, keeping his mind free of regrets and despair, content in the pleasure of watching her. There'd be time enough for those later.

There'd been one difficult moment, when she'd seen his back. He couldn't know for certain, of course, but he could well imagine what it looked like, and her gasp only reminded him. The scimitar scar that ran diagonally across his back from his shoulder to his buttock was long healed and logical enough—she knew he'd been on crusade. But there were newer scars from the whip, and a myriad of tiny scratches from the hair shirt he'd only just abandoned.

"What happened to you?" she gasped.

"I fell afoul of an Arab sword, but I survived."

"I don't mean that. I mean the marks. Someone's hurt you. Someone who wanted to inflict as much pain as he could."

She was far too close for comfort, but he couldn't

tell her he'd inflicted that pain himself, to drive the Devil from his body. And that he'd failed.

So he made do with the faint smile he'd perfected as Prince William the deviate. "The giving and receiving of pain can bring an intense pleasure unlike anything else. You have to be careful not to go too far, or people might die, but if you judge it correctly it can be quite…delightful."

Her expression of horror was just what he expected, and yet it still pained him. "Do you want to hurt me?"

What would she do if he said yes? He found he didn't want to know. He suspected if his hands were on her, his cock inside her, then she'd let him do just about anything. But she didn't need to know that about herself.

"That's a more advanced study," he said smoothly. "You're still on baby steps."

Her eyes widened, and he half expected her to lash out at him. Instead she turned and dove away from him, and he walked out of the water, knowing that for one brief moment he'd done the right thing.

He had dressed quickly, only to realize she was watching him from the water, surveying his nude body with unabashed curiosity. When he caught her looking she turned away with a haughty gesture, and he almost had to smile.

He must have dozed off in the hot sunlight—little wonder given his active night. The sound of the water woke him, just in time to see her emerging from the river like a pagan goddess, the water dripping off her breasts, down her flat belly, nestling in the red curls between her legs.

She walked slowly, taunting him, and then stopped, reaching for the discarded robe before he could move. At one point last night she'd put the chemise back on, and he'd torn it off her, rendering it useless. He hoped the rough weave of the monk's robe wouldn't be too harsh on a body already scratched from the feel of his unshaven beard.

He rose, grateful for the disguising nature of his own robe. He could tell by the way she moved that she was mad at him, as she had been through most of their acquaintance, and he told himself he was glad.

"We need to be away from this place," he said as she came toward him. "If we keep moving we might reach the shrine by nightfall. The sooner you're among the good sisters the better."

"Why?"

"Because you have no other place to go," he said flatly. "Unless you wish to return to your father."

"What makes you think the nuns will accept spoilt goods?"

"Because I'll pay them enough to take you." He put it more cruelly than need be, but it was nothing less than the truth. They would take her, no matter what shape she was in, because of the hefty dowry her father had paid, and as a favor to the man who had given his entire holdings to the church. Peter de Montselm.

She had pale skin to go with her red hair, but it

turned whiter at his cruel words. He had no choice, he told himself. She would hate him soon enough— why delay the inevitable?

"Are you ready? I find I'm weary of delay. This entire journey has been one disaster after another, and I can't wait until I'm back in court." He wasn't sure if he was overdoing his part, but she seemed to swallow it.

She took a step away from him. "You'll make better time if you go on alone," she said in a flat, unemotional voice.

Yes, he had overplayed his part. "I thought I made this clear days ago. I'm not leaving you behind."

"Why not? I'm more than capable of finding my way to the shrine, and you walk faster than I do. No one will interfere with a mendicant monk, even if he travels alone, and you appear to have had your fill of me. We'll both be much happier traveling alone."

"No." He had no idea why he insisted, when in truth he could make it to the shrine in half the time without her in his company. In time to send someone back for her, in time for him to have already gone in search of the missing prince.

And if she ever need speak of the last few hours, she would blame Prince William, and that would be the last of it. Prince William wouldn't be held accountable for the rape of a nun—it would be the least of his crimes. Assuming the man was still alive.

Except that Peter was certain he was. William came of an evil too old and powerful to give up life easily, and the world would feel lighter once he had left it. Right now it felt as heavy as lead on his shoulders.

"What if you're with child?" he asked suddenly. "How are you going to explain that?"

"A virgin birth?" She said it to shock him, and he almost had to smile. He was a hard man to shock. "Or I could say I was set upon by bandits and cruelly raped, but that I managed to escape. The subject is unlikely to come up, however. It's the wrong time for me to get pregnant."

He blinked. "Is there ever a right time?"

"I am skilled in midwifery, my lord. Have you forgotten? I know about birth and conception, and I know a woman is most likely to become pregnant midway between her monthly courses. I just finished mine, and am therefore relatively safe. And why aren't you turning green? Most men do when women discuss their womanly functions."

"I'm strong enough to withstand the idea," he said lightly. "In that case, there is no reason why I shouldn't see you safely to the shrine. There'll be no proof that I amused myself with you."

He'd gone too far then, and he knew it. He'd hoped she'd dissolve in silent tears. Instead her green eyes flashed fire.

"Amused yourself with me, you foul-minded, indolent, rapacious son of a bitch!" she cried. "Where the hell is my knife?"

He'd already scooped it up from the riverbank, a wise precaution since he had every intention of making her angry. Not, however, this angry.

"Behave yourself, lady," he drawled. "What more did you think it was?"

She came at him like a charging boar, so fast he barely had time to fend her off. She kicked at him, but since she hadn't put her sandals on, it did little good. She tried to knee him, but he managed to stop her, catching her wrists, turning her and pinning her against a tree. She was crying, certainly, but they were tears of rage, and she moved her face down and bit his hand, as hard as she could.

He didn't release her. Didn't dare. "If you don't calm down I'll truss you up like a plucked chicken and leave you here."

"You'd like that, wouldn't you? Leaving me helpless. Well, I'd rather you do that than spend another moment in your royal-pain-in-the-arse company. Let go of me!" She tried to kick him again, and he had no choice but to pin her against the tree with his entire body. Making her fully aware of the state of his arousal.

She looked up at him mid-spate, shocked and suddenly stopped fighting him. He leaned his forehead against hers. "Sweet scold," he whispered. "My foul-tempered angel, I'll never get my fill of you. But I have no choice—I have to take you back there. And the more I touch you, the harder it gets."

He'd stopped holding her wrists, and she reached down and put her hand around him. "Yes," she said, pulling on him lightly, so that he almost spilled in her hand. "The harder it gets."

He couldn't help it. He shoved the robe she was

wearing aside, pulled his up and lifted her, bracing her against the tree as he filled her with one deep thrust.

She came immediately, tightening around him with a hoarse cry, putting her mouth against his, kissing him as she rode him. He could feel the hardness of her nipples through the rough cloth, and the ease with which he'd entered her told him she was as aroused as he was.

She surged up, then sank down on him, riding him, riding the wave of pleasure, and when the peak came she sank her teeth into his shoulder and bit him, hard, through the heavy fabric.

The sharp pain was the finishing touch, and he let go, pressing her against the rough bark of the tree, filling her with his seed, shocked at the way her body clung to his, drawing him in deeper, jealous of every bit of him.

They stayed that way, her legs locked around his hips under the enveloping robe, her arms around his neck, his body within hers, as their breathing slowly returned to normal. He was going to say it, and nothing on this earth could stop him, even though the words would only make things worse.

"Sweet Elizabeth," he whispered against her ear. "I love—"

"Ahem!" The voice was like an explosion in the forest, and Peter jumped back, the enveloping robes falling around him, to turn and face the apoplectic expression of someone he knew far too well.

"Brother Jerome," he said in a resigned voice. "How did you find us?"

Elizabeth had sunk back against the tree, decently covered by the robe he'd thrust aside so eagerly. How long had the men been standing there? They'd been so caught up in their rage and lust that a small army had approached and they'd been completely unaware.

There were a dozen armed men accompanying Brother Jerome, as well as horses snorting in the warm air. "We've had search parties out for the last day. The prince also sent his own men, but Bishop Martin insisted on sending a guard, as well, and we were the first to find you." His eyes narrowed as he peered at Elizabeth. "That's not Brother Adrian," he said in a suspicious voice.

Elizabeth reached up and covered her head with the hood of her robe, hiding her face, and Peter resisted the urge to touch her, turning instead to the new-comer. If Brother Jerome hadn't realized Elizabeth was a woman, what in Christ's name did he think they were doing locked together like that?

And then his words sank in. "Bishop Martin is at the shrine?"

Jerome nodded. "As is your charge. It was nothing less than a miracle, Brother. The prince managed to escape those cutthroats and find his way through the forest alone. God must truly bless his pilgrimage to have spared him from the carnage. Of course, the robbers had no idea the prince was posing as a lowly monk, but that didn't seem to stop their slaughter. Thank heavens you managed to escape, as well."

"Thank heavens," he echoed faintly. He couldn't see Elizabeth's face, couldn't be sure she'd taken in all that she was hearing. He should have told her the truth himself. Long ago, before he'd touched her. But then, there was no good way for her to find out he'd been lying to her all this time.

As if wanting to drive a final nail through him, Father Jerome said in a cheerful voice, "And I see you've already managed to get back in your proper garb. It must be a blessing to be free of such an imposture, Brother Peter. I warned Bishop Martin when you first suggested such a thing. You were the obvious man to take the prince's place, but the risks were too high. We can only thank God you've been returned to us safe and sound."

"Yes," he said in a muffled voice. "Safe and sound."

"And who is this young man?" Brother Jerome was trying his best to sound avuncular.

There was no way around it. "This is Lady Elizabeth of Bredon. She's to join the sisters of Saint Anne."

Jerome looked between the two of them. Peter met his stern gaze fearlessly. "I see," he said, and the sorrow in his voice was sharper than a sword. "We've only brought one extra horse. We thought you were alone. Lady Elizabeth can ride with one of the other men."

He didn't object. Brother Jerome held out his hand. "My lady?"

Elizabeth stepped forward, keeping her head down

as she moved past him, careful not to let even the hem of her loose-fitting robe touch him. She looked smaller, somehow, not like the long-legged goddess who strode through life bringing babies into the world and cursing him. Her narrow shoulders were slumped beneath the robe, and she looked small and defeated. And if suicide were not a mortal sin he would have cut his own throat there and then.

Instead he simply followed after them, head bowed low.

Adrian woke abruptly. He looked out the small, unshuttered window, trying to gauge the time. It was dangerously close to daylight. The village was already awake, but full light would make escape even more difficult. He could hear the sound of bridled horses—horses that could only mean Prince William's men had reached the village. For the sake of their hosts they needed to be gone, with no trace of them, no word as to which direction they were headed.

But of course, that would be obvious. The only place they would be safe, Joanna would be safe, was the Shrine of Saint Anne. They just had to make it there while avoiding Prince William's hunting party.

He looked down at the woman sleeping by his side, about to wake her, when he paused for a moment. She looked so peaceful, so serenely beautiful, that he regretted disturbing her. She lay on her back, still and silent, and he was reminded again of the tomb of his grandfather. He and his wife were depicted in marble atop the crypt, lying side by side throughout eternity, in stone and bone, and for the first time he began to understand the legendary bond that they'd held between them. The peaceful, calm knowledge that they would never be separated.

He shook himself. Now was not the time to be distracted by sentimental thoughts, any more than by lust. Now was the time to run.

He touched her shoulder, and her eyes flew open, staring up into his. There was instinctive fear in her gaze, a fear that vanished and was replaced with only mild wariness.

"We have to go," he whispered. "William's men are approaching the village, doubtless looking for us. We're going to have to make a run for it."

"But how will they know we're here?" she protested, rising nonetheless and pulling on her leather slippers. "Will they seek out every traveling pilgrim and his wife?"

"They'll be asking for a woman of uncommon beauty. That will give us away every time."

He expected her to look pleased at his backhanded reference to her charms, but she merely nodded, taking it in her stride. "Then you should go on alone. I don't know how you managed it, when the night before you were at death's door, but you seem to have regained enough strength to make it on your own. Leave me behind."

He shook his head. "You're a witness, as well, my love." The instinctive use of an endearment was a mistake—she looked startled, and he quickly went on. "They'll kill you, but they'll make life very unpleasant for you beforehand. Another drawback to being so beautiful,'' he said lightly, looking out the window. He could hear the sound of William's men, moving from house to house, and sooner or later someone was going to mention the pilgrims.

''You can't be certain.''

''Are you willing to take that risk? Because I am not. We're going out the window now. Don't argue with me.''

The window was not overlarge, but she managed to swing one leg over it, pulling her gown up to reveal white, beautiful legs.

''Stop staring, Brother Adrian,'' she said sharply. ''And I think the sooner you get back to your monastery the better off you'll be. You've become far too worldly of late.''

He cursed himself silently. When he shed the borrowed robes of the monk, he had begun to forget that it was still, indeed, his purported role in life, at least as far as Joanna was concerned. It was enough to drive a man mad—a knight pretending to be a monk pretending to be a pilgrim. What would his next layer of deception include?

He followed her out the window, and a moment later they had disappeared into the forest, with not a soul to see them.

21

The tub of water was blessedly warm, even if the soap was rough, and Elizabeth sat in the middle of it, soaking, trying to concentrate on useless things. It was astonishingly easy to wash her short-cropped hair, though it felt very odd beneath her fingers. When it was long the heavy weight of it had pulled it straight, but cropped short, it curled around her face.

Her body ached—it had been a fast, hard ride to the shrine, and she'd had no choice but to sit astride, her arms around the waist of one of the burly soldiers. It was little wonder her hips felt…

She ducked her head under the water, to wash away the malicious memory. The nuns had welcomed her warmly, whisking her away from the presence of the men, asking no questions but taking her to a warm bath, then offering a cup of wine and a meal to follow.

She had thought she was famished when the day began, but now the very thought of food made her nauseous. She hadn't lied to…to the man who had been with her. She was in little danger of being with child, and it took a number of weeks before morning sickness began.

No, her stomach was protesting the unpalatable

truth of her situation. She'd been lied to, unmercifully. She had lain with a monk, done things no decent woman should do with her husband, much less a holy man.

But a man who lied and kissed and…and…as he did was far from holy. At one point he'd told her he was no monster.

He was wrong.

She ducked under the water again, trying to concentrate on the warmth. Maybe she could just stay there, hold her breath until she passed out and then drowned. That way she'd never have to see Brother Peter again. Never have to answer questions, never have to think about anything…

Except mortal, unforgivable sin, far worse than copulating with a monk. Suicide was a coward's way out. She may be a blind, trusting fool, but she was no coward.

She came up for air finally, taking in great gulps of it, only to find Mother Alison sitting beside the tub, a calm expression on her face.

At least it wasn't the mother abbess, a stony-faced woman who took one look at her and probably knew to the last detail what she'd done with the lying monk. Mother Alison was in charge of the novitiate, and it was her duty to see to the new members of the order. Her duty to tell her she was no longer welcome, Elizabeth thought glumly.

"I wondered how long you were going to stay under the water," Mother Alison said in a comfortable voice. She was a tiny creature, small and slender and almost elfin, with the kindest eyes in the world. Elizabeth looked at her stonily, determined not to cry. "I'm very glad you decided to come up for air. I wasn't looking forward to diving into the tub to rescue you."

"I wasn't going to drown myself, Mother," she said.

"I never thought you would. But you might have fallen asleep. You've had a very busy few days, and it's little wonder you're exhausted."

"Yes," she said, not wanting to think of what the last day or so had entailed.

"We were all praying for you when we heard your party had been set upon by bandits. Once we knew there were no women among the victims, and that Brother Peter had disappeared, we were reasonably sure you were safe. Brother Peter would never let harm befall an innocent."

"Brother Peter is…" She stopped herself in time, silencing the rage and pain that bubbled just beneath the surface. She had been so stupid, so abysmally stupid. Bad enough that she'd been blinded by a deviate prince. Far worse that she'd become entangled with an unholy monk.

"Brother Peter is a good man," Mother Alison finished for her. "A troubled man, but a good one. I'm not as convinced about our royal guest. Nothing seems to affect Prince William, not the death of those who accompanied him nor his recent ordeal."

Better to talk of the real prince than think about his

wicked impersonator. "How did he manage to escape and find his way here?"

"I'm certain he'll wish to tell you the story himself. It does seem to change with each telling, but one does not contradict or question the king's son. Especially now that his penance is complete and he is absolved of his sin, made new again."

There was no missing the touch of asperity in Mother Alison's voice. "You don't believe in the power of absolution?"

"I do. For those who truly repent. Why don't you come out of there before you're wrinkled up like a prune? The prince is counting on your company at dinner. He wishes to apologize for the masquerade and any harm that might have come to you."

"I don't want to." She sounded like a little girl on the edge of a temper tantrum and she didn't care.

"You can't stay in the tub forever, my dear."

"I don't want to join the prince for dinner. I don't want to have to see a man ever again."

"In which case you'll die unshriven and go to hell, since only priests can hear confession," Mother Alison said in a dispassionate voice. She rose, bringing a heavy sheet of toweling to the side of the tub. "Come along, my child. You needn't worry about seeing Brother Peter. He's keeping vigil in the chapel. I only hope he'll show some sense for a change."

"I couldn't care less what he's doing. And he strikes me as someone eminently sensible."

"Except for the burden of guilt he bears. You've seen the scars on his back, have you not? He mortifies his flesh with whip and hair shirt, fasting and sleepless vigils that last for days. I worry that he'll push himself too far in his zeal.''

''I wouldn't worry about him,'' Elizabeth said. ''He's in no danger of becoming a saint anytime soon.''

''So I gather.'' She held out the towel. ''Come, Sister Elizabeth. If you are to join our ranks, one of the first things you'll have to learn is obedience to the rule.''

Obedience had never been her strong suit, but Mother Alison was astonishingly forceful. Elizabeth had no choice but to climb from the tub, wondering if her wet, naked body betrayed her.

But the nun was looking tactfully away as she held out the toweling, and Elizabeth took it and wrapped it around her, shivering slightly in the cool room.

''I'm surprised you're allowed to talk to me. I was told this was a silent order.''

Mother Alison laughed. ''Who told you such a lie? In truth, we have our times of silence and meditation as any order does, but we are usually a fairly talkative bunch. We are women, after all.''

The spring night had turned chilly, and Elizabeth moved closer to the heat emanating from the brazier.

''I brought you something to wear. It's a bit short, but if you decide to stay you'll be able to make yourself a habit that reaches your feet.''

''If I decide to stay? Why wouldn't I? I've traveled for days, risked death and worse, to get here. Why should I change my mind?''

"Change is always possible, my child. And this is not an easy life, for all its joys. You don't strike me as someone who's made for humility and obedience."

"I can learn. And I wasn't looking for an easy life. I doubt such a thing exists."

"True enough."

"And a woman's life is about blind obedience, to a father, to a husband, to a king. I'd rather my allegiance be to God and to the brides of Christ."

Mother Alison surveyed her with compassion. "Did you want to tell me anything, Lady Elizabeth?" she asked.

"You said it yourself, you cannot hear my confession and give me absolution."

"No. But sometimes it helps just to talk about your problems with someone who won't pass judgment. I came to my calling later in life, my dear. I am not unknowing when it comes to the world."

For a moment hope sprang in Elizabeth's heart. She wanted to tell Mother Alison the truth of what had happened. She wanted someone else to tell her what to do, whether to join the order and repent, or leave this holy place and find some kind of life for herself.

Her only possible choice would be to return to her father's household, and she would rather die. She shook her head. "No, Mother. I have nothing I wish to talk about."

If the tiny nun was disappointed she didn't show it. "Then you must dress and join the prince for dinner. He is a very charming man, but even if I had not heard rumors, I would guess that he is a man who does not like to be crossed. Will you need help dressing?'' She nodded toward the pile of simple gray clothing on the bench. ''You won't be wearing a veil yet, and the robe is simple enough.''

Elizabeth reached an instinctive hand to her short hair. ''I thought it would be covered.''

''Not yet, my dear. And there was no need to shear it off quite yet.''

''I wanted to do something to show my willingness to eschew the world and join the cloister,'' Elizabeth said.

''Perhaps. But I think it even more likely that you thought cutting your hair would make it impossible for you to change your mind. You can always change your mind, my child. If the cloister is not for you then you must say so. To consecrate yourself to God with only half a heart is a greater sin than not coming here at all.''

''There will be nothing in my heart but God, Mother Alison.''

''Indeed.'' She didn't look convinced. She reached out and patted Elizabeth's hand. ''Best dress quickly, before the prince becomes impatient. He was about to leave when you and Brother Peter arrived, and I expect he'll plan to depart as soon as he has thanked you.''

Elizabeth tried to picture the sweet, smiling Brother Matthew in princely robes, but all she could see was Peter's lying face. Above her, blocking out the light, kissing her.

"You promise I won't see…Brother Peter?" The name came hard to her lips.

"I promise. Now, hurry along, child. We'd all be happy to see the last of the prince and his men, no matter how charming he appears to be."

He wanted her. Joanna had enough experience of men to know that the sweet monk walking by her side wanted to lie with her. It should have come as no surprise. Most men took one look at her and wanted to touch her. It wasn't vanity on her part, simply observation. In truth, she cursed the beauty that had been her lot in life. Her older sister had been stout and plain, married off quickly to a yeoman farmer, and almost as quickly the mother of three.

But with his beautiful daughter Elric found he could look higher, and instead of offering a dowry he could pick and choose, lose a daughter and gain in property.

She couldn't really fault him. The husband he'd chosen was the wealthiest of the suitors, as well as the oldest. But he was kind and gentle, seldom interested in matters of the flesh, and for a number of years she'd been content. By the time she'd been widowed her father was dead, his land passed on to his nearest male heir, a second cousin who bore no affection for women in general and his pretty cousin in particular, and she'd had no choice but to marry again, quickly. That time she hadn't been so lucky.

Over the intervening years she'd learned that most men were easily led by the promise in her body, and she'd always managed to hide her distaste for the process. But right now, on her way to a convent for a period of rest and reflection, she didn't have to lift her skirts for anyone. And certainly not for a celibate monk who would never dare act on his amorous feelings.

It wasn't the poor boy's fault—it was probably misguided gratitude for her saving his life. And he would never dare act on it, if he truly did have lustful feelings for her.

The odd thing was, for the first time she was starting to wonder what it could be like. She knew better—she'd endured it often enough to know the act was designed for a man's pleasure and a woman's degradation. She had been blessed to be spared the pain and the dangers of pregnancy, she'd always told herself. But following in Adrian's footsteps, she found herself thinking once more of sweet-cheeked babies who had beautiful eyes like his.

He had walked a few feet ahead of her, and she surveyed him covertly, the grace of his body, the way he moved. She was still in awe of his healing powers—yarrow was an effective treatment but never had she seen someone recover so quickly. He was much stronger than she suspected beneath his humble monk's robe. Smooth-skinned, strong-muscled, he had the body of a warrior, not a monk. Perhaps he'd gone on crusade, then returned to take his vows.

But he looked too young for the last crusade. And as the hours, the days passed, he was looking less and less like a monk and more like a man. And she couldn't help thinking of him as such.

Thank heavens there was nothing to be done about it. For all that he moved and talked like a man of the world, he had vows of chastity and obedience that he wouldn't break lightly. She still wasn't convinced that they were in any particular danger from the prince—she'd looked into his eyes and known instinctively that he was a good, fair man with a shadow on his soul, and she could not imagine him sending a hunting party out to kill them, no matter what Adrian insisted.

But it meant they had to keep moving, with little time to talk, and no energy to think of other things.

So why did she keep thinking of him?

Perhaps it was his undeniable physical grace and beauty. Perhaps it was the knowledge that she was entirely safe to dream about him and what his touch would feel like, because nothing would ever come of it.

It didn't matter why. As long as they kept moving she could daydream all she wanted. And perhaps, when they arrived at St. Anne's and he left her to rejoin his holy order, she'd reward herself with a kiss from his undeniably beautiful mouth.

This time they heard the sound of the cart from far away. Adrian turned swiftly, taking her hand and pulling her toward the woods, when the old gray horse appeared, plodding steadily along the rutted track.

"There you two are," Odo, their farmer friend from yesterday, greeted them. "We were wondering where you two had gotten off to. I was going to offer you a ride the rest of the way to St. Anne's. I'm due there tonight with this load of corn, and I thought I'd spare you the trouble.'' He pulled to a stop, looking at them. ''The two of you can ride in the back. There's room there amid the straw, and some rough sacks that once held flour. If, say, you wanted no one to see you, the two of you could lie back there and cover yourselves with the sacks and no one would ever notice.''

''Why would we care if someone saw us, Odo?'' Adrian moved warily toward the cart, still holding Joanna's hand firmly in his. She suspected his other hand was on his knife, just in case.

''Oh, I don't know,'' Odo said. ''But when a man and his woman sneak out the back window when no one's looking, and when armed men come around looking for a beautiful woman and a wounded monk, I begin to wonder. Being as how I'm a curious fellow and all. But then, I've seen no monks around here, and certainly no one appears to have suffered any kind of wound. And while you're pretty enough, my lady, you can't hold a candle to my Roseanna.'' He sat back on the rough seat. ''Well, are you two coming? I haven't got all day.''

''We're coming, Odo. Thank you.''

Adrian lifted her onto the back of the cart, his strong hands around her slender waist, and if the gesture pained him he didn't show it. Climbing in after her, he started rearranging the sacks as the cart moved forward.

"We'll be out of the woods in about an hour. You'll want to be out of sight then, I'm thinking."

Lying with him in the narrow bed at the miller's house was one thing. Lying on the bed of the rough cart was far worse, since the most space he could make was one person wide.

"I'll be on the bottom," he said, picking up one of the discarded sacks. "I'm heavier."

"You're wounded," she said flatly. "Even if you're healing quickly, you still don't need to aggravate it. Besides, I'm used to lying beneath men."

She said it deliberately, hoping to shock the gentle monk. But he was no longer a gentle monk, he was a man, and he simply looked at her. "It tends to be a woman's lot in life," she added.

"Lives can be changed."

"Are you meaning to save me from my life of sin, Brother Adrian?"

She must have imagined the flush of color on his high cheekbones. "You're in no need of saving, my lady. I'll lie on the bottom…"

It was too late, she had already stretched out in the small, coffinlike space he'd arranged. "Keep your weight on your elbows and we'll be fine," she said calmly.

It was more difficult than she had imagined. He settled down on top of her, as gently as possible, pulling the rough sacks over them before resting his arms on either side of her. The sacks smelled like flour and honey—they blotted out the light, enclosing the two of them in muffled darkness. She could feel him stretched along the length of her body, even though he was doing his best not to put his whole weight on her. The position was miserably uncomfortable, with her face in his shoulder, trying not to breathe in the intoxicating scent of his skin.

They rode in silence for a bit, and when he spoke his voice was very quiet in her ear. "I hesitate to say this, my lady, but we'd fit better if you moved your legs."

She had her knees locked tight, up against his legs. "To which side?"

He simply put his knee between her legs and pried them apart, setting his legs more closely against her. She wanted to squirm away, but she was trapped in this boxlike space, with nowhere else to go.

"This is not a good idea," she whispered.

"What else do you suggest? There are layers of clothing between us and a driver within a foot of us. Between the two it should manage to keep us relatively chaste. We can lie here in pious reflection, thinking pure thoughts."

He was lying. She could feel him against her, the hard flesh that couldn't be mistaken, pressing against her intimately. The motion of the carriage rocked him against her, and a little shiver ran over her body. She closed her eyes in the enveloping darkness and tried to pray.

Bump...bump...bump... The friction was gentle but insistent, and he seemed to become bigger still, harder, and she knew it wasn't her imagination. The rhythm of the wagon was setting an age-old rhythm in their bodies, and there was nothing she could do to stop it.

She put her hands on his shoulders, pushing at him. "You need to get off me," she whispered. "This isn't right."

Bump...bump...bump.... She was shivering, not quite sure why, cold and hot at the same time. She had no idea what was going on with her body, only that it was sinful and wicked and out of her control. *Bump...bump...bump....*

"Hush, love," he whispered in her ear. "Just let go."

She couldn't. She could hear the noise of a village now as they passed through, and if she moved, said anything, it would give them away. All she could do was lie there and feel the strange, clutching fire move from her breasts to her loins, to the spot between her legs where he was pressed.

It was growing worse, far worse, and she tried to shift him, but he covered her like a second self, only that one part of him was so different, so demanding. And she wanted to slide her hand down between their bodies and touch him. Which shocked her far more than it would shock even a gentle monk.

Bump...bump...bump.... She couldn't stop shaking. She was past speech, her heart was hammering against her chest, her breathing so labored she thought the world could hear.

He put his long fingers over her mouth, to still her. "Don't cry out," he whispered. His own voice was strained, and no wonder. Any other man would have spilled his seed on her. Any other man would have lost control long ago. *Bump…bump…bump….*

"Bite me when you come," he whispered. "That way no one will hear you."

"What?"

"It's going to happen whether you like it or not. Go ahead, love. Find your pleasure."

She couldn't find the words to tell him he was mad. That he didn't know what he was talking about. But his fingers silenced her mouth and she could no longer speak and *bump…bump….*

Her body went completely rigid beneath his, as a thousand tiny sparks of light raced beneath her skin. She tried to cry out, but his hand kept her silent. It seemed to last forever, and then she went limp beneath him, afraid she might faint.

He took his hand from her mouth, turned her head to face his and kissed her mouth. And for the first time in her life, without thinking, she kissed someone back.

22

_____

"Lady Elizabeth." The true Prince William rose from his seat at the table and came toward her. "You do me great honor. I cannot express how sorry I am about the dreadful deceit that was forced upon me. Not for the world would I have you be the victim of such a lie, but alas, these things were out of my control. I had no choice but to obey the monks, and Brother Peter insisted." He took her hand in his soft one and brought it to his moist, soft lips. "I crave your forgiveness."

She'd forgotten the melting sweetness of his smile, the dark warmth of his eyes. She'd been so besotted by the tall, dark-eyed man that she'd failed to remember her instant attraction to kindly Brother Matthew. Not the kind of attraction that tricked and betrayed her—no, she was drawn to his gentleness.

A gentleness that must be in question, if he had done all that they had said he had done. But then, who could she trust to be who they said they were?

She removed her hand, gracefully, and dropped a polite curtsey. "I am sure it was no fault of yours, my lord. And there is nothing to regret—I'm here, safe and sound, and so, praise God, are you."

"But alas, so many other people died in the slaughter. I saw the young monk, Adrian, butchered before my very eyes. And the lady…" He shook his head. "It was a sad, sad day, my lady, and I rejoice that Brother Peter knew to desert his charge and save you."

The urge to defend him came unbidden but failed to reach her lips. Maybe finally, at long last, she was learning discretion. "Brother Peter was…most helpful."

"I imagine he would be. But let's not talk of him, my lady. Come join me in a cup of this house's excellent wine, and we will decide what we'll do with you."

She took the goblet and the seat beside him, wondering why she felt so uneasy. The hall was crowded, though of the good sisters only two were present, Mother Alison and the mother abbess with her sharp, disapproving stare. And herself, of course. The group of men eating in the corner were loud and boisterous, and the prince followed her gaze.

"My father sent some of my men to bring me home in my newfound state of grace. They have been out looking for you and Brother Peter, but the abbot's party found you first."

She took a sip of the wine, smiling at him faintly. He smiled back, but for some reason the warmth didn't reach his pale blue eyes. "I've got more men combing the countryside for any trace of Adrian and the doxy. I doubt they survived, but it would only be right to bring their bodies back for Christian burial.

After all, they died on pilgrimage. Perhaps even the leman's sins will be washed clean.''

''You're certain they're dead?''

''Quite,'' the prince said firmly. ''There is nothing more we can do for them but say a prayer for their souls. In the meantime, we have more important things to speak of.''

''We do?'' she echoed doubtfully. ''My lord,'' she added hastily.

''Those garments ill become you, my lady. You were not made to wear drab gray.''

She looked down at the plain habit with its loose surplice and ornate cross. ''A holy sister does not spend time contemplating which colors are best, my lord.''

''Indeed. Which makes me think you are ill-suited for the cloister. You've seen little of the world, my lady. Before you decide to eschew it completely you should at least have a taste of it.''

''I think I've tasted enough,'' she said.

''Traveling with a penitent? A holy, passionless monk? I think not. You will bear me company back to court, where my father can thank you himself.''

''Thank me for what?'' Her unruly tongue hadn't been completely tamed.

''For helping to bring me safely to this house of God where my soul has been washed clean. The mother abbess has given her permission, albeit with reservations. She agrees with me that a vocation tested is a stronger one. We'll leave in two days' time. Long enough for them to find suitable clothes for you—you can hardly attend my father's court dressed like a nun. And you will see whether or not you find the world worth living in.''

She cast a nervous glance toward the waiting mother abbess, but the stern-faced woman merely nodded her acquiescence. Mother Alison looked less certain, but she simply bowed her head, accepting the inevitable.

As she must do, Elizabeth thought. After all, the prince was everything a royal son should be—charming, handsome, considerate and strong. He wasn't a true son of the king, only a bastard, and rumor had it that the young queen had become pregnant once more, and this time they were hoping it wouldn't be terminated too early by an unexpected fall, or stillborn with no warning.

If she were in the king's court she could see to it that this time the babe would be born safe and whole. The king's gratitude would be boundless, and there was no telling what might happen. Perhaps even marriage to a royal bastard. Her bloodlines were good enough, extending back to the first wave of William the Conqueror's men, and even if she were too tall and too red-haired, one man had found her enticing.

She quickly drank another deep gulp of the wine and turned to look into the prince's melting eyes. She was taller than he was, but then, she was taller than a great many men. If she wished to find a husband tall enough for her, then her choices were limited indeed, and the only tall man she knew was out of the question.

But she could be married, she knew that now. Another man could touch her the way…he had touched her. Another man could bring her pleasure and make her fall in love with him as easily as her deceitful companion had.

Oh, not that she was in love with him. She'd been fascinated by him, that was all. Deep inside she must have sensed the conflict and lies beneath that enigmatic exterior, and it had weakened her usually strong defenses.

It wouldn't happen again. When she found another man who made her feel as he had, then she would take him.

"I would be honored to accompany you, my lord."

And William took her hand in his beringed one and kissed it, slowly, lingeringly.

A strange shiver ran down her spine, far removed from delight. She wanted to snatch her hand away from him, tell him she was staying here, where she belonged. And then she felt his eyes on her.

She looked up. Peter stood at the far end of the great hall, and her eyes met his for the first time since she'd found out who he was.

There was nothing there. No regret, no passion, no anger, no love. He might well have been a statue, with eyes carved out of stone.

She turned back to the prince, giving him her most bewitching smile. "I will count the hours."

"There's no sign of them anywhere, my lord," Rufus said. William had seen Rufus kill men barehanded, had seen him sack and pillage and rape with the kind of brutality that only he could admire. It always amused him that he was the one person who could terrify Rufus. He wasn't afraid of death. Death was easy. Dying was hard.

William looked at him slowly. "You mean you couldn't *find* any sign of them, don't you? Sir Adrian is not that good at subterfuge, and he has a lady with him. A doxy, who'll doubtless whine and complain every step of the way. And yet you say you can find no trace of them?"

"Jenkins thought they might head toward the sea rather than circle around this way," Rufus said somewhat desperately.

"And who, pray tell, is Jenkins?" he said in his most dulcet tone. The one calculated to make Rufus turn even paler.

"One of the men, sire."

"And is he gifted with the sight? Did the Holy Virgin come down and tell him where my enemies have gone?"

"No, my lord. It was just a guess."

"I have no great fondness for guesses, Rufus. And no great fondness for wagging tongues. You will go back out, into the rain, and find them. They will try to approach this place—your Jenkins might have his doubts but I do not. They will approach this place, and you will kill them. You'll kill them quickly— now is not the time for leisure in such matters—but you will cut off his head and bring it to me, so that I may be certain his tongue will never betray me."

Rufus started backing toward the door, almost tripping over his huge feet.

"And Rufus?"

"Yes, sire?"

"You wouldn't make the mistake of failing me again, would you? I've managed to convince the good sisters that I'm a reformed soul. We wouldn't want anything to suggest otherwise until we're well away from here."

"We, sire?" Rufus knew perfectly well that the prince would never deign to include his men among his pronouns.

"I'm taking the girl with me. The overgrown one with the red hair."

"Begging your pardon, my lord, but she scarcely seems the kind of woman you fancy. Wouldn't she be more trouble than she's worth? The good sisters wouldn't like it if anything were to happen to her."

"The good sisters won't be able to do anything about it. Anyway, I'm not particularly interested in her one way or the other. She's merely a means to an end."

"Sire?"

"Brother Peter. Saintly, judgmental Peter de Montselm will come after her, because he knows just what I will do to her if he doesn't get there soon enough. And I'll be able to finish what I started. I've owed Brother Peter a debt for seven years, and it's past time I paid it."

"My lord?"

"None of your business, Rufus. Go and find me

that wretched knight and the whore, and be quick about it. You do have a sister, last I hear. It would be tragic if anything were to befall her.''

Rufus disappeared, practically falling in his haste to leave. William leaned back, toying with his jewel-handled knife. He had nicked the blade when he struck Adrian, probably hitting a rib. Which meant that it hadn't been a killing blow, more's the pity. If it had, his men would have already found the body, and that of the woman, as well.

They'd almost reached saintly Peter and his strange whore, as well. In the end, he was glad the abbot's men had forestalled them. There would be little pleasure in simply hearing of Peter's death. He wanted to be there, to watch. To deliver the killing blow.

He rubbed his shoulder absently. It still hurt him, the skin stretched taut over his body. So long ago, and yet he would never forget. Other men had been burned in the fire that engulfed the seraglio, with less severe consequences, and they had died, anyway, some by their own hand, unable to bear the pain. Crusaders should have been made of sterner stuff. But then, they hadn't had hatred to keep them alive.

William had chosen to live. To heal. The ruined half of his body was well hidden by his clothes, and very few knew how deep the flame had burned. Destroying his very manhood, so that his only joy was in the granting of pain.

And he knew whom he could thank for that particular gift. The man he'd gone on crusade with, the man he'd fought with, the man who'd pushed him off the building where he'd been watching the conflagration. The man who pushed him into the fire. Peter of Montselm.

All the remorse in the world wouldn't wash Peter's soul clean, but it somehow galled William that he saved all his guilt for other things. When he set his eyes on the king's son he betrayed no emotion at all.

But then, what could he expect from the man who'd set the fire in the first place? Burning hundreds of women and children to death.

In another instance William might have applauded the act. Peter had stood on the adjoining roof of the sultan's palace, his face blank, as the flames were mirrored in his eyes, and the screams rose to heaven.

He'd moved suddenly, turning to the man who stood watching in silence. "We have to stop it," he'd said in a ragged voice. "We can't kill them...."

"That is your holy charge," intoned the priest who'd blessed the firing of the building. "Let them burn now—they will burn throughout eternity in the fires of hell reserved for the unbelievers."

"We can't..." he'd cried, drawing his sword, and everyone drew back. Sir Peter de Montselm was taller, stronger, and a far better fighter than most of them. To meet his blade was to court death.

But William had no such fear. Hadn't he gone through the Crusades without a scratch on him? His father had sent men to look out for him, and he seldom put himself in harm's way, but the heat and noise from the flaming building was too delicious to stop.

"Get back, Sir Peter," he'd said calmly, drawing his own sword. "What's done is done."

He was totally unprepared for the savagery of Peter's attack. Within moments he was flat on his back on the roof, his golden, jeweled sword broken like a toy. "Anyone else?" Peter had said in a hoarse voice. "Or will you help me save who I can?"

From his vantage point on the ground William could see them wavering, and even the priest could not influence them the way Peter always could. They were going to do it, he thought. They were going to take the coward's way out, put a stop to the fire.

He moved so quickly no normal man should have heard him coming. He grabbed the jeweled scimitar he'd taken from a fleeing infidel and brought it down on Peter's back, slashing into skin and muscle.

He whirled around, and William staggered back. It was supposed to be a killing blow, but he barely seemed to slow down. He took another step backward, still clutching the bloody scimitar.

"Don't come any closer!" he'd cried in a high-pitched voice. "Or I'll cut your head off."

The screams were fading now, fading into the dull moan of the dying. "I would advise against trying it," Peter had said, advancing on him.

He would have run, but he couldn't look like a coward in front of the others. He'd already made the mistake of attacking Peter from behind, and they frowned upon such things. Peter would never kill him—of all things he was loyal to his uncle and, by default, his father. It would be safe enough to charge him.

Or so he thought. Peter knocked the scimitar from his hand with his own sword, and the blow swung William around. In the next moment he was flying off the roof, through the air, like some doomed bird, crashing into the center of the burning seraglio.

Rufus had gotten him out, though not in time. Dragged him, half dead, over the charred bodies stacked ten deep.

But he had survived. And it had taken seven years, seven years while Peter locked himself in a monastery and bewailed his sins, but revenge was almost at hand.

It was almost time to leave.

23

"You there! Where do you think you're going?"

Joanna woke with a start, but Adrian's hand was already over her mouth, stilling any noise she might have made. She couldn't believe she had slept, his body covering hers, not after that astonishing occurrence. She was no fool—she'd seen enough men at the peak of their pleasure to know that it must be something very like what had happened to her. She just didn't understand how or why. Women were put on earth to suffer men's touch, not enjoy it. And it had been barely a touch, just the inadvertent rubbing of two bodies together.

Though not so inadvertent. She could see his eyes in the shrouded darkness, and she knew he'd intended it. Knew that he was hard and wanting, and she knew what to do about it.

She'd slid her hand between their bodies to touch him, stroke him, but he'd stopped her, pulling her hand up to his mouth and kissing it before he set it back down beside her.

"Much as I appreciate the thought, my lady, I think we'd best forgo that for the time being. I need my wits about me, and that might get a bit messy."

She'd been beyond comprehending him. A man who gave her pleasure and asked for no release of his own? A man whose body clearly demanded that release?

"But…"

He'd kissed her mouth, silencing her, and this time she hadn't fought him. She'd simply closed her eyes and slept, only to wake now in the smothering darkness with his hand on her mouth and his body tight with tension.

"Got a delivery for the holy sisters, my lord," Odo said. "Tithes from the villages here about—corn and wool and the like."

"Which villages?"

"Aldenham and Whithall."

"Not Beckham? It should have been on your way."

Adrian moved, very slowly, and Joanna knew he was reaching for his knife.

"Not Beckham, my lord. They're a lazy bunch, born sinners. They wouldn't give the good sisters a crumb that they could use themselves."

"So you did not travel through Beckham?"

"Not this time, my lord. I came straight down the market road."

"And who did you see on this road? Anyone of interest?"

"Indeed I did, my lord. There were several groups of armed men moving about the countryside, looking for something. I have no idea what they wanted, and they didn't come near me, but they were right suspicious, if you ask me.''

''I know of the hunting parties,'' the man said in a rough voice. ''I want to know if you've seen anything unusual. A wounded monk, perhaps, accompanied by an uncommonly beautiful woman.''

''Hunting parties? What would they be hunting around here? The game is sparse after a long winter—they'd be unlikely to find much to eat....''

''They were hunting the people I was asking about, you fool!''

''To eat?'' The driver's voice was the perfect blend of gullibility and incredulousness.

''To kill!'' the interrogator snapped. ''And you haven't answered my question. Have you seen them?''

''Why would they want to kill a monk and a beautiful lady?''

''They're murderers and traitors. They tried to kill Prince William.''

''Who's Prince William? Never heard of him, and if the king had an heir you'd think word would reach us....''

''He's a bastard.''

''Then he's not a prince, is he?'' Odo said. ''So if someone tried to kill him it's plain murder, not treason. Doesn't matter, though. I've seen no monks, wounded or otherwise.''

''He might be traveling in disguise. Have you seen any recently wounded men at all, be they serf or knight, alone or with a beautiful woman? And if you don't give me a quick answer I'll cut out your tongue.''

''But then you won't get any answers at all,'' Odo said reasonably. ''No, my lord, I've seen no strange men, no beautiful women, no traitorous murderers. Only you and your hunting parties. May I go on up to the convent now? It's been a long day and I have to deliver my goods before I can rest.''

''Not tonight. No one's approaching the shrine tonight. There are guards patrolling, so don't even think to try another way. Your goods can wait.'' There was the steely slide of a sword being drawn. ''Do you have a problem with that, vassal?''

''Not at all, my lord. It won't be the first time I've curled up and slept under my wagon, and I doubt it will be the last. What about tomorrow?''

''What about it?''

''Will I be allowed to enter then?''

''If the prince has left. In the meantime you can either wait or go elsewhere.''

''Where are all these men you say are guarding the perimeter, my lord? You're the only one I can see.''

''They'll be making their rounds soon enough. Why, do you think you can overpower me, peasant?''

Joanna knew what was going to happen, knew there was nothing she could do to stop him. His body was coiled, ready to spring, and his hand still covered her mouth, silencing any protest or warning she might have given.

And then his hand was gone, the rough covering thrown back to the night sky, and Adrian rose, his knife in his hand. "He might not, Rufus," he said, jumping down from the wagon. "But I can."

Joanna scrambled to her knees, only to moan in despair. Their unseen interrogator was a huge man, far bigger than Adrian's slender form, and he was heavily armed. Adrian had only the knife.

"I should have known," the man said in a grim voice. "The prince was right not to trust you! Things would have been so much easier if you'd been privy to the rescue party, but he said you would never allow it. You've gotten squeamish, Sir Adrian. It doesn't matter—you know I'm not going to let you pass."

"Then I'll have to kill you, Rufus."

"Now, why would you want to do that? We've fought side by side over the years. We're both the prince's men."

"There's a difference. You follow him, I keep watch over him."

"We both do his bidding."

"He tried to kill me, Rufus."

"That's right, you're wounded. I almost forgot. That'll make my job that much easier. I promise to make it fast, for the sake of our time together. A clean slice to the throat and you'll be dead in moments."

"I don't think so. The man you follow is a monster."

"Aye. And what do you think he'd do to me if I wasn't able to stop you?"

"I don't want to have to kill you."

"Better you than the prince. But you haven't a

chance in hell of even pricking me with that little toy you're holding.''

"You think not?'' He kept his eyes firmly fixed on the larger man. "Joanna, I want you to run to the convent. Go fast, keep low, and you should make it. I'm hoping Peter has made it back, but if he hasn't, find someone, anyone who might be in charge. The mother abbess, the father abbot, anyone.''

"And they'll take her word over the prince's? Don't be daft, man.''

"Then why are you so determined to stop us?''

"They might listen to you. A trull is another matter.''

"She's no trull.''

Rufus's laugh rang out in the night. "Don't tell me you've fallen in love! You are a fool, Adrian, for all that you're a good fighter. If you've fallen in love with a whore you're better off dead.''

"Run, Joanna. Find Father Abbot and warn him.''

She scrambled out of the wagon, hesitating only a moment. She couldn't see how he could possibly survive, so mismatched, and she knew she would never see him again.

"I love you.'' She had no idea where those words had come from. She'd never given them to a man—no man had ever wanted them.

But there was no missing the blazing smile on Adrian's face. "I love you, too. Rufus is right on that one thing. Now run!''

She picked up her skirts and ran, through the trees, dodging the overgrown bushes as she listened to the sound of steel against steel. He was going to die, and she wanted to run back, to save him, to hold him as he died, but she kept onward, tears streaming down her face as the noise of the fight grew ominously still.

She expected there'd be guards at the front gate, but it was unattended. She staggered through, her heart ready to burst, her breath tearing at her chest, to fall weeping into the arms of the first person she saw. Someone who could only be the father abbot.

"Child, what is the matter?" he cried.

"Adrian! We came here to warn you...the prince...Adrian..." She gasped out the words.

"The prince is safe and well. He's completed his penance and has been absolved of his sins. He leaves tomorrow to start a new life."

"No!" she cried. "He's a murderer. Those were his men who attacked the party. His men who slaughtered the monks."

The abbot pulled back. "Those are very serious accusations."

"Don't let him leave. We have to help Adrian. That man was going to kill him."

"Sir Adrian is here? The prince told me he perished in the battle."

"The prince lied. We have to help him, Father. It may not be too late. Please!" she sobbed.

By this time a large crowd had gathered round them. "There, there, child. Mother Alison will take you someplace to rest. Brother Mellard, send my men to the front gate..."

"The side gate..." Joanna gasped.

"And have someone see to the prince. I wish to talk to him before he sets out for London."

"Yes, Father."

"But…" Joanna said as strong arms closed around her.

"Go with the sisters, child. And trust in God."

And Joanna had no other choice.

The cell Elizabeth was given was small and spare, but the bed was the first real one she'd had in what seemed like a lifetime. It was far too narrow to share with anyone, and she could spend the rest of her life in such a narrow bed and never notice the lack.

All the lies she'd been told over the last few days beat around her head like the wings of a thousand birds. She wanted to fling herself down on that narrow bed and weep. She wanted to hit someone, preferably Peter, and maybe herself, as well.

She had known. If she examined it honestly, she had known deep in her heart of hearts that he wasn't the true prince. But she hadn't wanted to consider who he could be, and who the real prince was.

It was odd. In his own way, the man she'd traveled with was far more princely than the king's son. And sweet-faced Brother Matthew fit the role of monk better than a man like…Peter, with his tortured eyes and simmering anger.

Prince William, the *real* Prince William, would look after her. And while she couldn't discount the stories that had sent him on a journey of penance, she knew that she would be safe from him. Brother Peter might have a taste for long-legged, flame-haired women, but the prince would have more exacting tastes. He'd have no interest in someone like her—she'd be perfectly safe traveling with him, even if the stories turned out to be true. And she couldn't believe he could be the monster he was rumored to be. You only had to look into his gentle blue eyes to know he could be trusted.

If she stayed in this tiny cell until it was time to go she might never have to see Peter again. That was what she needed—time and distance. Her wounded heart would heal, eventually, and her newfound knowledge of the world would help her. Knowledge and experience, no matter how bitter, were always a good thing.

The lone candle sent long shadows around the narrow room. She went to the barred window to look out over the moonlit landscape. She could hear noise in the background, a woman crying out, the sound of soldiers, and she climbed onto the ledge of the window, trying to see out, but it was to no avail. She turned to climb down, and saw Peter standing there, the door closed behind him.

He was wearing new robes, of a finer weave than the ones they'd both worn on the road. His face was freshly shaven, as well as the crown of his head, and she realized belatedly that the supposed prince of England hadn't been balding after all. His tonsure had been growing in.

She didn't like it. Didn't like the robe, didn't like the man. "What are you doing here?"

One of the things she hated most about him was his ability to mask his feelings. She had no idea whether he felt shame, anger, sorrow, lust or pity. He looked so different from the man she had first seen in her father's hall, the indolent, wicked prince with his strong face and mocking mouth. Now his eyes were dark and unreadable, his face impassive. Even the mouth that had done such sinful, glorious things to her was set in a grim line.

"Those robes don't become you. You aren't made to be a nun," he said.

"Not any longer, I suppose," she said. "Fortunately the holy sisters seem willing to accept soiled goods, and I find this robe to fit me very well indeed. I'll ask you one more time and then I'll call for help. Why are you here?"

"I came here to warn you."

"Against rapacious men? Too late. Get out or I'll scream, and no one will think of you as saintly Brother Peter any longer."

He didn't bother to defend himself. "The prince is not who he appears to be."

She had to laugh at that. "And what man is? In the last three days no man has been what he appeared to be. Next you'll be telling me that Brother Adrian is no monk."

"He isn't. He's the king's man. And my cousin."

In the bare cell there was nothing to throw at him but angry words. "Go away, you deceiving, miserable wretch of a human being. I'd rather converse with a rabid dog."

A small smile softened his mouth. "Your mouth will get you into trouble."

"As will yours." And, unbidden, the thought of just what his mouth had done on her body brought a rush of color to her face. Ensuring that he knew what she was thinking about, as well.

"Elizabeth, it doesn't matter what you think of me. I cannot let you go anywhere with Prince William. He's everything you heard and more."

"You have no say over what I will or will not do."

"A word to the mother abbess will keep you here."

"And if you did, I would see to it that that word would be followed with a detailed account of what happened between us during the last few days."

He raised an eyebrow. "A detailed account? Mother Abbess would never recover from the shock."

Rage swept through her. "Do you think this is funny?"

"Unlike you, I don't pass judgment, nor tend to think people are infallible. People do good and bad things. They make mistakes, commit sins, and pay for them as best they can."

"Go to hell."

"Without question. But you're not going with Prince William. He doesn't want you, you know. He's just trying to get to me, and he'll use anyone he has to."

That was the final straw. "Of course he doesn't want me. Why should any man want me? Lord knows you must have been completely desperate after God knows how many years of celibacy."

"*Desperate* is a good word for it," he said softly.

"And why would he want you? Don't try to tell me his tastes run to other men—I wouldn't believe you."

"His tastes run to nothing at all. He wants to kill me."

"And who can blame him?" Elizabeth said sweetly. "You bring that out in the best of us."

He laughed. "I'm glad to know you consider yourself among the best of us."

"Hardly. That doesn't mean I don't want to kill you with my bare hands."

It was the wrong thing to say. He walked toward her, slowly, giving her time to duck away, but the room was so small there was no real place to run to, so she stood still, meeting his gaze calmly.

"Then put your hands on me," he said softly. "Do it."

She could do him little harm and they both knew it. She had strong hands, but not strong enough to strangle him, as tempting as the notion was. She had no weapon, and in the convent neither did he, so she couldn't stab him. She was barefoot—she could hardly wear the monk's sandals and her feet were too big for any of the footwear at the abbey.

But she had her fists. She slammed one into his stomach, hard, surprising him, hitting him so hard it hurt her hand.

"You can do better than that," he murmured.

She punched him with her other hand, but this time

he was prepared, and his stomach was so hard he must have barely noticed.

"I hate you," she said.

"Of course you do."

And she began pounding him, on his chest, beating against him with all her strength as she called him every name she could think of and more besides, hit his unmoving body, his unflinching face, hit him until her arms ached and her hands were numb and she could do nothing but cry as he put his arms around her and held her.

She could no more move away from him than she could fly. "I hate you," she sobbed again.

He kissed her. It was the last thing she expected, his mouth hard on hers, but the greater shock was that she kissed him back. Kissed the monk, knowing who and what he was.

She had no idea what would have happened next. Whether she would have been proved wrong about the narrowness of the bed, when someone knocked on the door, and by the time Mother Alison opened it he was across the room from her, shrouded in darkness.

"There you are, Brother Peter. Something's happened—Father Abbot wants you immediately. He's in the great hall." She turned to look at Elizabeth, and there was no way she could miss seeing the tears on her face. "Dear child…" she said.

"Leave her be, Mother," Peter said. "She'll be fine. But she won't be going anywhere with the prince."

"I think that's very wise," Mother Alison agreed.

Elizabeth opened her mouth to protest, but she shut it again, knowing nothing would come out but a helpless sob.

And in truth, Peter was right. She was going nowhere. There was no place for her in a world without Peter. There was no place for her in a world *with* Peter, either, but the cloister would be a start. God would quench the fire that was right now burning in her blood.

If it took the rest of her life.

24

"My lord, there's trouble."

Prince William turned slowly, covering his scarred flesh. Winston was his second in command, without the brute strength of Rufus but with far more cunning. "Where's Rufus?"

"Dead, my lord. There are new arrivals—Sir Adrian and the woman managed to get through, and they're talking."

"Of course they are," William said in a furious voice. "The question is, does anyone believe them?"

"Bishop Martin has requested your presence immediately. When I said you would probably be asleep, he told me to wake you."

"How dare he?" William said in an icy voice. "I have played their silly games long enough. If he wishes to rescind his absolution, then so be it. We'll leave immediately."

"Sire?"

"They won't dare stop me. Tell the holy father that I'll attend him within the hour. Get the men ready and the horses saddled. And alert Lady Elizabeth that our plans have changed."

"She won't go, my lord. The mother abbess said

to tell you she's changed her mind and wishes to stay at the convent."

"She's not allowed to change her mind. Do what you have to do, Winston. We'll leave immediately, and she'll be coming with us. You can silence her, but just don't kill her. Do you understand? If Rufus is gone, you'll have to take his place. And you know I'm not happy when my wishes are thwarted."

"We'll meet you at the west gate, my lord. That's the one least guarded, and it's heading south. They wouldn't expect us to leave that way."

"Very wise, Winston. I think you'll do quite well."

Elizabeth had managed to doze off, though she wasn't quite sure how. Her brain was whirling with confusion, and the worst part was, why had she kissed him back? For that matter, why had he kissed her? He was back now, in the life he had chosen, where there was no room for a woman even if he wanted one, and yet he'd come to her room and kissed her. And if Mother Alison hadn't interrupted, God only knows what would have followed.

She would have hoped she'd have had the sense to stop him. Stop herself. But there was no guarantee that she could have.

She rolled onto her back, heaving a sigh of frustration. Things had grown quiet for a bit, but now she could hear the sounds of horses being made ready, the muttered voices of men. Who could be leaving at such an hour? With any luck it would be Peter, knowing that there was nothing but temptation left behind.

When she woke he'd be gone, and she could start her new life, one of prayer and repentance and obedience.

She closed her eyes. She wasn't going to sleep, she knew it. It felt as if a sword were hanging over her head, ready to fall, and if she weren't alert enough it would slice through her brain and her heart.

Or perhaps it already had. Neither of those seemed to be working properly—her brain had melted the moment Peter had put his hands on her, her heart had shattered when she found out his true identity.

No, her heart had shattered when she knew she loved him. Because even then, she'd somehow known only grief awaited her.

She rolled onto her stomach. The good sisters' beds were austere, with no pillows or freshly laundered linen coverings. She would learn to sleep this way— it was at least better than sleeping on the floor.

But the last time she'd slept on a floor she'd been in his arms, and she could have slept on hot coals and not cared.

She had to stop thinking about him. About his betrayal, which he seemed perfectly willing to repeat. The only way she would sleep would be if she could clear her mind, and the only way she could clear her mind was to pray.

She didn't even know how to begin, her sin was so great and so unrepented. All she could mutter was, "Please, Lord, give me a sign. Save me."

She didn't hear the door open. Her eyes were closed, and she didn't see the shadow steal across the room. All she knew was the hood coming down over her face, smothering her.

She tried to scream, kicking out, but the rough fabric got in her mouth. She knew the blow was coming, but she didn't feel it. She thought this was not the sign she wanted.

And then everything turned black.

He lived. Adrian lived, they told her so, and Joanna almost collapsed.

"You are welcome here among us, Dame Joanna," Mother Alison said, but she couldn't quite believe her.

"I am a great sinner, Mother," she said. "If I had anywhere else to go…"

"There are none of us here who are without sin. As to whether or not you qualify for greatness in the matter of sinning, that's a matter for God and your confessor to decide. In the meantime we'll have a room made ready for you. I am certain you'll want to rest after your ordeal. We can talk of sin tomorrow."

"Adrian…"

"He lives, and should continue to do so for many years. The young man is impervious to things that will kill most hardened soldiers. Do you wish to see him?"

"No!" Joanna said swiftly. The sooner she parted from him the better. But she couldn't resist asking one last question. "Then he is not a holy friar?"

"Sir Adrian? Good heavens, no! I can't think of a

man less suited for the cloister. I'm certain his wife would agree.''

For a killing blow it didn't even make her sway. She'd survived worse blows. Hadn't she? ''He's married?'' she asked in a deceptively even tone.

''As good as. He's been betrothed to Baron Leffert's daughter these past three years. I believe they were just waiting until he finished his service for the king to wed. I imagine tonight's work will have put an end to any welcome he might have at court.'' Mother Alison looked at her closely. ''There was nothing between the two of you, was there? No promises?''

No promises, she thought. If only this blessed numbness would last. She felt encased in ice, and she never wanted to feel warmth again.

''Nothing at all,'' she said. ''He's a young man and I'm a woman of the world. We have little in common.''

The tiny nun made a quiet noise, one that might have been agreement or not. ''Well, you will probably want to see him and give him your thanks after you're better rested. He saved your life, after all, rescuing you from that horrible attack.''

She thought of the long hours, dragging his bleeding body through the forest on her cape, and she almost thought she could smile. Almost. ''Indeed. Though I think a period of solitude and prayer might be the best for me.''

''You're as bad as Brother Peter. I find that those most likely to atone for their sins are quite often those whose sins are merely human. The true monsters of this world seldom truly repent.''

''Are you speaking of Prince William?''

''I would never dare speak thus of my king's son,'' Mother Alison said smoothly. ''I'm simply saying that those who appear to sin quite often are not nearly as bad as they think, and those who appear blameless can be instruments of the Devil. Sister Agnes will show you to your room. You'll be on the left side of the cloister with the guests—I hope the noise won't bother you.''

''Isn't there room in the convent for me?''

''Do you wish to take the veil, child?''

''I would scarce believe I am worthy.''

''All God requires is a willing heart. Stay with us for a time and see if you think this might be the life for you. If in time you come to feel that way, we would welcome you with all our hearts.''

A week ago, even two days ago, she would have had no hesitation. Even now, when harsh reality settled in on her momentary adolescent dreams, she should know the wisest, safest, best course. Because in truth, no man was ever going to touch her again, if that man was not Adrian.

Would he need a mistress? Many married men had them, but even if he were willing, she would not be. It was a hard lot for a wife, even if she were spared the labor of fornication. And with Adrian, the loss of conjugal duties might be a greater sacrifice than she had previously thought.

The room they brought her to was small and neat,

at the end of a corridor. She bathed and changed into the plain chemise they'd brought her and climbed into bed with the vague notion of crying herself to sleep.

Moments later she rose, pulling her blanket around her narrow shoulders, and stepped out into the hallway.

The stone floor was icy beneath her feet, but the hall was deserted. She had no notion of who might be resting in these rooms, but she had every intention of finding out, if she had to wake half the abbey.

She found Adrian in the third room, sound asleep, fresh bandages on his wounded shoulder and across his belly. He'd been hit on the head, as well—she could see the bruising that extended to one eye, and she wondered what would happen if she blackened the other one. She was feeling strangely violent, she who had always been so passive, and her anger was directed at the beautiful man-child sleeping so peacefully when she was so troubled.

Or not sleeping. He opened his eyes to look at her, and his smile would have melted a harder heart. "They told me you were safe," he said. "But I couldn't quite believe it until I saw you."

She moved into the room, her face stony. "You seem to have survived your battle in good order," she said in a cool voice. "I thought he was going to slice you to ribbons."

His smile had faded. "You look like you wish he had. Have I done something to offend you, Joanna?"

"Apart from lie to me about who you were? And…and take advantage of me in the wagon bed?"

she said. She'd long ago lost the ability to blush—the heat in her face must have come from some other source.

He slid to a sitting position, wincing, and it was all she could do to keep from rushing to his side to help him. She wanted him to hurt, she reminded herself. She wanted him to hurt in his body as she hurt in her heart.

"I don't know that I received any great benefit from our moments in the miller's wagon. If anything it made my life a great deal more difficult."

"Then you should have kept your hands off me."

"It wasn't my hands that made you climax."

She didn't flinch. "I'm a whore," she said carelessly. "It's easy enough to do."

"I killed the last person who called you that. Even you aren't allowed to do so. And it seemed to me as if you had not the slightest idea what was happening to you as you lay beneath me. If it wasn't so farfetched I'd think you'd never known real pleasure from a man."

She looked away. He was far too perceptive, and lying had always been difficult for her. "Far-fetched indeed," she said. "Mother Alison said you were to be married when you returned home. I hope your wife knows what a liar you are."

His look of confusion smoothed out and his smile returned. "So that's what's going on! I wondered what turned you into such an icy witch."

"There is nothing going on. I was going to thank you for saving my life and bringing me here safely, but since I saved your life earlier I expect we're even. Goodbye, Sir Adrian.''

"Not so fast, my lady. Come back here.''

She'd reached the door, but his voice stopped her. Her eyes were filled with unshed tears—she'd learned long ago that they were no real weapon against the fists of men, but they seemed beyond her control.

"I'm going back to my room....''

"Turn around, Joanna, and come back here. I have something to say to you.''

She should run, she told herself. Anything he might say would only make it worse. But she turned, anyway, blinking back the tears. He was holding out his hand, as if he actually expected her to take it.

She walked across the room, keeping her hands at her sides. He simply reached down and caught one, pulling it against his chest. "You're not joining the holy sisters,'' he said in a calm, decisive voice. "You're coming home with me.''

She tried to yank her hand away, but he held it tight. "No,'' she said sharply. "I won't do that to another woman!''

"I don't want you to do a thing to another woman. Only with me.''

She fought back the treacherous weakening. "I will not be your whore while your bride sits alone.''

"I would tell you I'm man enough for both of you, but I doubt you'd be amused. I have no wife. The girl I was pledged to died of a fever two years past. I barely knew her, so it was no great sorrow, but as of this moment I am planning to marry no one but you.''

She froze. "That's very cruel of you," she said in a small voice.

"To marry you? I promise you, I won't make that bad a husband."

She realized he was serious. Which could only mean the blow on his head was worse than she thought. She put a quick hand on his brow, checking for fever, but it was cool and dry. "You're mad," she said. "I'm probably ten years older than you, I'm barren, and I don't even like being with men."

He smiled up at her, very sweetly. "You're not more than five years older than me, and I'm very mature for my age. I intend to show you more pleasure than you can even begin to imagine, and we'll have beautiful children together. Now, get into bed with me."

"You've been wounded...."

"I'm not going to show you that pleasure now, lady. I'll wait till I'm mended and we're married. I just want to lie next to you. I sleep better that way, heal faster that way."

He was mad, totally and completely, but one should humor madmen. And there was nothing more she wanted than to lie next to him on that narrow bed and feel his body next to hers.

Without another word she climbed up onto the bed beside him, and he made room for her, pulling the blanket she'd brought around them both as he settled her against him. "Your feet are cold," he said.

"Yes."

"You think I'm mad." He kissed her nose, and she let him.

"Yes."

"You'll marry me, anyway."

"Yes," she said. "Yes."

Peter lay facedown on the cold, hard stone of the chapel. He hadn't moved for hours, determined to keep his mind empty, his senses shut down. He heard the uproar from a distance, the shouting and the noise, but he ignored it. He was too busy listening for an answer.

He'd spent seven long years atoning for a sin that could not be forgiven. Hundreds of innocents had perished in that fire, women and children. The fire he had ordered set. In the end, the only one to survive had been William, his body burned and broken as his soul was already twisted. He should have died in that fire. As Peter should have died.

But they'd both lived. Peter to spend the rest of his life in penance for a crime too horrifying to live with. A sin committed without knowledge was still a sin. William had told him the building was empty of all but a few soldiers, and Peter had ordered the place torched. William had lied.

It made no difference. He was the man who'd given the order. He was the man who'd flung William off the adjoining roof, into the midst of that conflagration, wanting him to suffer.

But God had spared William, as God has spared Peter. And for the first time Peter wondered if God knew what the hell he was doing. *Blasphemer,* he mocked himself. He groaned, hitting his head against the hard stone floor in frustration.

The sound of voices was an insistent buzz at the back of his head. The chapel doors slammed open and a breeze made the candles sputter. Peter closed his eyes, ignoring the booted footsteps coming down the nave. If it were William or one of his men come to dispatch him, he'd welcome it. He'd be one step closer to forgiveness.

"Brother Peter." Adrian's voice came from close at hand, but Peter ignored him. There was nothing Adrian could say that would make any difference.

"Leave him alone, Sir Adrian." Brother Jerome was there, as well, his voice chill with disapproval. "Bishop Martin said he was to be left alone with his devotions. There is no need to disturb him—all will be well."

Adrian ignored him, bending down and putting a hand on Peter's shoulder. "Peter," he said urgently. "Get up. There's trouble."

"There is no trouble," Brother Jerome snapped. "And if there were, Brother Peter has no need to be involved. He's been out in the world too much—he needs solitude and reflection, not a mad journey to save a woman who has no need of being saved. The prince has repented and vowed to live a chaste, good life, and even if he had not, do you truly think he would waste his time with someone with hair that color and so freakishly tall? When he could command the greatest beauties of the kingdom? Brother Peter…''

Peter had surged to his feet in one swift movement, ignoring Brother Jerome. ''She went with him after all?''

''We believe it was against her will. No one saw them leave—the prince chose to sneak out in the middle of the night rather than face Bishop Martin. But there was definitely a struggle in her room—the place was torn apart.''

''When did they leave?''

''They can't have been gone more than a few hours. We can't be certain which way they've headed.…''

''I can,'' Peter said grimly.

''Brother Peter, I refuse to allow you to leave. If Lady Elizabeth is in any sort of danger Bishop Martin will dispatch a group of my men to return her here, where she belongs. I'm sure he'll even let Sir Adrian lead them if his concern is so great. But you have been among worldly temptations too long. You will stay here and pray for their safety and the good of your soul.''

Peter ignored him. ''Have you got horses?''

''Waiting for us. How many men will we want?''

''An army would be slaughtered. Just the two of us.'' He moved past Brother Jerome, brushing past him as if he were nothing more than a ghost.

''If you leave, Brother Peter, there'll be no place for you. You will be damned to hell for all eternity. What woman is worth paying such a price for?''

"Do you want me to hit him?" Adrian asked calmly.

Peter shook his head, opening the chapel door. "We don't have time." It was full light outside—when he'd last seen Elizabeth it was before midnight.

"I have clothes waiting—"

"I belong in these clothes," he said, indicating his robes. "Whether or not Brother Jerome agrees."

"Can you fight in them?"

"Yes. If need be I can even kill in them. But they'll remind me not to if I can help it."

"Not kill William?"

"I'll leave that joy up to you," he said.

"You'll be damned for this," Brother Jerome cried after him. "There'll be no hope left for your miserable soul."

Peter paused for one last moment in the doorway of the chapel. "Then the price is worth it," he said. And closed the door behind him.

25

Elizabeth waited until the sun was high, the covering was off her head and she'd been dumped off the horse by the odorous soldier carrying her before she decided to throw up. She'd been contemplating the notion for the long, horrible hours since she woke, her body trussed and imprisoned against someone's unbathed body, her head aching as if it had been split by a mace, her stomach roiling in rhythm with the mad pace of the horses. Her head was covered with something that smelled of wet sheep and mold, so that she couldn't see a thing, but she could tell by the thunder of hooves that there were a great number of them.

She'd landed on hard stone paving, fighting her way out of the enveloping covering to find herself in the middle of a small courtyard, surrounded by armed men far more interested in their horses than their abandoned captive. She could either make a run for it, fast, before they remembered she was there, or she could throw up.

Unfortunately her body made the decision. When they let her go, she managed to crawl off a little way, and then she emptied what little was in her stomach.

The sun was high overhead, beating down on them.

It was no wonder the hours had been endless—they'd been riding forever. At least she had the blessing of being unconscious for part of it.

She moved a little farther back and lay her face down on the cool stones, taking deep breaths. They had stopped at some kind of house—smaller than a castle, larger than an ordinary house, clearly belonging to someone of wealth and property. Someone who might help her?

Except that grass grew between the paving stones in the courtyard, the windows of the house were barred and shuttered, the place deserted long ago. There would be no help for her here.

A pair of legs appeared in her line of vision. Fine legs, in elegant embroidered hose. She looked up, squinting into the sun, into the blandly smiling face of Prince William.

"It's a good thing Brother Peter can't see you now, my lady," he said in that dulcet voice. "His infatuation with you is beyond my understanding already, and if he saw you looking like a drowned, overgrown kitten he would have no reason to rescue you. And then this would all be for nothing."

She blinked. The words sank in, but they made no sense. She pushed herself to a sitting position, staring around her. "What is this place?"

"This place is what is so deliciously fitting about the entire enterprise. Why I knew it must be ordained. This was Peter's family home. They owned most of the land between here and the shrine, and even the land the abbey lies on was once in their possession.

A very wealthy family indeed. But they all died. A fever overtook most of the countryside while he was conveniently away on crusade, and when he returned his family was gone, half the farms deserted. Coming back to this area would already have been painful for him. Dying here will have a sweet poetry.''

He held out a gloved hand, jewels sparkling in the leather cuff. She stared at him, uncomprehending, so he simply grabbed a fistful of her short curls and hauled her upright.

She rose to her full height, looking down at him. For the first time her size gave her a perverse pleasure. "What do you want from me?"

"Not a thing, lady. You're simply the means to an end. A way to lure Peter away from his precious God and into my trap. I have a score to settle with him, one that's long overdue. Are you going to be ill again?" he asked, peering at her suspiciously.

He was very finely dressed, and she would have liked nothing more than to have vomited once more, over his rich clothes, but her stomach had already resorted to dry heaves when he approached her, and she knew she was past that point.

"No."

"'No, *my lord,*'" he corrected.

A lifetime ago the false prince had corrected her. The annoying, deceiving, seductive monk masquerading as the prince. But Elizabeth was past tears.

"No," she said stubbornly.

There was surprising strength in that gloved hand that whipped across her face, sending her sprawling onto the stonework once more. One of the jewels must have grazed her, because she could feel the wetness of blood running down her face from beneath her eye. A little bit higher and she might have been blinded.

The prince turned his back on her, dismissing her presence. "Bring her into the house," he ordered. "We're bound to have a bit of a wait for Brother Peter. He'll have to search his soul, pray for deliverance, change his mind three times before he comes for her. Because he knows he'll be coming to his death, and a man always thinks twice about such things."

"What will we do with her, my lord?" asked one of the villainous-looking soldiers.

He let his eyes skim over her as she lay on the pavement, blood dripping down her face. "Why, anything you please. Just don't kill her. We need to save that until Peter arrives."

Rough hands took hold of her, dragging her out of the sunlight. She was too terrified to scream, and they threw her on the floor of a small room, the bunch of them crowding in.

"Who's first, lads? Shall we draw for her? She's not that pretty, but they're all the same between their legs, and I'm more than ready to take my turn at her. Especially after being around all those damned nuns."

Elizabeth scrambled away from them, into the corner like a trapped rat. But she was no helpless female, and she would be damned if she'd let them touch her.

"Not all the same," she said in a breathless voice as one man approached her, his filthy hands fumbling with his hose, cheered on by the laughter of the men crowding into the room.

He held up his hand to silence them. "What do you mean by that?" he asked suspiciously.

She hadn't spent years among the midwives of Bredon without learning more than she ever wanted to learn. "You'll find out soon enough. The symptoms take about three days to show up. I expect I'll be dead by then, but I'll leave you all something to remember me by."

"You're telling me you have the pox? You're too young for that," the man said, but he nevertheless took a nervous step back. "And it takes years for it to show up, not days. I've had friends die from it." He gulped.

"There's more than one kind of pox. Why do you suppose my father sent me to a convent? To make certain there was no risk of contaminating the people of Bredon. It comes from the Holy Lands, an illness derived from the Saracens, who have carnal relations with animals and boys. Your privates shrivel and fall off as if they were leprous. Boils cover your skin and you begin to vomit black blood. It takes a few days to die, but it feels like years to the afflicted."

"You lie. You have no sign of such an illness." He took another step back, anyway, coming up against his now-silent company.

"Women show no sign of it. It festers inside them, where no baby will ever grow. Some say it's a curse made from Saracen witches, others say it's God's will for not taking back the Holy Lands as the crusaders promised. The reason matters not, only the outcome. Touch me, and you will die a horrible death.''

"I don't believe you. How would you have gotten such a foul disease? You look to me like a virgin.''

She didn't have to manufacture her bitter laugh. "Far from it. The knight who brought it to Bredon Castle was dead within a week of his arrival, and who's to say where he got it from? It spread so quickly that my father lost a dozen of his best fighting men in short order. He had the infected women strangled, but he always had a soft spot for his only daughter. He spared me, hoping the plague could be stopped if I were kept celibate.'' She summoned what she hoped was a suitably wanton smile. "But it makes little difference to me. The prince has said I'll die today, and I may as well enjoy myself before I go.'' She began inching the skirt up her long legs. "Who's first?''

They turned and ran, the bunch of them, slamming and locking the door behind them. She wanted to laugh, to throw back her head and laugh until tears poured down her face. But she knew that once she started she would not stop.

The prince was a fool. Peter would never come after her. If he had any sense at all he'd be glad she was dead, so he'd never have to suffer such an illogical temptation again. And Peter was very wise.

She leaned her head against the rough wall. It was no wonder he'd managed to find that empty farmhouse, no wonder he knew his way around the countryside so well that he'd managed to avoid the prince's hunting party. He'd managed to keep her safe. Long enough to break her heart.

She needed to view her very short future with equanimity. She would die, painfully, she expected, but at least she'd ensured that she wouldn't suffer rape at the hands of a dozen rough men. And at the very least, she had known what love was.

Not that Peter had loved her, of course. Seducing her had probably been one more piece of self-loathing, along with his hair shirt and his self-flagellation.

No, she'd had the gift of loving him, whether he deserved it or not. And damned if she didn't love him still.

She was a pragmatic woman—she'd seen too many deaths and births to think that one's allotted time was fair or expected. She would die, and most likely spend a fair amount of time in hell for her sins.

And remembering that endless night on the bed of cedars, the morning by the cool stream, the heartbreak of his kiss beneath the very roof of the holy sisters, she decided that it was a small price to pay.

William hummed softly beneath his breath, his humor sweeter than it had been in a long, long time. The great hall of Peter's abandoned house had seen better days, but the warmth of a fire offset the cool spring night, candles glowed everywhere, he'd eaten well of venison and roast rabbit, and he was going to have the sublime pleasure of torturing and killing Peter and his outsize whore.

He hadn't yet decided who would go first. He knew Peter would die slowly, by fire. In truth, the night wasn't so cool that he'd needed a fire set, but he had other plans for those bright orange flames.

He would unman him, as well, though not by fire as he'd been unmanned. A knife was more thorough, and he wasn't sure which would bring him more pleasure—to watch while he screamed in pain or to wield the knife himself. A dull knife.

Which would cause him more agony—to have his little nun watch him as he died, or to witness her painful death and have the memory of her screams join his own? So many delicious choices—it was hard to choose.

Only one thing marred his happy anticipation. He hadn't heard the screams he'd expected from his hostage. His men could hardly have been tender in their affections, and no matter how stalwart she might have intended to be, she would break beneath their abuse. But there had been no shrieks echoing through the abandoned household. No coarse male laughter as each took his turn.

Had they killed her? He would be most displeased, and someone would pay for not following his instructions. They were all terrified of him, his band of rough mercenaries, and he couldn't imagine they would dare go against his wishes. Accidents happened, however, as he well knew. He hadn't meant to kill the baron's daughter—he had more sense than that.

If Lady Elizabeth hadn't survived her afternoon of pleasure, then he would simply have to improvise. He'd have them drag her bloodied body to the hall and lay it out in front of the fire. He would be cheated of half his vengeance, and his men would pay for it.

"Winston!"

"Yes, sire."

"The girl's dead, isn't she?"

"I don't believe so, my lord."

William looked at him suspiciously. "Bring her here, then. I need proof. And entertainment. I'm tired of waiting for her noble rescue."

"Yes, my lord. Shall I bring your knives?"

William smiled serenely. "Yes, Winston, do that. And drag her here, then, man. I'm bored."

And he leaned back in his chair, smiling in sweet anticipation.

The tiny room was pitch dark, her stomach was roiling again, the pain in her head now joined by a deep throbbing beneath her eye. Elizabeth put up a hand to touch the wound, only to pull it back swiftly. It was swollen and painful, and she suspected she wouldn't be able to see clearly out of it. Not that it mattered in this dark pit.

She wasn't even given the blessed relief of sleep. She spent the endless hours huddled in the corner of the room, prepared to spin another wild tale if anyone should decide to risk such a horrible death.

But no one came.

And no one would come, certainly not Peter, no

matter what Prince William might think. After their last encounter it would have proved to him that he dare not be anywhere near her. The best solution to his problem would be her death.

No one would care if she died, she thought gloomily. The good sisters would keep her dowry, her father and brothers had already forgotten her, and to Peter she was the temptation incarnate. Even the twisted Prince William didn't want her—she was simply a means to an end.

Too bad she was no longer a virgin—had she been so she might have qualified for sainthood eventually, had her own shrine. To do so she would have to perform miracles after her tragic death, but Elizabeth had no doubts that she'd be able to do that. She'd always had the ability to do almost anything she set her mind to. If she missed hell and landed in purgatory she might spend her days walking this empty land, performing kind deeds for strangers.

A lovely thought, but she was no suffering, gentle Madonna. If her spirit were left to walk this land she'd plague Brother Peter for the rest of his life, and raise holy hell for Prince William. Could spirits kill? They could drive people mad, but it seemed fairly certain that Prince William had already taken that particular road. Perhaps she could talk one of his men into killing him.

There would be a great deal to learn as a ghost, but she was open to new adventures. At least this way no one could hurt her, no one could touch her. Kiss her, put his hands on her breasts and...

The door opened, letting in a shaft of dim light, and she stiffened. Planning an eternity as a vengeful ghost was all well and good, but she wasn't looking forward to the transition. Particularly with the memory of Peter's hands fresh in her mind.

"Come along. He's wanting you."

Oh, sweet Jesus, she hoped not. The very thought of sweet Brother Matthew touching her was more than her weakened stomach could bear.

A wave of dizziness swept over her as she rose. Her bare feet were freezing, her head throbbing, and she almost considered sitting down again and announcing she wasn't going to leave.

But she didn't want to die in darkness, in a cold, dank room. So she steadied herself, leaning against the wall for a moment before moving forward.

The prince had made himself at home. It was a pretty-enough room, Elizabeth thought as she stumbled after her captor. His man had tied her hands together in front of her and was leading her like a fractious mare. The prince sat alone in the huge room, by the fire, the flames dancing across his pretty face. She saw the knives then, and her stomach lurched.

"You look quite good for a woman who's just entertained a dozen soldiers," he said, frowning.

"They let her be, my lord," the man who brought her said warily.

"Why? She's no great beauty, 'tis true, but I wouldn't have thought they'd be so picky."

"She's got the pox. She told them their privates would shrivel and fall off if they took her."

"Nonsense. Why am I surrounded by idiots?" he asked plaintively.

"I'm not quite sure, my lord...."

"That was a rhetorical question, Winston! I was not expecting an answer."

"Yes, my lord."

"Any sign of our expected guest?"

"No, my lord. None of the men seem to be around—they must be guarding the approach. I'll seek them out and see if there's word."

The prince sighed. "He'll show up sooner or later. Trust Peter to be late to his own demise. Leave the girl with me, Winston, and go fetch me some wine. I grow weary of waiting."

"You'll have a long wait," Elizabeth said. Her one eye was swollen shut, but she could see more than she wished to already. "He's not coming."

"I know him better than you, my sweet." He took the end of the rope and tugged her forward, so abruptly that she fell on her knees. "He'll be here. But don't make the mistake of believing it will be out of love for you. He's atoning for his sins, he'll atone till Judgment Day and beyond, and he'd come if you were the sour-faced mother abbess."

"That's because he's a good man," Elizabeth said.

"That's because he's a fool. I almost regret doing this. Killing him might be a mercy, freeing him from that crushing load of guilt. But I console myself with the knowledge that I'm sending him to the eternal torments of hell and then I am at peace."

"You're the one who'll spend eternity in hell," she

said. "You're a sick, evil monster. A killer of the innocent, a despoiler of everything good…"

"Oh, I am a mere infant in the annals of destruction compared to Peter. Am I not?"

For a moment she had no idea whom he was talking to. And then she heard the footsteps behind her, and knew with a dreadful sinking feeling that Peter had walked into the trap after all.

26

His beloved looked like holy hell, but she was in one piece. *His beloved?* When the hell had that happened? Sometime during the endless ride he'd come to the conclusion that there was no saving him. He was doomed to love her, whether it made sense or not, and the more he fought it the more powerful it became.

"I'm surprised you managed to get in here without setting off some kind of alarm. My men had orders to let you pass, but they were going to at least apprise me of your arrival."

"Your men were…indisposed," he said, moving forward into the light. He was trying not to look at her—William would take advantage of any weakness, any lapse in attention. She would simply have to remain that way, on her knees.

"You must not have come alone, then—there's no blood on your sword, and my men wouldn't have given up without a fight."

"True enough. But it's easy enough to sneak up on a stupid man and disarm him, and your men are very stupid."

"I won't argue with you on that one. I, however,

am not stupid. And I'm wondering why you even bothered to carry that sword in here, when you and I both know you aren't going to use it.''

''You think not?''

''I know not. You're still beating your breast over those infidels we torched in the Holy Lands. You took an oath before God that you would never take another life unless your own is threatened, and you've held to that, haven't you?''

''Yes.''

''So you think you're going to kill me in cold blood? In front of your overgrown trull? I doubt it, not if I don't attack you first. Sit down, Brother Peter, and have some wine. Or are you still Brother Peter? Somehow I doubt it, even though you're still wearing your monk's robes.''

It would be so simple to kill him, Peter thought. To slash through his throat and send his head flying. As he'd seen William kill so many times before. Infidels, he'd said. Worthless enemies of Christ who deserved to die. And in such inventive ways.

''No wine.''

''Surely you don't think I'm going to let you take the girl and walk away? Not after I've gone to so much trouble to get you here. If you hadn't set that wretched Adrian to watch over me I would have cut your throat the first night out. You're damnably hard to kill, Peter.''

''I always have been.''

''But not this time.'' William gave a sudden hard jerk on the rope he held in one soft hand, and Elizabeth collapsed at his feet. A moment later he was on his knees beside her, holding a knife to her throat.

"She bleeds quite easily, Peter," he said cheerfully. "I was thinking I would cut her in a thousand places and watch the life blood drain from her."

It was Peter who felt cold, bloodless. "Let her go, William."

"Think of it this way. If you hadn't given that order no one would have set fire to the seraglio. All those women and children screaming into eternity, weighing on your conscience. Don't you think the only fair trade is to lose the woman who, inexplicably, is so important to you? You're a great one for sacrifice and denial. Why not make the greatest sacrifice of all. Her life as payment for the lives of all those women."

"I believed the seraglio was empty when I ordered it burned. You know that."

"Of course I do. Because I was the one who told you no one was inside. You were so pathetic, trying to rouse the other crusaders into stopping the fire. There was no way to stop it—the building was dry as dust. The people inside died far too quickly."

"But you didn't."

William pressed the knife against Elizabeth's throat, hard enough that a trickle of blood snaked down her pale skin. "No, I survived. As a grotesque, impotent creature, a monster, not a man."

"No, William. You were a monster long before I flung you into the fire."

He smiled, a saintly expression. "If you try to save

her you'll be condemning her. Come any closer and I'll plunge the knife into her throat and watch her strangle on her own blood.''

"You'll kill her if I don't try."

"But you can't be certain of that. As long as she still lives there's hope." He dipped his finger in the blood on her neck and brought it to his lips. "Which do you love more, Peter? Your immortal soul? Or this wretched female?"

"Let her go. You'll have a great deal more pleasure killing me."

"No, I won't. You'd sacrifice yourself for anyone—it's what you've been trying to do since you returned from the Holy Lands. No, this time you'll have to watch your loved one die, and the only way to stop it is to kill me. When I know that you can't break your holy vow." William put his hand on her chin, drawing her bruised face up to his. "Let's see, where shall I begin?" He put the bloody tip of his knife blade against her pale lips.

"Don't!" Peter's voice was anguished.

"You can't do anything about it, Peter. One of England's most gifted killers, and your holy vow is more important than your lady fair. Shame on you. Did you really think to argue her freedom? Appeal to my better nature? I have no better nature."

"No," he said.

"So tell me, which do you choose? Your immortal soul, or your lady?" He drew the knife down her cheek to the pulse below her chin.

''The lady,'' Peter said. And he flung the knife, straight and true.

The look of shock on William's angelic face would have been comical, if it weren't for the knife embedded in his throat.

And then he smiled. ''I won,'' he choked, slashing the knife he still clutched toward Elizabeth's throat.

But she rolled away, and he pitched forward, driving the knife deeper in, and his own weapon skittered across the stone floor.

Peter picked it up, moving slowly across the room to cut the ropes that bound Elizabeth's wrists. He didn't even look at her, but past her to William's corpse. The blood pooled beneath him, spreading upward, around him like a halo.

He stared down at the lifeless victim and raised his voice. ''Adrian!''

He'd been waiting, alert. ''You've finished it, then?''

''Yes.''

''What's to be done?''

''Take Elizabeth back to Saint Anne's. I'll see to the body.''

''And the men?''

''We'll leave them be, trussed and helpless. Sooner or later they'll free themselves, and when they discover their lord is dead they'll disappear.''

''And you?''

Peter looked at him blankly. ''What about me?'' He walked over to Elizabeth and put his hand beneath her chin. His skin felt like ice, like that of a man already dead. His eyes roamed her face. "There used to be a woman living near the market cross not far from here. If she's still there she could tend to her wounds. If not, get her back to Saint Anne's as fast as you can and she should be fine."

"And you?" This time it was Elizabeth's turn to ask.

The faintest of smiles curved his lips. "Goodbye, sweet scold." And he walked away, out of the hall, out of her life forever.

27

It was on the very edge of summer. The apple blossoms had fallen away to bright green leaves, the sweet scent of lilacs filled the air, and the Shrine of Saint Anne bloomed with early roses and sweet william. And Elizabeth waited.

She'd lost count of the days since that terrible night when Peter had walked away, the blood of Prince William staining his monk's robes. No one spoke of him, and she asked no questions. She simply spent her days at the convent, doing her best to follow the order of the house, quiet and obedient for the first time in her life.

The disappearance of the bastard prince was quickly forgotten. Queen Isabella was with child again, and there would be no untimely falls to bring an early end to the pregnancy. A true heir would be born, and England would thrive.

And Elizabeth moved through the cloistered halls, meek and silent, a ghost of Peter's sweet scold.

She was living in a state of uncertainty, her mind blank, her heart numb. She knew she should make her vows, take the veil and all it involved, but even that step was too strenuous for her. She spent her time in the gardens, tending to the tiny shoots that were peeking forth from the rich soil, and Sister Marie Felix, the head gardener, set her to work, asking no questions, letting her grieve in silence.

Queen Isabella was not the only one with child. Joanna and Adrian were married before they left the shrine, and within a month she was already pregnant. Elizabeth could imagine her, glowing with joy, but imagination was enough. Nothing could make her leave the safe haven of the cloister, the daily round of prayers and duty. There was no child for her, as she'd known there wouldn't be, but for some reason she almost wept when her monthly courses came. But she wasn't one to weep.

The summer days grew long and hot, and still Elizabeth toiled beneath the sun, tending the garden, letting her pale skin burn beneath her short hair. It was slowly growing back, the same stubborn red she'd hacked off. Perhaps when it grew back completely she would stop thinking about what she must not think of, and make up her mind.

It rained for the first half of June, almost drowning the tiny plantlings. The first day the sun came out Elizabeth finished her morning prayers. It would still be too wet to garden, and she was lost.

She was sitting in her room, staring absently at the tiny barred window, when Mother Alison knocked at her door.

"You look like a ghost, child," she said. "Haven't you mourned long enough?"

"I'm not mourning," she said. "No one has died...have they?" Sudden terror filled her. Had Peter's despair overtaken him at last, and had he put an end to his life? Ensuring the eternal damnation he was so convinced he deserved?

"No one has died, child," Mother Alison said. "Only your spirit."

"I was always told I had too much spirit. Surely it's better that I finally learned to be meek."

"Are you longing to inherit the earth, my child?"

"I have no wishes."

Mother Alison shook her head. "You worry me, my dear. I think it's past time for you to make up your mind. Do you feel the fire calling you, to join us as a holy sister? Or do you think your lot is a different one?"

"I have no other choice."

"You always have a choice. If you did, what would you choose? The veil, or the world?"

"The world is full of violence and pain," Elizabeth said.

"It is. It is also filled with joy and love."

"Not for me."

Mother Alison made a clucking sound. "I forget how very young you are," she said. "Wounds heal. Things change."

Unconsciously Elizabeth touched the mark on her throat William's knife had made. She could no longer feel the faint trace beneath her fingers, and its loss was somehow like a knife wound to her heart.

"I would join the holy sisters and live my life in obedience to the rule," Elizabeth whispered.

"Would you, indeed? We would welcome you with all our hearts, child, if that is what you truly wish. But why not think about it a bit longer? The rain has stopped, the sun is shining. Go for a walk in the orchards—there will be no one there to bother you, and you can think in peace."

"I would rather stay inside...."

"And I would rather you walk to the orchard," she said firmly. "If you plan to practice obedience then now is the time to start. The walk will do you good."

There was no way she could protest. "As you wish, Mother."

The tiny nun made the sign of the cross on her forehead, an unexpected gesture. "Go in peace, child. I'll expect you when I see you."

It was going to be a warm, sultry day, and Elizabeth pulled off the light veiling she usually wore as she made her way down the neatly marked paths of the herb garden. She usually kept her devil's hair well covered, but today she wanted to feel the damp wind in it.

She passed no one as she made her way up the hill that led to the bounteous orchards. It was sext and the household would be at worship. How unlike Mother Alison, to send her out at such a time. She was a stickler for attendance, and yet she'd set Elizabeth free.

The apple and pear trees spread out over the top of

the hill, sweet smelling in the bright sun. Small green apples had begun to appear, a bounteous crop. Perhaps by the time the apples ripened and fell she'd be over her pain.

She would go sit beneath an apple tree and think about her future. The ground would be wet from the rains, it would soak through her plain robe, and maybe she'd catch cold and die and then Peter would be sorry.

Ridiculous, she thought, trying to smile, but her face felt stiff from lack of trying. It was too hot a day to catch cold, and she was made of stronger stuff than that, and he'd forgotten all about her.

Except that he stood at the top of the hill, waiting for her.

She halted, her heart suddenly hammering in her breast. He was wearing leather and wool, no longer the humble monk's robe and not the vain garb of a prince. He stood there watching her, his face still and unreadable.

She moved again, coming forward. He wouldn't be able to see how fast her heart was beating, she told herself. He must have come for a reason.

"You look like a ghost. Mother Alison was right. Have you been eating?"

"You've been talking with Mother Alison?"

"She sent you here, did she not?" he countered. Now that she was closer she could see the difference in him. The shadows in his eyes had faded. Not gone entirely, but no longer owning him.

"Yes, she sent me here. What I don't understand is why."

"It's time for you to choose."

"Choose what?"

"The veil, or life."

She said nothing, staring at him. "There's no need for this," she said in a quiet voice. "Clearly I'm not with child."

"I didn't think you were."

"Then why are you here?"

"To give you a choice. You can take the veil, or you can come with me, back to the place where you nearly died, and make a new life."

"Why?"

"I owe it to you."

Wrong answer. "I choose the veil," she said in a cool voice, turning away.

"Is that all you have to say?"

"It is," she said over her shoulder. Why did she have to start crying, now of all times? After months of dry eyes and a dead soul, why had everything burst into life once more?

Because he was here. She kept walking, head down, tears spilling onto her robe, furious at him. At herself and her stupid weakness. When she looked back, he was gone.

She sat down in the middle of the path and let out a howl that could wake the dead. No one would hear, and the hell with them if they did. She was desperately, hopelessly in love with him, and she'd been fool enough to send him away. She should have taken what he had to give, even if he didn't love her. Maybe she loved him enough for the two of them.

She was crying so loudly, with such enthusiastic gusto, that she didn't hear his horse until it was right beside her. He didn't climb down, he simply sat there looking at her tear-stained, woebegone face.

"Give me your hand, Elizabeth."

She stopped crying. She rose to her feet, holding up her hand, and he pulled her up in front of him. "I thought I'd marry my red-haired witch, not a weeping maiden," he said in a gruff voice.

She took a deep, shaky breath, a little fight still left in her. "If you think I'd marry such a lying, deceitful wretch who'd abandon me when I most needed him and spends all his time brooding…"

His smile stopped her. "I think you will do just that. Where else can you find a man who loves you and is willing to take such abuse?"

"It's only because you enjoy abuse that you…you love me?"

"As you love me. Though I expect you're not going to want to admit it as long as you can berate me."

"If you marry me I'll berate you for the rest of your life."

"I expect no less."

She caught his dear face in both her hands and kissed him. The touch of his mouth was heaven, and she closed her eyes. "Perhaps I won't berate you right now,'' she said with a happy sigh. ''Give me a year or two.''

''A day or two. I love you, sweet scold. Though I don't deserve you.''

''You're right about that. But you can spend your life trying to be worthy.''

And his laugh rang out on the hot summer day.

**From the *USA TODAY* bestselling
author of *Getting Lucky***

Susan Andersen

Were things getting
too hot to handle...?

When Victoria Hamilton's "no strings, no last names" vacation
fling resulted in a baby, she knew she had to begin a new life
far from her family's corrupting influence. Now her father has
been murdered, her half brother, Jared, is the prime suspect
and Tori has no choice but to return to Colorado Springs with
her six-year-old daughter. She'll do anything to prove Jared's
innocence. But confronting her past when she opens the door
to her new private investigator and comes face-to-face with
John "Rocket" Miglionni—the former marine who rocked her
world six years ago—sure isn't what she had in mind....

"BRIGHT, SMART, SEXY, THOROUGHLY
ENTERTAINING."—JAYNE ANN KRENTZ

*Available in August 2004
wherever paperbacks are sold.*